D0252508

PEOPLE WHO KNEW ME

PEOPLE WHO KNEW ME

KIM HOOPER

St. Martin's Press New York

This is a work of fiction. All of the characters, organizations, and events portrayed in this novel are either products of the author's imagination or are used fictitiously.

 Printed in the United States of America. For information, address St. Martin's Press, 175 Fifth Avenue, New York, N.Y. 10010.

www.stmartins.com

The Library of Congress Cataloging-in-Publication Data is available upon request.

ISBN 978-1-250-07798-1 (hardcover)
ISBN 978-1-4668-9030-5 (e-book)

Our books may be purchased in bulk for promotional, educational, or business use. Please contact your local bookseller or the Macmillan Corporate and Premium Sales Department at 1-800-221-7945, extension 5442, or by e-mail at MacmillanSpecialMarkets@macmillan.com.

First Edition: May 2016

10 9 8 7 6 5 4 3 2 1

I read somewhere that one of the most common fantasies
is running away and starting a brand-new life.

This book is for all those people—cowardly and courageous—who
dare to imagine leaving it all behind.

PEOPLE WHO KNEW ME

ONE

People who knew me think I'm dead.

The words rolled around the back of my throat, like clothes in a slow spin cycle. I'd just hailed a taxi, settled into my seat, its seams split to reveal yellow foam beneath. The cab smelled like pine. I expected to see one of those air fresheners hanging from the rearview mirror, but there wasn't one.

The cabbie's name was Angel Rivera. According to the identification badge on the dashboard, that is. He was forty-something, with a gold chain around his neck and a faded sticker of the Puerto Rican flag on his glove compartment. He looked straight ahead, didn't dare make eye contact with me via the mirror. A week before, planes flew into buildings and people died. The ones left behind—me, Angel Rivera, all of us—responded by either embracing everyone or trusting no one.

I trusted no one.

"Newark Airport, please," I said. He didn't respond, just nodded and navigated his way to the Henry Hudson Parkway, my road out of everything.

I had my purse under one arm, an overnight bag under the

other. To Angel Rivera, I must have looked like a woman committed to her career, flying off to a business meeting in Philadelphia or D.C. or Boston or some other place requiring just an overnight bag. Maybe he resented the tight bun on top of my head, the height of my heels, the obvious expense of my blouse and perfectly fitting skirt—the same blouse and skirt I'd worn the day before those buildings fell. He didn't want to be there, driving around someone like me. He wanted to be home with the family I pictured him to have—a few kids and a wife who cleaned apartments or waited tables or worked as a nanny for women like me, overnight-bag-carrying women who left their loved ones for big-city meetings. He wanted to hold that family close because we'd all learned a week before that anything could happen.

There was none of the usual traffic leading to the Holland Tunnel. We drove right in. I closed my eyes, like I used to as a kid, making wishes in the darkness. As I said good-bye to New York, my only wish was for everyone I left behind to forget me.

Forgiveness was too much to ask for.

Light filled the cab as we exited the tunnel. I opened my purse and counted the cash discreetly. I'd cut up all my credit cards and my ATM card, flushed the bits down the toilet. I kept my driver's license. I'd need it as identification to get on the plane. There was no way around that. Renting a car would have required ID, too. I'd briefly considered stealing a car, but was sure I'd screw that up. I'd end up in jail, begging the cops to keep me there forever instead of calling my confused husband to bail me out. They'd write me up as a mental case, which I probably was. So I decided to fly, to be one of the brave few to board a plane so soon after what had happened. The uniformed guys at the security gate would be on higher alert than ever before, but my ID wouldn't raise any eyebrows. Nobody would be checking for an Emily Morris catching a flight from New Jersey to California. Emily Morris was dead.

I stared out the window as we took the Pulaski Skyway over the Passaic and Hackensack rivers. I grew up there—in Jersey. My mom still lived in Irvington. I'd never see those rivers, or her, again. Even though we weren't close, my mom and I, the finality of it all should have brought me to tears. But I just sat tight-lipped and unblinking. I was already becoming a different person, a colder person.

I'd cried over so many smaller things before. I'd cried at the sight of dead dogs on the side of the road, their fur fluttering in wind generated by passing cars. I'd cried when that gymnast busted her knee in the 1996 summer Olympics. I'd cried when I sold my first car, a run-down 1985 Honda Civic. The tears weren't for the vehicle itself, but for the memories associated with it—driving out to Coney Island during the summer before college, stuffing all my belongings in the hatchback for the move to the dorms at NYU, kissing the guy who would become my husband in the front seat after seeing *City Slickers* in a second-run theater with sticky floors from spilled sodas. He didn't have a car. That's why he drove mine.

But I couldn't cry in Angel Rivera's cab. I'd cried all my tears in the days leading up to the decision to leave. Tears for love lost when the buildings fell, tears for necessary choices, and tears for me—because, after all, I had died.

TWO

It was fourteen years ago when I got into Angel Rivera's cab. *Fourteen years*. Sometimes it feels like yesterday. Sometimes it feels like a dream.

I wasn't alone in that cab. My daughter was growing inside me. I'd thought long and hard about ending the pregnancy. My plan to move across the country and begin a completely new life made no sense with a baby. I would be lost. I would be utterly alone. Maybe that's why I wanted to keep her, so I wouldn't be.

"Current temperature of seventy-three degrees. Can't beat the weather," the overly peppy flight attendant said when we landed in Los Angeles. I'd always wanted to go to California. And it had the added bonus of being the farthest away from New York that I could get without crossing an ocean or leaving the country. In California, people meditated and grew avocados in their backyards and kept bathing suits in their top dresser drawers. In New York, blood pressure ran high, produce arrived in trucks tired from cross-country journeys, and bathing suits, if owned at all, were tucked away with old Halloween costumes. I thought of California as being full of transplants like me, people starting over, anew, again. I could get lost in crowds of people also trying to get lost.

People think it's easy to be anonymous in New York. It's not. The subway system creates an intimacy that even the coldest New Yorker can't avoid. California has highways full of people hiding in cars behind tinted windshields and knockoff sunglasses.

That first day when I arrived, I checked into a Motel 6 in downtown Los Angeles, next door to what might have been a crack house. I got a hamburger from McDonald's and flipped through the classifieds, looking for rooms to rent. I was convinced there were bugs in the sheets, so I stripped the bed and lay flat on the mattress. The room smelled like cigarette smoke. I apologized to my pregnant belly.

I couldn't sleep. I tossed and turned. What kind of future would I be able to offer my child? I had enough cash to secure an apartment and hold me over for a few weeks, but then what? I had no prospects. I couldn't return to the career I'd started as Emily Morris. The promising life she had was dead. In the midst of my panic, I started singing "Twinkle, Twinkle, Little Star" and, somehow, I became calm, eerily calm. Life would be simpler, I thought. I'd strip it down to its bare essentials, change my definition of happiness to include just food and shelter for my baby and me. On the plane ride, I sat behind two backpackers embarking on a trek through Yosemite. They were talking about the simplicity of leaving everything behind, only having to worry about the weight on their backs. My focus could be similarly, pleasantly narrowed. I said, out loud, to my future child, "It will be okay. Just you and me now."

Connie Prynne. That's the name I chose. My reasons were juvenile, really. I picked the first name of my favorite book character, Connie Chatterley in *Lady Chatterley's Lover*, and the last name of my second-favorite, Hester Prynne in *The Scarlet Letter*. I'd been a literature major in college—or, rather, Emily Morris had. Connie is from Florida. She graduated from Miami Central High School but never went to college. She moved to California when she was eighteen, following a boyfriend who had a pipe dream of becoming an actor. They broke up, he went back to

Florida, she stayed. Her parents died in a freak boating accident when she was twenty-two. She has no siblings. Connie Prynne is a person without strings. In other words, free.

I assumed I'd find someone in a back alley to make me a fake ID. I'd use that to open accounts, start my life. Just like in the movies. It'd be as simple as switching from signing checks and forms as Emily Morris to signing them as Connie Prynne. But I realized I'd run into trouble when I got a job, when my name and paperwork would travel to the government for tax purposes and some old lady at a desk cluttered with Styrofoam coffee cups and pictures of grandchildren would scratch her head, unable to find evidence of my actual existence. I'd be locked up for some kind of fraud. I'd have taken the risk if it was just me, but I had Claire. That's what I named my little girl—Claire.

So I did it the legal way. It's always bothered me that there's evidence somewhere of who I used to be. For those first couple of years, I was convinced someone would find me out and come knocking on the door. My nightly lullaby was the reminder that nobody from my past would put out an inquiry for a woman they believed had died. I only had to worry about people in my present, which was why I vowed not to allow any people in my present.

Just Claire and me.

I didn't want friends. I didn't want lovers. I wasn't willing or able to take on anyone else. I was still mourning the people left behind in New York, the people who knew me. I was full-up with them. There wasn't room for someone new. That's what relationships are, after all—making room for other human beings, with all their requisite feelings and needs and demands and expectations. And it's always a risk. People can disappear at any moment.

The problem is, no man is an island. Ironically, I'd written a college paper about the John Donne poem containing that very line. Turns out that overly used, trite phrase bears an annoying truth. You can't go it alone, no matter how hard you try. Over the past fourteen years I've acquired a couple of people in my life, in spite of myself. One is JT. One is Al.

Those first eight months in California, I rented a crappy apartment in a not-so-great part of Canoga Park, in the Valley. Claire was born on May 9. The week after I brought her home, there was a gang-related homicide on our block. With those new-mother hormones coursing through my body, I considered going back to New York, I really did. But then I came across an ad in the classifieds for a cottage in Topanga Canyon. It seemed too cheap and good to be true, but I called anyway. The next day, I went to see the place and meet the owner, JT. It was one of Claire's first excursions into the world. I had her strapped to my chest. I called her my "roo," my little kangaroo.

JT had deep lines in his face, evidence of six decades of life. A long gray ponytail trailed down his back, likely growing nonstop since his hippie days. He was missing a front tooth.

"Is there some kind of catch?" I asked him. It was only $1,100 a month—half the price it should have been, at least. It was—still is—perfect: two bedrooms, two bathrooms, a small kitchen, a small living space, and a possibly rotting back deck, complete with a fraying hammock.

"No catch," he said. "I just don't want to sell it. Need someone good to look after it."

We stood there on the deck, the wind chimes doing their musical thing. Claire was dead asleep on me, drooling on my shoulder. JT squinted in the setting sun. I wanted to hug him.

"You're my savior," I said.

He laughed and said, "I've been told I look like Jesus."

Maybe that's what the *J* stood for.

In addition to offering me a place to live, JT suggested I check out his friend's bar for a job. I'd been working part-time at a daycare center, mostly because I could bring Claire with me and leave her there when I worked my other job—waitressing at a fancy steakhouse in Malibu. I ventured to Malibu with the hope that rich people would leave me decent tips. Turns out most rich people aren't generous; maybe that's how they became rich.

"It's close to home," he said. "I bet he'd let you bring the baby, let her sleep in the back room with some whiskey on her lips."

I couldn't tell if he was joking—about the job or the whiskey. But I went to check it out anyway. It was called just Al's Place. Al himself was a large man—six and a half feet tall with a big belly and hundreds of tattoos, but gentle as could be. He said he needed someone who would "basically run the place" with him. I was honest, told him I had no bartending experience. He said, "If JT sent you, I'm willing to give you a shot." Because it was more of a managerial role, it was well-paying. Eighteen bucks an hour. When I asked about health insurance for Claire and me, he said, "I suppose I could look into that if you stick around."

Al didn't ask for references. He didn't do any kind of background check. He had to assume that people who want to work in a dimly lit shithole don't want to talk about their past. He had a southern drawl and once mentioned that he used to live in Tennessee, but got into "some trouble" out there. I've never asked him questions because I don't want him to take any reciprocal interest in me. We have an unspoken truce.

Shortly after I showed up at his bar, he called me from across the room: "Connie." Then again: "Connie." This happened a lot the first couple years—when I forgot my new name. Eventually, he came right up to me and said, "You deaf or somethin'?" When I shook my head, he looked at me strangely. But he didn't say anything more, in accordance with the truce, I guess. There are times, still, when I forget my name—like when the receptionist at the dentist's office calls me back for my teeth-cleaning, or when I'm introducing myself at a PTA meeting. I'm not always sure who I am.

JT was right when he said Al wouldn't mind if I brought Claire to work. In fact, Al made part of his back office her play area, stocked with blocks and stuffed animals when she was a baby, then coloring books and Barbie dolls when she was in elementary school.

It's cans of Coke and DVDs now. Al adores Claire, which is amusing, since Al looks like the type who doesn't adore anyone. Sometimes I wonder if he pines for his own family, his own children. He would never say as much.

The bar has been Claire's second home since she was a baby. She's never minded coming along with me—never whines or asks when we're leaving. Even as an infant, she rarely fussed. It's like she knew I had to make money for the two of us. When she got older, she just did her homework back there, quietly. I meet her teachers every year, listen to the accolades they give her. They think I must have something to do with her straight A's, her curiosity, her obedience. They don't know that she just came to me that way. It's like the universe knew I couldn't handle a difficult kid.

Now, at thirteen, Claire comes to the bar sometimes, but she doesn't have to; she can stay home alone. This fact still startles me. I comfort myself with the knowledge that I am less than ten minutes away. Claire says I worry too much. She still believes the world is truly kind. I dread the day she realizes it's not.

It turns out I'm a pretty good bartender. As the stereotype goes, I listen to other people's problems to make me feel better about my own. Divorces, affairs, job losses, broken hearts—there's a different story with every drink. Al's Place has no pretense; people know their secrets are safe here. And with all that's happened in my life, I don't judge. I nod along, never truly surprised by any of the stories. People take comfort in the fact that I accept their poor choices, their sob stories. I have to, because mine are worse.

It's not unusual for guys to ask me out on a date after they've confessed their sins and spilled their truths to me. I suppose that's what we all crave—sharing our darkest selves and having another human say with their eyes, *I understand*. My refrain is always the same: "I don't date." They say, "Oh, come on." They roll their eyes. They laugh nervously. They think I'm bluffing. I'm not.

Claire says I should date. She's at that age when dating seems glamorous and alluring. I'm a mystery to her. She's more social than me. She has friends. She goes to sleepovers at Heather's house. She hangs out with a girl named Riley. She mentions a boy—Tyler. She's more outgoing than I ever was, signs up for teams and clubs. It's because of her that I'm not a total recluse. I've taken her to all the classes that come with each passing interest—gymnastics, tap dancing, painting. She's into soccer now.

It's only a matter of time before she has her first boyfriend. She's a beautiful girl, and I think that's an objective assessment, though a parent never knows for sure. She has the long, wavy brown hair I used to have, until I got pregnant and the hormones shocked my system so much that my hair went forever straight. I dyed my hair blond when I moved to California, as a just-in-case disguise. Claire must assume it's my natural color. Sometimes it bothers me to think how little I've let her know me. She has my mouth—small, but with full lips. From the nose up, she looks like her father. It's been impossible to forget him because of her.

She asked me about him once, when she was six. I was surprised to hear the question: *Mom, who was my father?* I shouldn't have been, though. It was around the same time she was asking all kinds of questions I didn't know how to answer: *Why are there so many homeless people? If tomatoes are a fruit, why aren't they in a fruit salad? Why are tears salty like the ocean?*

She wanted a good story, a love story. So I came up with one, long ago, in preparation for the day she asked me. When people lie, they tend to embellish and go on and on, so I kept it short and sweet. I told her he was my high school sweetheart. I told her we wanted to live happily ever after. I told her he died in a car accident when I was pregnant with her. I told her she had his eyes—big and blue. I told her his name was William.

Most of those things aren't true.

"Do you have a picture of him?" she asked me, those big eyes of his looking back at me.

"No, sweetie, I don't," I said.

That was true.

I hated lying to her, I really did. But the guilt faded over time. Living with my lies has become easy. I don't even notice them anymore. They have become, in a sense, my truth.

She never asked about her father again. She never seemed bothered growing up with just me. Even now, in the midst of what's supposed to be a bratty adolescence, she still hugs me before she goes to bed, still kisses my cheek and says she loves me. But I never should have let myself think that I've done okay at all this. That somehow it will always be okay.

It was just a few weeks ago that I was thinking about the upcoming anniversary of 9/11 and how I could finally relax in this life that still feels new. It's been fourteen years, I told myself. *Fourteen years and at last I can exhale.* But I can't, because the universe, or whatever it is that keeps track of these things, seized that moment to say, *Silly Connie, or Emily or whoever you are, did you really think it would be that easy?* See, last week, everything changed. Last week, the universe decided the karmic equilibrium had been off for too long. Last week, my doctor said, "It could be cancer."

THREE

To understand how I ended up in California, you have to go back to 1992, to an autumn Saturday at New York University. I was just twenty years old, starting my senior year, majoring in literature because I thought I could have a life of just reading and talking about it. I lived in an apartment off La Guardia Place with Jenny, a girl I'd call my best friend for a few years, until we'd lose touch completely. One day, I'll tell Claire this is just what happens in life—people come and go.

Fate put Jenny and me together as roommates freshman year. When a girl in our dorm got mugged, Jenny's parents freaked out and bought the La Guardia Place apartment for her. They said it was a good investment opportunity for them and they liked that there was a gate with a security intercom. It would let them sleep at night, they said. Jenny was from a small town in Minnesota. She'd been homeschooled on a farm. She'd never seen a black person before coming to NYU. Her parents didn't want her to live alone, so she asked me to move in with her. I didn't have to pay rent, just half the utilities. My room was the size of a large closet, with just enough space for a twin bed, a small nightstand, and a dresser. I had a round window next to my bed, about a foot in diameter, like a porthole on a ship, and on winter mornings I'd watch the snow fall and write poems that I thought could rival Emily Dickinson's. It's that delusion that makes youth so sweet.

"Have you met the guy next door yet?" Jenny said, coming in the front door and taking off her boots. She threw her coat over the armchair and sat next to me on the couch—a hideous plaid thing from the seventies that came straight from her parents' garage. She was excitable like this at least three times a week, and it was almost always boy-related. Jenny was a virgin. She was determined not to be by year's end.

"I haven't," I said, pulling my knees to my chest. "Cute?"

She took her book bag off her shoulder and set it on the coffee table with dramatic flair.

"*Cute* is an understatement," she said. She put her hand to her heart as if it weren't there anymore, as if he'd already taken it from her.

"Did you introduce yourself?"

I wasn't boy-crazy. Not like Jenny. I'd had a boyfriend through most of high school. Danny stayed over, slept in my bed. My mom was hardly ever around. She was either working one of her many odd jobs or spending the night with one of her many odd boyfriends. Even when she was around, she didn't care. Danny and I had sex on my sixteenth birthday. We used condoms my mom kept in a Duane Reade bag in her nightstand drawer.

By the time I started college, I didn't want to be tied down by anyone. I still dated, but sporadically. In freshman year, there was the guy in my biology class—Lawrence, never Larry. He refused to dissect a frog—because of fear, not morals—and I lost all attraction for him. In sophomore year, I hooked up with Tony, a twenty-four-year-old wannabe-guitarist who worked the counter at a butcher shop. In junior year, I had an on-and-off "thing" with Alex, whose high-school-sweetheart-of-a-girlfriend went to Boston College. They broke up every other week and, as a testament to my stupidity, I thought it was somehow romantic to be "the other woman." Then he told me it was over. I thought he meant with her, but he meant with me. I feigned apathy and committed myself to being alone and reading all the books by the Brontë sisters.

"I was way too shy to say anything but hello," Jenny said. She hit herself in the forehead with the palm of her hand to express her regret. Jenny majored in theater.

"Well, if he lives next door, we'll see him again."

"Let's make up a reason to go over there," she said.

"Like what—'Hey, do you have a cup of sugar?' "

Jenny shrugged and said, with all seriousness, "That could work."

"Jen, seriously?"

She laughed, trying to play it off like she'd been joking. Jenny needed me, relied on me to call her out on her naïveté. As a young, still-insecure kid, I needed to feel smart and savvy. We were good for each other.

"Let's just ask if he wants to grab pizza with us," I said, standing up, pushing down my rolled-up-to-the-calf sweatpants and gathering my hair in a loose bun.

"*Now?*" she said.

"Why not? It's almost dinnertime."

She looked up to me from her cross-legged seated position on the couch, something like admiration and terror in her eyes.

"Are you even going to change first?" she said. It was like she was from the 1950s, when girls only presented themselves to boys while wearing poodle skirts.

"Jen, come on."

I had my hand on the doorknob when I remembered:

"Shit, I have a date with Gabe tonight."

I turned around and she was right there, on my heels.

"Ooh, Gabriel?" she said, with a trying-to-be-ethnic accent.

Gabriel—Gabe—Walters was one of those guys on campus almost everyone knew, and for that very reason he wasn't my type. He was handsome enough to make me feel self-conscious, and that was a turnoff. Jen assured me I was attractive, even "on his level."

I never saw myself that way, though. I was thin, "like a model" according to Jen, gangly and scrawny according to me (and the handful of boys who teased me in junior high). When I was thirteen, I resorted to supplementing my meals with those protein shakes created for elderly people who don't have the ability to chew anymore. I had long brown hair, wavy if I didn't blow-dry it, which I almost never did. I knew my big brown eyes were my best quality, so I accentuated them with too much eyeliner and multiple coats of mascara, hoping people would look there and not notice that my chest was flat, my legs were twiggy, and I wore the same pair of jeans every day because, truthfully, I was a poor kid on scholarship.

"Is this an official date?" Jen asked. We sat back on the couch.

"I guess so."

Gabe flirted with me for months in junior year. I didn't give him much attention—partly because I was involved with Alex throughout that year, and partly because I assumed he flirted with all the girls. When the school year was coming to an end, we had a brief conversation about summer plans. He was going to Puerto Rico, to stay with his mother's family for a few months. Gabe's mom was Puerto Rican and his dad was white, which explained the juxtaposition of his brown skin and bright blue eyes. Jen called him "exotically handsome"—or was it "handsomely exotic"? His family had a place near Aguadilla and he claimed he was going to surf eight hours a day. He said I should come along, and I laughed. He said he was serious, and I laughed more. I told him we should probably have dinner first, before getting on a plane together. He suggested we go out that very night. I said, "Look, if you still want to have dinner with me when you come back, I'll go." He said it was a deal. I assumed he'd forget about me. He'd get tan and even more muscular and he'd find a beautiful Puerto Rican girl to distract him. Come fall, I'd never hear from him. And I'd never have to worry about seeing him. He was a business major; we wouldn't share any classes.

But that's not what happened. One night in the dining hall

with Jen during the first week of the new school year, I felt a tap on my shoulder and turned around to see him there.

"Emily," he said, a dopey smile on his face. Nobody ever called me by my full name. It was always Emmy or Em.

"Yes, Gabriel?" I said, not missing a beat.

"I believe you said you'd let me take you out to dinner."

"Did I?"

"You did. I wouldn't be confused about something that serious. You can pick the place, as long as it's not on campus."

Jenny looked like she was about to jump out of her seat and accept the invitation herself.

"When is this alleged date?" I asked.

"Saturday? I'll be by your place at eight?"

"Here's the address," Jenny said, scribbling madly on a Post-it note withdrawn from the depths of her book bag.

"At least someone is looking forward to it," he said. He winked at Jenny in a way that probably made the hairs on her arms stand up. I gave him a stiff smile. Jenny berated me for ten minutes after he'd left, saying I needed to be more polite, show more enthusiasm.

"A guy that good-looking doesn't need my enthusiasm."

"Where are you guys going?" Jenny asked.

"Mexican place on Bleecker."

"You don't even seem excited." She crossed her arms over her chest, profoundly disappointed in me and my disinterest in joining her in acting like a giddy schoolgirl.

"How I feel before the date shouldn't matter. We'll see how I feel after."

I stood up and went to the door.

"Where are you going?"

"Next door. Gabe won't be here for an hour. You wanted to say hi to the cute guy, right?"

Standing at their door, we could hear muffled music within—

Nirvana. The *Nevermind* album had come out the year before; "Smells Like Teen Spirit" was on all the alternative radio stations. We knocked twice and, as footsteps approached, Jenny let out something of a squeal.

The door opened to a shaggy-haired guy, at the forefront of the grunge look. This couldn't have been the guy Jenny was raving about; her version of "cute" was very clean-cut, very JFK, Jr. I thought he was cute, though. His hair was dark, almost black, his eyes crystal-blue.

He looked at us expectantly and I remembered that we were the ones knocking on their door and not the other way around.

"Hi," I said, more tongue-tied than I wanted or expected to be. He smiled, which just made me more uncomfortable. He had a sly grin, the type of grin that suggests he's up to something.

"Well, hello," he said, totally at ease.

"I'm Emmy Overton," I said, feeling immediately dumb for using my full name. That was my last name then, the one I was born with—Overton. "And this is Jenny."

"Emmy and Jenny," he repeated, saying it like the two of us were hosts of a variety show.

"Hi," Jenny said over my shoulder.

"We just wanted to introduce ourselves. We're your neighbors. Next door," I said.

"Right, I thought you looked familiar. I'm Drew," he said, sticking out his hand. He had a firm shake. My palm was sweaty—it always is when I'm nervous—but his wasn't. "And my roommate is . . ."

He turned around and shouted, "Hey, Brian, come meet our neighbors."

The "cute" one came to the door. Brian looked like he had been class president in high school. Even relaxing in his apartment, he was wearing a collared shirt and khaki shorts, like he was prepared to play golf at a moment's notice.

"Hey," Brian said. "Nice to meet you." He was overly nice, well mannered.

Drew welcomed us inside and cleared off their couch, which was covered in books and binders. In the next fifteen minutes, we found out that Brian's parents owned the apartment (to which Jenny, desperate for commonalities, said, "My parents own our apartment!"); Drew and Brian met in a chemistry class and became lab partners first, then friends; and they were seniors ("Like us," chirped Jenny), Brian majoring in political science and Drew majoring in liberal arts.

"What do you plan to do with that?" Jenny asked, sounding like her mom, who asked if Jenny was still majoring in theater every time she came to visit.

"Be liberal and artsy," Drew said.

Jenny laughed too hard, even slapping her knee, and Drew smirked at me as if to say, *This roommate of yours is a character.*

I gave myself permission to peruse their bookshelf: Jack Kerouac, Kurt Vonnegut, Ray Bradbury, Henry Miller, Ernest Hemingway, Leo Tolstoy, T. S. Eliot, George Orwell. There was a random palm-reading book, too.

"Let me guess—the liberal arts major is the reader of you two?"

"Guilty," Drew said, raising a hand.

"And whose music taste does this reflect?" I asked, waving my hand to indicate the Nirvana that was filling the room.

"That would be me, too," Drew said.

"Nirvana," I said. "I approve."

He nodded. Jenny and Brian looked at each other.

"Nirvana?" Brian said, confounded. They were pop music types, those two.

"I don't know them, either!" Jenny said.

It was clear where the attractions were. Brian looked at his watch and said he was heading out to a party. He asked Jenny if she wanted to come along and she skipped out of the apartment by his side, giving me a too-obvious wink on the way out. Drew and I sat on the couch, staring at anything but each other—the ceiling, our feet.

"You're a Scorpio, aren't you?" he said.

I am, born October 28.

"How did you know?"

"Just a vibe," he said.

"Oh, god, you're not an astrology weirdo, are you? Is that your palm-reading book on the shelf?"

He laughed. "It might be."

He stood and went to the shelf, pulled out the palm-reading book. He flipped through it, scanning, then looked up and said, "I'm a Scorpio, too. I know my kind."

This excited me, irrationally. I was never one to believe in astrology. I'd been known to call it stupid.

"I read this back in high school," he said, putting the palm-reading book back in its spot. "Here, give me your hand."

He sat next to me again, taking my hand like it meant nothing. I got chills from the bottom of my spine to the top.

"Tell me my fate," I said with a cynical sigh, trying to sound disinterested. At that age, apathy is cool.

He traced his finger along the lines of my palm. Oh, how I wanted to kiss him.

"You're going to live a long time," he said.

"Would you tell me if I wasn't?"

He nodded. "I couldn't lie to you on the first day I met you. That's just wrong."

"Okay, go on, then."

"You'll experience a lot of love. You're lucky that way."

I smiled and dared to look him in the eyes.

"You're really beautiful," he said.

I felt my face get hot and averted my eyes from his. That's when I remembered the time. Gabe. My date. I had to get ready.

"Shit," I said, standing hurriedly and heading for the door.

"What?"

"I forgot. I have to go. To this dinner thing."

"Dinner thing?" he said curiously. "Like a date?"

I didn't want to tell him, which had to mean something.

"Kind of. I guess."

He laughed like it was no big deal at all, like he wasn't the slightest bit jealous. This disappointed me, warned me that maybe I was the only one getting chills up my spine.

"Have fun, then," he said. "And I would love to take you out sometime, but only if you don't call it a 'dinner thing.'"

"I'd like that."

He opened the door for me, and we stood there on the threshold. If life were a movie, we would have kissed, but it isn't, and we were shy. And I had a date expecting me. Drew just smiled that smile of his and I tried not to stumble over my own feet on the way out.

When I picked out my clothes for the date with Gabe, I imagined I was dressing for a date with Drew. I stepped into a flowing black skirt I'd bought at a flea market in Bensonhurst that summer. It was still warm enough for a purple tank top, as long as I wore my favorite black cardigan over it. The cardigan looked gray in comparison to the skirt. I'd worn it so many times that there were perpetual balls of lint attached to it. I hung dangly earrings from my ears and fastened a silver bracelet around my wrist.

I sat on the couch, waiting, and then felt agitated that I was waiting. Gabe wasn't even late. It was ten minutes before eight. I was just antsy. I wanted to go next door, spend the night talking to Drew.

I picked up the phone and dialed Gabe's number. It rang a few times and then he answered.

"Gabe? It's Emmy."

"Hey, there, I was just on my way over."

"Good, I was hoping to catch you before you left."

"What's up?"

"I know this is strange and you will hate me forever, but I have to cancel."

I expected a reaction or at least a question, but he was silent. I thought the connection was lost, but then I heard him breathing.

"I'm sorry," I said.

"Are you sick?" he asked.

I knew I could say that, but then he'd want to reschedule. Or bring me soup.

"No, I'm fine. It's just—I met someone."

"You met someone? In the few days since I asked you out?"

"I know, it's weird. It just happened. I wasn't expecting it."

He sighed. I imagined him stepping on the heel of his dress shoe with one foot, then the other, taking them off, resigned to a night of staying in.

"Well, bummer," he said. "If it doesn't work out, let me know."

"I will. Thank you for understanding."

"He's a lucky guy, whoever he is."

"Thanks, Gabe. I'll see you around."

And that was that.

I was relieved for just a moment, before I got so anxious that I had to pee. I rifled through the drawers in the bathroom, in search of Jenny's perfume. I spritzed myself twice, on each side of my neck.

My knock was tentative. Drew opened the door, surprised to see me.

"I canceled."

He smiled like it was the best news he'd gotten in years, flung his arm out to the side, and said, "Come in!"

He was in the middle of boiling a pot of water for pasta, which was impressive cooking according to my twenty-year-old self.

"I'm assuming you need to eat, then," he said.

"Yeah, no more 'dinner thing' means no more dinner."

He dumped a box of noodles into the water.

"What you did right there—that's more cooking than I've ever done," I said. "All of my eating is very microwave-based."

"I cooked for my mom growing up. I'm used to it," he said. "If I can't read for a living, maybe I'll be a chef."

He's a dreamer, I thought.

I sat at the barstool, resting my elbows on the kitchen counter, chin in my hands, and watched him. In a separate pan, he melted butter and added flour until it became a thick paste.

"A roux," he said.

"Fancy," I said.

Within minutes he had some kind of cream sauce simmering while the noodles cooked.

"Was it just you and your mom?" I asked him.

He nodded. "I saw my dad about once a year. He had a whole other family after us. My mom raised me. She's paying for college. My dad—he'd show up to a baseball game, school awards ceremony, that kind of thing."

"School awards ceremony, huh? You a smarty pants or what?"

"I went to public schools in Jersey. If you could count to ten, they'd put you in the accelerated learning classes."

I laughed. "I grew up in Jersey, too."

"I knew we had a lot in common."

He sat on the barstool beside mine, and rested his elbows on the counter. We filled the next few minutes talking nonstop, leapfrogging from one topic to another.

"Close to your mom?" he asked.

"Nope, not really," I said, and he didn't press further. I could tell already that he was close to his mom, a quintessential mama's boy.

"Dad?" he said. I shook my head. I never met my dad. My mom said I was the product of a one-night stand. That fact was given to me when I was too young to know what a one-night stand was. I protested once about not knowing my father and she said, "I never knew mine, either. You'll get over it."

"Ever been in love?" he asked.

I laughed uncomfortably. "You get right to it, huh?" I said.

"May as well."

I shrugged. "I don't know if I have. You?"

"Yes. I was six. And she was my first-grade teacher. It didn't work out."

I rolled my eyes. "Quite the jokester," I said, giving him a playful punch in the arm, as an excuse to touch him.

It's like he took that touch as a sign, because, without warning, he leaned from his barstool over to mine and kissed me. It was spontaneous, fast, and simple, as if it were the nine hundredth kiss he'd given me, as if we'd known each other for years already. I was dumbstruck.

Then the timer beeped and he leapt up to drain the pasta. By the time he presented our gourmet-looking fettucine alfredo, too much time had passed since the kiss, so I didn't say anything about it. I just hoped it would happen again.

I took small, careful bites and he did the same, following my pace.

"It's delicious," I said.

"This is nothing. There's a lot more where this came from," he said. Then: "You'll see."

You'll see? Did he know, psychically, that we would have more nights like this? That we would fall in love?

"We should drive out to the Jersey Shore together. See a movie. Eat bad food."

Dumbstruck, again.

"That sounds fun," I said.

He looked at me, stunned, like he wasn't sure he'd actually presented the idea out loud, like he'd been fantasizing and the verbalization of that fantasy was purely accidental.

"Tomorrow?" he asked tentatively. Seeing his apprehension, his fear of rejection, made me less nervous. He liked me as much as I liked him. There was comfort in that equality. "Unless tomorrow isn't good . . ."

I'd planned to spend most of Sunday writing an essay for my feminist literature class. Ditching feminist lit responsibilities for a boy? I couldn't resist the irony.

"No, it's great," I said.

"Crap," he said, and my heart sank. I thought he was going to cancel. "I don't have my car here anymore."

"Oh," I said. "I have mine." I was one of the only people I knew who had driven her car from home to campus. I didn't feel right leaving it with my mom. It felt like leaving a part of me there when I really just wanted to be gone completely.

"You have a car?" he said, delighted.

"It's a piece of shit, but yes."

I liked the idea of driving somewhere with him—to another state, no less. It felt grown-up, like a mini-vacation.

"My mom's car broke down over the summer, so I left mine with her," he said.

"That's nice of you." There was something sweet about a guy who loved his mother so much, who had that kind of loyalty. I'd never known a guy like that.

"I'd do anything for her. It's pathetic, really."

"It is pathetic," I teased, "but sweet."

"Will you let me drive, at least? I can't let you drive on our first date," he said. A proper gentleman. I'd never known one of those, either.

"Sure," I said.

"We'll go to my favorite ice-cream parlor. I'll buy you a cone, as a thank-you for the car. It's only fair."

"I'm all about fairness."

"Start thinking about your ice-cream flavor choice," he said. "I'll judge you by it."

I already knew I'd get cookies and cream. And I knew he'd kiss me after and that it would be sweeter than any dessert.

I woke up to find Jenny eating Pop-Tarts on the couch, a book cracked open in front of her, which she was thoroughly ignoring in favor of a *Saved by the Bell* rerun on TV.

"So. How was it?" she asked, eager for details.

"Great," I said. I tried to prevent the corners of my lips from curving upward, but they betrayed me.

"I knew it!" She lurched forward in her seat, like she was about to jump up and hug me. I must have looked overwhelmed by her excitement. "Look at you—playing coy."

"I just don't want to jinx it."

"Fair enough." She reclined back into the couch.

"How was your date with Brian?" I asked her.

She rolled her eyes and playfully slapped the air between us. "Oh, that was nothing. I went with him to this dumb party. He was hanging out with all these guys. I left after an hour."

"Did he say he wanted to hang out again?"

"He said, 'See you around.'" She was disappointed, but trying to act like she wasn't. I'd seen this from her before.

"Well, you *will* see him around. He lives next door. You never know. See what happens."

"It doesn't matter. At least one of us has a boyfriend now."

"I wouldn't say that," I said, though I wanted her to say that, over and over again.

"Do you have another date planned?"

"We're going to the Jersey Shore today."

"The Jersey Shore?" She said it like I'd suggested our date would be in the bottom of a trash Dumpster.

"It'll be nice. Drive out, see a movie, get some food."

"A road trip already, huh?"

"Can I tell you something?" I said. I had to tell someone. I was bursting with it. Jenny nodded, like I knew she would. "This is going to sound crazy, but I think I found the guy I'm going to marry."

It was a thought that had kept me up from one o'clock in the morning, when I got home from his place, until I left my bedroom at nine o'clock, giving up on sleep. It was the beginning of something. I would have given up sleep forever to feel the anticipation of that something.

Jenny's eyes were huge. Marriage was one of her goals in life, right there at the forefront of her mind.

"I can totally see it—Emily Walters."

See, she thought I'd been out with Gabe. Gabe Walters.

"No, not Gabe," I said. "Drew."

"Drew?" She looked perplexed. "The guy next door with the hair?"

"Yeah. I hung out with him last night. Instead of Gabe."

"Really?"

She thought I was crazy, clearly.

"We just clicked."

She composed herself, resigned to being the supportive friend.

"That's great, Em. Really."

"I think so."

"So. What's *his* last name?"

"Morris," I said.

She nodded approval. "Emily Morris," she said. "Emily Morris."

FOUR

It was just a few weeks after that first official date at the Jersey Shore that I moved my clothes to Drew's apartment and started spending all my nights there. His roommate, Brian, didn't care. Jenny did. I told her I wasn't really living there; I was still her roommate, technically. But that technicality fell by the wayside, and by second semester she got a new roommate. Drew and I shared his little twin bed at night and spent every waking moment together during the day. We were mutually self-absorbed, the way only young people can be. We delighted in each other's morning breath, spent midday study breaks in bed tracing the veins on each other's bodies with mesmerized fingertips, took showers together and shampooed each other's hair. We used the term "soul mate."

After graduation, Brian moved to Boston, which meant we had to find our own place. Drew, like me, had been paying next to nothing to live in the city. The real world, with its real apartments and our lack of real income, was cruel.

We sold my car to secure a lease on a place in Brooklyn—a one-bedroom that cost three-fourths of our take-home pay every month. This was twenty years before Brooklyn became cool, before the hipsters took over, before couples in skinny jeans moved in and started popping out kids named Atticus and Clementine. Brooklyn was run-down then, a place for people who just couldn't afford the city. I had a job at a coffee shop, shifts starting at four in the morning six days a week. Drew worked at a shipping yard. Not because it interested him in the slightest, but because they paid him overtime under the table. If one of us could pick up an extra shift, we would. We rarely saw each other. But we told ourselves it was for our future. We told ourselves we were happy. And we were.

It had character, that apartment. We put up a folding panel to separate our small kitchen space from the couch and TV. We created the illusion of rooms. The plumbing was shoddy, but the bathroom had a claw-foot tub that I'd fill once a week with bubbles. The creaky wood floors were chipping around the yellowing-white baseboards. They were original, from the 1920s, according to the landlord—a fifty-something chain smoker who owned the liquor store below us. We "cooked" on a hot plate because the stove was broken and the landlord always had some excuse for not getting us a new one. We had to stuff piles of clothes under our bed because the one closet barely had enough room for our winter coats. We couldn't fit (or afford) a dresser. But we were relentlessly optimistic. We told ourselves the lack of a dresser was good because it would curb our shopping habits. And it did. I went a whole year without buying a single article of clothing—not even underwear.

We put shabby chic curtains in the windows that made me smile every time I turned the corner of our street and saw them. They were white lace with pale blue roses. We threw a cool paisley sheet over our couch to cover up the tear in the middle cushion and the stains on the side ones. I sewed decorative throw pillows—lopsided with cotton stuffing from the craft store. Everything felt charming and personal and full of love. We were young and invincible. And we had a plan. I would go to grad school, become a literature professor at a big-name university. Drew would go to culinary school, become a chef and open a restaurant where reservations would be booked months in advance. We had dreams, all contained within the walls of that tiny Brooklyn apartment.

I was sitting on our couch, drinking the broth left in a bowl of soup, listening to Depeche Mode, when Drew came home. Behind him, at the end of a shiny new black nylon leash, was a dog, a golden retriever, wagging his tail so hard he nearly whipped himself in the face. He was too big to be a puppy, but had the energy of one.

"Em," Drew said, "meet Bruce."

He knew I'd always wanted a dog. My mom had a strict no-pets policy when I was growing up. Her rationale: "I can barely feed *you*, Emily." I brought home a stray once—an emaciated mutt I named Scruff—and she took him to the shelter while I was at school the next day.

I hesitated in getting up, in going to the dog, in nuzzling his face, in becoming instantly attached to him.

"Is he ours?" I asked.

"He sure is."

This was Drew's style—spontaneous. Just the week before, he'd called me at the coffee shop, convinced me to feign illness so I could meet him at the flea market and see this "amazing lamp" he'd found. It was sixty dollars. I told him we couldn't afford a sixty-dollar light source.

"Shelter says he's about a year old. Deaf out of one ear."

That explained the spontaneity. It was likely Drew just went to look. And then he saw Bruce and chose him because he feared nobody else would.

I approached Bruce with my palm out for him to sniff. He skipped that getting-to-know-you step, though, and started licking my face. I laughed uncontrollably, the way little kids do when getting tickled.

"Why 'Bruce'?" I asked, tilting my face away from the dog's overly friendly tongue.

Drew shrugged. "He just looked like a Bruce."

We went to the pet store that night, strolled the aisles, filled our cart with tug-toys, stuffed animals, meat-flavored treats, and a forty-pound bag of kibble. Drew had just gotten his first credit card. He used it freely, convinced we would pay it off in one fell swoop when we were rich. I believed him because I wanted to.

Bruce waited in the backseat of the car while we were in the store. He yelped when we came out, as if he already recognized us, as if he already knew we were his parents, the three of us a family.

"He's like our little kid," I said, reaching over the center console to scratch his nose on our drive home.

"He is," Drew said.

Then: "We should make it right."

"Make what right?"

"Be a proper family."

I didn't know what he meant.

"We should get married," he said.

I looked at him and he took his eyes off the road quickly to meet my stare. He glanced back and forth—road to me, me to road, road to me—several times. He was exhilarated, like a skydiver jumping out of a plane.

"What?" I said.

"We should just do it, start our lives together officially."

"Are you serious?"

"Of course I'm serious. I mean, we love each other, right? Why are we waiting? We should just do it."

There was no ring. That's how I knew it was a spur-of-the-moment impulse versus an orchestrated event. Maybe that was more romantic. Maybe the bended knee was overrated. *We should just do it.* He didn't even propose, really. A proposal comes with a question. He made a statement.

Concerns swirled in my head—*we don't have actual jobs yet, we can barely make rent, we're too young.* Drew always called me a worrywart. I knew that's what he would have called me right then, if I'd vocalized my thoughts, so I just said:

"Okay."

Then: "I need a ring."

He smiled—the very smile that made me fall in love at first sight—and said, "Let's stop by the mall on the way home."

And that's just what we did. We went to one of those chain jewelry stores that had commercials on television about "special deals for that special someone." I picked out a half-carat, round-cut diamond on a gold band. We put it on his card.

The following week, we applied for a marriage license and made an appointment for our "I do's" at the city clerk's office downtown. That's what they called it—an appointment, not a ceremony. Drew picked the date—September 26, exactly two years after the day we met.

"That's romantic, right?" he said.

I bit my lip. "It's a Monday."

I bought a dress at Macy's—an above-the-knee casual white dress more adequate for a champagne brunch. It was discounted as part of an end-of-summer sale. On September 26, we showed up at the courthouse, me in the dress, Drew in his one and only suit with the pant legs a couple inches too long. We should have splurged on hemming.

I hadn't talked to my mom in a year or so, but Drew insisted we invite her. Surprisingly, she showed up, in a blue dress I remembered her wearing years before, during the short phase when she dated a guy I called the Gambler. He took her to fancy dinners around the city until he ran out of money and disappeared completely. The dress no longer fit her, since she'd gained weight in her middle. I could see the side seams stretching. Drew's mom came, too. She brought a bouquet of pink carnations. We waited in line, between two ropes, like at a fancy Manhattan club. Drew's mom stood behind me. I could hear the carnations rustling in their plastic wrapping. She'd started having tremors in her left hand. The doctor gave her the name of a specialist to see. She didn't go. She said the doctors didn't know anything, that she was just having muscle spasms from gardening too much.

We had to fill out one form. Just one. We had to raise our right hands and swear that everything on the form was correct. And we had to pay fifty bucks, for the processing of the paperwork. The lady behind the desk told us we were next. She looked bored. I wanted to ask how many of these appointments she saw every day.

The door to the ceremony room opened and two people—a woman with badly bleached hair, dark roots showing, and a man with a gaudy gold chain around his neck—fell out of it, tonguing each other in wedded bliss. The officiant poked his head out and said, "Your turn."

The room was about five feet wide, eight feet long. No windows. It could have been a storage closet at one time, a place to keep janitorial supplies. Drew and I stood at the front of the room, with the officiant, facing each other, holding hands. The whole thing took less than ten minutes. We repeated after him, as instructed, said the usual vows regarding sickness and health and richer and poorer, exchanged the gold bands we'd bought from a wholesaler in Queens, and then we were married. Drew's mom cried; my mom did not. The only times I ever saw my mother cry were when she was drunk and heartbroken. We took a few pictures outside, in front of the courthouse. When it started drizzling, we left for dinner at the Old Homestead Steak House on Ninth Avenue to celebrate. I got my first-ever martini, two olives.

"What about a honeymoon?" my mom asked, all of us drunk or on the verge of drunk.

Drew and I hadn't even talked about a honeymoon. We had no money.

"We'll do a trip later," I said, dismissing her.

"We have more important things to do first," Drew added, winking at me like we were partners in crime, in on something together. I'd never felt so mature, so hopeful.

"Important things?" my mom pried.

"I want to go to culinary school," he said. He was sipping scotch. The ice cubes rattled in his nearly empty glass.

"He's going to be a chef!" I said, too loudly. I was excited, after all. And I wanted to rub it in my mom's face that I'd found what she never had—a husband with a plan.

"And Em is applying to grad school at Brooklyn College," he said.

"How are you going to afford that?" my mom asked. She was always the bearer of bad news. On my prom night, she told me that my hair—arranged in some kind of fancy bun—put too much attention on my face.

"There are scholarships," I said. "People make it work."

My mom didn't look satisfied and, to compensate, Drew's mom raised her glass with her shaky hand.

"Here's to the future," she said.

I looked at Drew as our two glasses clinked. He'd told me once that it was bad luck not to make eye contact when saying "cheers." Maybe it was the drunkenness, or the distraction of our mothers, but his eyes didn't meet mine. I didn't think much of it. We ordered another round. Neither of us would remember how we got home.

FIVE

When I moved to California, one of my first orders of business was finding an OB/GYN. I went to Planned Parenthood—which should be called Mostly Unplanned Parenthood—because I had no money, no insurance, and they didn't ask questions or pass judgments. Dr. Tan was a just-out-of-medical-school doctor. When I asked why she chose to work at Planned Parenthood, she said she wanted to make a difference with her practice. I wondered if tending to a pathetic thirty-year-old pregnant woman was the kind of difference she wanted to make.

Dr. Tan no longer works at Planned Parenthood. She works with a medical group in Tarzana. I still go to her for my routine annual exams. Well, usually they're routine. Last week's visit was not routine.

"How long has it been like this?" Dr. Tan asked. She was staring at my right breast, touching it lightly with her cold fingers. Usually she spent a quick three minutes on my breasts, checking for lumps before telling me to hop off and get dressed.

"Like what?" I asked, shifting around on my back, the paper gown crinkling beneath me.

"Red," she said. "It's very red."

It wasn't that I hadn't noticed. I had. It was kind of itchy, a little swollen. I thought I was having an allergic reaction to a detergent. I'd been on a luckless quest for a new detergent that wouldn't cause the rash.

"I don't know," I said meekly. "Is everything okay?"

"I'm concerned about this dimpling of the skin, right here," she said, pressing into a patch of skin on the outside edge of my breast, kitty-corner from my armpit. "I'm going to set you up for a mammogram."

I'm forty-three—forty-four next month. I had my first mammogram at forty because Dr. Tan said that's the protocol: mammogram every year starting at forty. "That must be when everything starts going downhill," I'd said. She'd laughed.

"All of my mammograms have been fine."

"I know. We should take a look, though, okay? I'll set up an appointment with the imaging center."

She forced a smile that was nothing like the genuine one she'd had when I'd joked about everything going downhill.

"What do you think it is?"

I didn't want to ask the more obvious question: *Could it be cancer?* I was sure it couldn't be. There was no lump—no telltale frozen pea under the skin. I've done the checks in the shower, just like they tell you to do. I've eaten well, for the most part. I've been a runner for years. It couldn't be cancer.

But then Dr. Tan looked at me seriously and said, "It could be nothing—maybe just mastitis. I can't know for sure. We have to take a better look." Then: "It could be cancer."

There are about twenty women in the waiting room at the imaging center. Some look bored, mindlessly flipping through magazines; some look antsy, crossing and uncrossing their legs, tapping their feet on the cheaply carpeted floor. A technician calls my name and I follow her to a small room. She explains that she'll be taking a couple pictures of each breast. She wedges the right one, the red one, between two metal plates. She doesn't appear troubled by the redness, which convinces me that Dr. Tan was overreacting.

It takes just a few minutes, as she promised it would. She leaves me in the little room so she can share the images with a Dr. Ferguson. I flip through the tattered pages of a two-year-old *People* magazine, just to have something to do. One article deems Gwyneth Paltrow the world's most beautiful woman. The next profiles the secret lives of the Boston Marathon bombers. The media has this way of making nonsense important and tragedy salacious. When I get to the back cover, the technician opens the door.

"Ms. Prynne, Dr. Ferguson would like to talk to you. Go ahead and put your clothes back on and I'll show you to his office."

I get that shaky, low-blood-sugar feeling as I step back into my jeans and button up my shirt. On the way to Dr. Ferguson's office, I chew off a thumbnail.

Dr. Ferguson is sitting behind a big oak desk, manila folder files spread across it. He has what I assume to be images of my breasts in light boxes on the wall behind him. They look fine to me, tumor-free, not that I know what I'm looking for. Maybe he's the kind of doctor who takes time to talk with each patient, even when there is no problem.

"Okay, Connie," he says, glancing down at my chart because he hasn't bothered to learn my name before I came into the room, "what I'm concerned about is the thickening of the tissue in your right breast."

He points to the right breast with the tip of his pen.

"Thickening," I echo back to him.

"With the red appearance your doctor noted, we might be dealing with inflammatory breast cancer."

We? He has already paired us on a team, against an enemy I don't even know yet.

"What does that mean—inflammatory breast cancer?"

He crosses his arms in front of him, leans back in his chair. This must be his lecture posture.

"It's extremely rare—about one to five percent of breast cancer cases," he says.

I don't move or say anything, so he continues.

"What happens is the cancer blocks the lymph nodes so you get redness, swelling, pain, itchiness, thickening of the skin."

"I thought it was a rash."

"That's the thing with IBC," he says, giving it a nickname when I'd rather he didn't, "many women don't recognize the symptoms as possible cancer."

"Possible cancer," I echo.

"I want to set you up with a core biopsy. Can you be here tomorrow morning?"

I was expecting him to suggest next week. Tomorrow morning presents an urgency I'm not prepared for.

"IBC can be very aggressive," he says. "We want to catch it early."

He doesn't say, *Or rule it out completely*. I wish he'd say that.

The list of things Claire needs from me, as her mother, gets shorter by the day. A ride is still one of them. I've always arranged my shifts at the bar so I can take her to school and pick her up. My own mother never took on that responsibility. I walked to elementary school and took the bus to junior high and high school. Sometimes I think being a mom is just a chance to show my mother how it's done, even if she's no longer paying attention, or never was.

I'm late today, though. The mammogram appointment went longer than I thought it would. I wasn't anticipating a closed-door meeting with a Dr. Ferguson. I wasn't expecting to need ten minutes, sitting in my car in the imaging center parking lot, to collect myself.

I turn the corner and see Claire before she sees me. She's leaning against the same light post as always, looking a little uneasy and worried that I won't show and she'll have to bear the embarrassment of waiting in the front office with the other forgotten kids. When she spots me, the relief is evident in her smile.

I can't have cancer. Claire's mother can't have cancer.

"Sorry I'm late," I say as she sits in the passenger's seat.

"No worries. I just came out. I was talking to Mr. Michaels about our math test tomorrow."

I have a core biopsy of my right breast. Claire has a math test.

"Math test already, huh?"

School started a week ago.

"I think it's more for him to see what we all remember from last year," she says with a laugh. Claire is an easy laugher. I hope she always will be.

Claire sets the table for dinner, our two usual place settings. It's our weeknight routine: she brings her school bag into the kitchen and sits in her designated chair, knees tucked underneath her, and does homework while I cook dinner—or, rather, arrange dinner. There is a distinction. I just place pre-made, store-bought items on a plate. Claire doesn't complain; it's all she's ever known. I had good intentions of being one of those moms who makes everything from scratch, an intention represented by the stack of cookbooks collecting dust on top of the fridge. I blame Drew. He was the cook, so I never had to learn. And then when I did have to learn, I was too busy raising Claire.

When she gets up for a glass of milk, Claire flips the calendar on the fridge from August to September. When she was little and didn't pay attention to calendars, I just skipped September completely—went straight from August to October the way elevators go straight from floor twelve to fourteen. It's silly. It's not like it helped me forget what happened that day. I always remember. Time doesn't heal all, no matter what they say. And tragedies don't make you stronger. That's another popular lie. They just make you more hardened, less surprised by misfortune. Then again, maybe I have healed a bit. After all, this threat of cancer startles me so much that you'd think I'd never been tested by life before, never known adversity.

I touch my breast, in the dimpled area that made Dr. Tan's brows furrow. It's warm in that spot, even through my blouse—or maybe I'm just imagining things? Wouldn't I feel ill if I had cancer? I feel fine. Last weekend, Claire and I ran in the sand and jumped through the waves at the beach. I wasn't even winded.

"Earth to Mom," Claire says, voice raised.

"What?"

"I've been asking you the same question for, like, five minutes."

I'm just standing there at the kitchen counter, a cooked chicken breast in my hand, my original, pre-distraction goal being to cut it up and throw it in a salad.

"Sorry, what?"

"Can. I. Go. To. Heather's. This. Saturday," she says, clearly irritated.

"Sure, yeah. Sure."

"You okay?" she asks, nervously biting down on the eraser end of her pencil.

I don't know if it's normal or good for a child to be concerned for her mother, to pick up on cues of angst. My daughter always has, though. As young as five years old, she brought me soup in bed when I was sick. There's an unspoken understanding that I am all she has, and vice versa. At least she has friends, though, Heathers in her life. Of course, Heather can't take care of her if I'm gone.

"I'm fine, just got some things on my mind," I say.

"Wanna talk about it?"

She bites her lip now, instead of the eraser end of her pencil. She pulls her knees up to her chest, wraps her arms around them. In that little ball she's made of herself, it's painfully obvious how young she still is.

"No, just boring adult stuff."

"Is it money?" she asks.

Despite all my attempts to shield her from money problems before, she's heard me on the phone with credit card companies, begging shamelessly for forgiveness of interest fees. She's heard me tell JT that I'll be late on rent because I just don't have it.

"I can babysit," she says. "I'm old enough now. Heather babysits her neighbor's kids and makes fifty bucks a night."

"It's not money, sweetie. We're fine," I say, which is true. The bar pays my bills and a little more if I smile big for tips and take a few extra shifts. I've never had a lot of money in my life. My mom lived paycheck to paycheck in good years. Drew and I had our struggles. There were so many adjustments coming to California, but thankfully I already knew how to stretch a dollar. Claire and I shop at thrift stores, like I used to do in college. I clip coupons. I pack all of Claire's lunches in reusable containers. I take toilet paper rolls from the bar to stock up at home. Sometimes I take a jug of orange juice.

"Okay, well, I'm here, if you want to talk," she says, releasing her knees and resuming her homework.

They'll do the biopsy tomorrow.

I'll have the results by Monday.

And then, if it's cancer, I'll have to change Claire's world as she knows it.

SIX

I started working when I was fifteen years old. Before that if you count babysitting the neighbor kids. My mom said I had to earn my keep, so I waited tables, tore tickets at movie theaters, folded clothes at trendy stores. But my first real job was a year after Drew and I got married, when we were forced to come to grips with the reality of being adults.

"You must be Emily Morris," the receptionist said as I walked through the doors of Mathers and James Advertising. She was my age, or even younger, with black hair, accented with random strands dyed red, and a big loop ring in her nose. I'd come to learn that it's hard to tell the difference between people on their way to a concert and people who work in advertising.

"That's me," I said.

"I'm Jessica." She stuck out her hand confidently, shook mine, and leaned in close, as if to tell me a secret: "We got, like, hundreds of applicants for this position. You are *so* lucky to be here."

I didn't feel lucky. I wanted to be at Brooklyn College, backpack on my shoulders, notebook in my hand. I'd been accepted into their grad school program for English. According to the welcome letter, I had a future of "immersion in literature from the

Middle Ages through modern day, studying and analyzing texts, using different critical and theoretical approaches."

But we needed money, Drew and me. One of us would have to get a job. A coin toss decided it would be me.

Drew had our monthly bills spread on the kitchen table when I came home from the coffee shop one night. He was biting his thumbnail.

"What's wrong?" I asked.

"I'm doing the math," he said.

Our plan was to live one measly paycheck to the next, to barely get by, in that romantic way young people do. I'd work at the coffee shop; he'd work at the shipyard. That would pay the bills while he went to culinary school and I went to graduate school. We would be poor, but *enriched*.

That was the plan.

I sat at the table, surveyed the bills.

"What math?" I asked.

He stared, wide-eyed and unblinking, as if the bills were tarot cards holding the secrets to our future. "I don't think we can both afford to go to school right now."

I had already been accepted at Brooklyn College and Drew had been accepted at the Culinary Education Institute. We would both get some financial aid, but not full scholarships. My mom said it was because we were white. I told her that was racist.

"School is expensive," he said, explaining his conclusion. "More expensive than we thought."

"Okay, what are you saying?" I asked.

"We should take turns. One of us goes to school, one of us gets a real job, then switch."

He was still staring at the bills. "We're twenty-three. Our programs are only a couple years. We could both finish school by twenty-seven, twenty-eight this way. In the meantime, we'll make more money as a couple, start saving, pay off our loans faster . . ."

He finally looked up at me. "We're a team now, right?"

I nodded apprehensively, forcing a smile.

"What's a 'real job'?" I asked.

"Salary, health insurance—all that responsible stuff," he said. Neither of us knew anything about being responsible. We were imposters.

"All right," I said. "Then who goes first?"

I was sure he would say I could go to school, live my dream, while he worked. He always let me have my way.

He didn't say that, though. He said, "Flip a coin?"

I laughed, he didn't. "Can you think of another way to decide? Neither of us will be happy putting off school. We both know that."

He was right. I couldn't think of any other way to decide, nothing "fair," at least. Any other way would lead to a fight, and Drew and I, as a couple, did everything possible to avoid fights. He grew up in a house where problems were actively ignored; for years, his mom told him that his father might come back. I grew up overhearing shouting matches between my mother and her boyfriends-of-the-moment. Both of us were terrified of conflict.

He took a quarter out of his pocket and I wondered for a split second if he'd put it there, knowing it would come to this.

"Call it?" he said.

The coin started flipping through the air and I acquiesced: "Tails," I said.

It landed on heads.

I thought he would see my disappointment, say, *Best of three?* But he just put the quarter back in his pocket.

Jade was the woman at Mathers and James who made the bizarre decision to hire me for the junior editor position. She was a tall, thin blond woman in her forties who held the title of creative director. She painted each nail a different color. If you saw her on the street, you wouldn't guess her to be the director of anything.

The interview was short. I did my best to appear somewhat disinterested, as I had in the other interviews I'd landed. I didn't really want a job. Jade said she had a good feeling about me, though, and proclaimed herself to be someone who went with her gut. She did all of the talking—yammering on and on about the opportunities for advancement within the agency. Then she complimented me on my sea-green earrings and said I'd hear back in a few days. Which I did. They offered me a salary of thirty thousand, a small fortune in my eyes. Drew hugged me when I told him, then ran downstairs to the liquor store below us and bought an eight-dollar bottle of red wine.

The punk-rock receptionist brought Jade out to greet me.

"So good to see you again, sweetie," Jade said, hugging me like we were old friends. She smelled like lavender.

I followed her to a tiny, empty cubicle. She waved her hands in front of it dramatically and said, "This will be your personal office."

There was just enough space for a small desk—with a computer and phone—and a chair. I set down my purse.

"Marni, sweetie, meet your new neighbor," she said, peering over the wall into the cubicle next to mine.

The face of a young woman—about my age, maybe a couple years older—peered back. She was wearing thick-rimmed glasses that appeared to be more for style than prescription.

"Hey," she said, and sat again.

"Marni's a junior writer here. You will be proofreading some of her stuff," Jade explained. "See how she's decorated her cubicle?"

Pages of magazines and photos had been tacked to the walls. Next to her computer, a goldfish swam in a small bowl with blue pebbles. A Post-it on the bowl read *Bob.*

"Feel free to decorate your cube, too," Jade said. "We encourage people to express themselves creatively here, right, Marni?"

"Truth," Marni said from over the wall.

Jade looked at her watch and said she had to "scurry" to a meeting. As soon as she was out of sight, Marni came around the corner and sat on my desk.

"Jade is such a fucking weirdo," she said, loud enough for me to look around to see who may have heard. Marni waved me off. "Don't worry, everyone here thinks that."

"I figured she must be crazy because she hired me," I said.

"She probably thinks you have a good aura," Marni said. "That's what she said about me, anyway. And it's total bullshit because my aura sucks."

I laughed.

"I'll give you and your aura the benefit of the doubt, though," she said. "You have to be better than the last guy. He talked to himself."

"Did he get fired?" I asked. "For talking to himself?"

"No, he quit. I think he wanted to pursue comic book writing or something."

I liked Marni.

"Have you worked here long?" I asked.

"Couple years. Started here right out of college. I was gonna go to grad school, but that would have been a grand waste of money."

"Funny you say that. I was supposed to start an English program at Brooklyn College. Today, actually."

"You made a good decision coming here instead."

"I want to go someday, in a couple years, maybe. Right now I'm working while my husband goes to school."

She stepped back, analyzing me up and down, blatantly.

"Forgive me for saying so," she said, hand on her hip with attitude, "but you look *far* too young to have a husband."

"I probably am," I said with a nervous laugh. "College sweethearts. We're about to celebrate our first anniversary."

"I guess that's cute, as long as you sowed your oats or whatever."

I didn't confirm or deny the sowing of oats. I barely knew her.

"Just be careful," she said. She stood and smoothed out a wrinkle in her magenta pencil skirt.

"Careful?"

She sat again.

"Things get weird when the woman is the breadwinner."

She could see I wanted her to explain. She exhaled.

"My ex couldn't handle it when I got promoted to copywriter—fifty grand a year if you twist Jade's arm a little," she said. My eyes got big. "It was like I cut off his dick."

I flinched at the word "dick." She must have sensed my discomfort, because she stood again and waved at the air, swatting away her theory like it was an annoying fruit fly.

"Actually, don't listen to me. What do I know? I just date a bunch of losers."

Her chair creaked as she sat. "I'll tell you about them—my losers—over drinks after work if you want."

"Sure," I said.

I waited until lunch break to go outside and call Drew to tell him I'd be home late. I didn't want Marni to hear me, to see me as a wife who needed to check in with her husband. I spent the afternoon reviewing ad copy, correcting typos, suggesting rewordings, and wondering if I'd ever want to go back to school if I was making fifty grand a year.

SEVEN

Marni and I were friends immediately, the best of friends after only a few weeks. So when she left Mathers and James a year later, lured by a 30 percent increase at another ad agency, we promised each other we'd continue to meet up for after-work drinks. As happens, we kept our promises weekly at first, then monthly, then sporadically.

She called me one Friday to say she'd been promoted to senior copywriter, so we had to celebrate. "Meet me at the Dive," she ordered. Marni always had a beat on the best new bars. And in New York City, there's always a "best new bar."

This one, true to its name, was grungy, even a little dirty. There was a jukebox in the corner, a flickering Budweiser sign, and a sawdust-covered concrete floor, just like at the bar in Jersey my mom used to frequent; she'd get whiskey and I'd get a Sprite. At first glance, it was the type of place where men broke each other's noses on a nightly basis. But when you looked closer, most of the people in the place were white-collar Manhattanites, slumming it for a night with stiff drinks and Bruce Springsteen through the speakers. Even so, it was a decent alternative to the usual pretentiousness of SoHo.

I sat at the bar, between two guys with ties tucked into their button-down shirts. Marni was late, as expected. I ordered a vodka tonic. I'd come into my own, alcohol-wise, ditching the cheap beers and wine coolers of college days and graduating to liquor—on the rocks. It would take a couple difficult years for me to fully appreciate anything straight up.

I'd developed a habit of sitting with my hands under my thighs in bars. It hid my wedding ring and gave me an opportunity to see just how desirable I still was. Marni knew of this game of mine. We played it frequently during our happy hour outings. I kept a collection of business cards and phone numbers scribbled on bar napkins in a desk drawer at the office. Marni said it was weird, that I was longing for the single years I never had. I told her I was just having fun. Maybe I was a little bored. Drew was so occupied with school and I was working long hours at the office. Still, it's not like I ever called any of the guys. And when Marni left Mathers and James, I threw away all the numbers, which makes me think I kept them around to impress her more than anything.

"Boo!" a voice said, so close that I felt warm breath on the back of my neck.

I turned to see Marni in an outlandish faux-fur coat—dyed purple—that went down to her shins. I knew it was faux because Marni had become a staunch vegan, which was somewhat revolutionary in 1997.

"Where in the world did you get that coat?" I asked, touching it.

"I'm doing well, thanks for asking," she said, pulling up a stool and squeezing in next to me, forcing one of the tie-tucked guys to move over. He scoffed, out of Marni's view, which was lucky, because she would have told him to move to the Midwest if he didn't like rudeness.

"Sorry, how are you? Blah, blah, blah," I said.

"Great. And I got this also-great coat at a thrift store near my new apartment. It's so freaking hot outside, but I had to show you." She took it off, elbowing the scoffer next to her in the process.

"New apartment? Geez, how long has it been since we caught up?"

"Last time I saw you, it was snowing outside, if that says anything."

"That's unacceptable."

"You're telling me."

She flagged down the bartender aggressively. Marni was born and raised in New York—the Bronx, to be specific. She was forthright and firm, with little understanding of boundaries or personal space.

"So. New apartment?" I asked her.

"Oh, right. I moved to Queens. Little studio on Shore Front. It takes me, like, ten hours to get anywhere, but I like it," she said. "You guys still in Brooklyn?"

"Same place," I said. When we chose our tiny apartment, I thought we'd be there a year, max. Somehow the months just passed and we just stayed.

"Em, it's time to move on up in the world and out of that shithole."

"Yeah," I said, folding the corners of my napkin distractedly. "So, congrats on the new position. How is it?"

She got her first drink—some kind of dark beer that I thought only men drank—and closed her eyes as she took her first sip.

"Stressful," she said. "Did I tell you they put me on the Durex account?"

"Condoms?"

She rolled her eyes exaggeratedly. "I mean, what am I going to write about condoms? I brought up the idea of just publishing photos of herpes as a campaign, and that didn't go over well."

"You don't say."

"Do they still have you writing about paper towels?"

I nodded. That had become my primary gig at Mathers and James. I'd worked my way up from a proofreading peon to a copywriter. I used the word "absorbent" more times on a daily basis than any one person should. The highlight of the year was when the brand came out with a perforated paper towel "for smaller messes."

"I don't even know why we're talking about work. That's boring. Tell me about you and your hubby." She said "hubby" with a tinge of disdain. Marni never wanted to get married, and had trouble hiding her skepticism of the institution. Once, she compared a husband to a mole: "You sort of just learn to live with it because getting it removed is a big hassle."

"Are you popping out kids soon?" she asked. She hated the idea of children even more than the idea of a husband. "I would strongly advise against it. I can give you free condoms."

"We don't need those," I said, "because we hardly ever have sex."

With Marni, I knew this declaration of accidental celibacy would be shocking. I wanted it to be shocking. I wanted someone to commiserate with me. Before Marni, I never really talked to friends about sex. She had no off-limits topics, a fact that intimidated me at first. I considered her crude, mostly because I was a prude and prone to embarrassment—blushing cheeks and all. But then I got used to her, came to appreciate her frankness. Every woman needs a Marni, someone who says "pussy" and uses "fuck" as an adjective, verb, and noun. She told me she'd use it as an adverb, too, but she wasn't one hundred percent sure what an adverb was, despite making a living as a writer.

"Unless one of you had some kind of genital injury, this is not okay," she said, speaking a little too loudly for my liking.

"We've been busy," I said.

"You're freaking twenty-five years old. You can only use the 'busy' excuse when you're thirty-five or older and have two maniac kids."

"It's true, though. I'm billing ten-hour days at the agency. Drew's finishing up cooking school . . ."

"Is he *still* in school?" she said.

"He just has one summer class left and he's done."

"Finally," she said. "But that's beside the point. Let's go back to the lack of sex. Is it really that exhausting for him to sauté crap all day?"

It was a thought I'd had myself, on the nights I managed to get home by seven and wanted him with all my twenty-five-year-old gusto. His usual refrain: "I'm beat."

"It's not just school. He's talking with his friend—this guy, Domingo—about opening a taco shop," I said, repeating the rationalizations I told myself. "It's stressful for him."

"Domingo? First of all, what kind of name is that? And second of all, tacos are never, ever stressful. For anyone."

"It'll be a gourmet taco shop."

"Oh, *gourmet*. Well, that's stressful," she said sarcastically.

"It's a big deal—going into a food business. They fail all the time."

"So do marriages."

"Oh, Marni, don't be such a cynic."

"I'm a realistic, Em. A *realist*."

She drained the rest of her beer and let the bartender know—with hand signals alone—that she wanted another one. I wasn't even halfway done with my vodka tonic. I guided my skinny cocktail straw around and around my glass with the tip of my index finger.

"Anyway," she said with a disapproving sigh, "what about you? What's next, then?"

"Next?"

"Yeah—what's the plan? I can get you in at my agency, if you want. Could be a pay increase."

"I don't know, I'm pretty happy as I am," I said. "Especially with Drew doing this taco shop. I don't want to shake up things too much."

A guy walked by and hit Marni in the side with his elbow. She glared at him, following him with her eyes all the way across the bar until he went into the restroom. She muttered, "Asshole," under her breath and turned her attention back to me.

"You know what you are?" she said. Whatever it was couldn't be good, judging by her tone. "Complacent."

"Maybe," I said. "Is that so bad?"

"Jesus, you're complacent about being complacent."

"Mar, my life is different from yours," I said, remembering why I let months pass between these meet-ups of ours. "I can't be free and crazy like you."

"I resent the 'crazy,' " she said.

We turned our attention to our drinks.

Then: "Do you ever think about going back to school?"

"I think I'm past that," I said.

And I was. It didn't make sense anymore. I was making good money at the agency. It made me nervous to leave, to put pressure on Drew and his tacos.

Marni looked off, above the top row of bottles at the bar, into a distance I didn't know.

"Don't you ever wonder about all the different paths we could take in life? Like, what if I had married Phil?" Phil was one of Marni's many guys who had come and gone. "Or what if you hadn't married Drew?"

"You could make yourself nuts considering all those what-ifs," I said.

"I'm already nuts, according to you."

"Then you could make *me* nuts."

I pulled a twenty out of my purse and set it on the bar.

"I've driven you away already?" she asked, as I stood.

"I have to go. We're having our moms over for dinner tonight."

Marni laughed a laugh reserved for comedy clubs.

"You don't even like your mother."

"It was Drew's idea," I said.

"You really are two old married farts."

I never minded the commute from Manhattan to Brooklyn. It gave me time to make my daily to-do lists and prepare for the transition from home to work (or vice versa). That's what it felt like—two different worlds, home and work, Manhattan and Brooklyn.

Drew offered to meet me for lunch sometimes, in the city. I said I was too busy, I had a client meeting, I was on a deadline. The truth was the hours between eight and six were my own. Creating taglines, preparing for campaign pitches, brainstorming with the art team. Drew didn't know any details of this and I preferred it that way. He saw me leave in the morning—in my pencil skirts and heels—and he saw me come home, tired. We didn't talk about the in-between. When it was just the two of us, we talked about just that—the two of us.

That night, like every weeknight, I caught the R train at Prince Street, got off at Fourteenth/Union Square, and took the L train the rest of the way. My stop was DeKalb. Home was just a short half-mile walk from there, at the corner of Irving and Menahan. Marni could say what she wanted, but I liked our little place. The subway station was close enough to walk to, even in the dead of winter. We had a favorite bakery down the street where the owners knew us by name. Drew was eyeing a storefront for lease on Knickerbocker, just a short walk away. He didn't want a long commute since he'd already be working long hours—at the beginning, at least. His priority was me, he said.

I took the stairs two at a time and unlocked the door to our apartment. We always locked it, even if we just went up the street for takeout. Inside, my mom and Drew's mom were sitting on our new leather couch—one of our proudest purchases as a couple. It wasn't *new* new, but it was new to us. The previous owner said he'd used it for only a year. He was moving in with his girlfriend and she insisted on keeping her own couch. So it goes.

"There she is," my mom said, the annoyance in her voice making it obvious that I'd kept them waiting. I dropped my purse, kicked off my heels, and hung my keys on a nail on the wall by the door. Bruce gave me his usual evening greeting—a jump that resulted in two clumsy paws on the front of my dress and slobber all over my hands.

I hadn't seen my mom or Drew's mom in months—"just so busy," I told my mom during our intermittent obligatory calls. In college, before I met Drew, I hardly ever called my mother. He was the one who said, "Come on, Em. You should try harder. Family is family." Any rebuttals I had—*She never tried very hard*, or *She should call me*—sounded childish. So I tried, begrudgingly.

Drew's mom looked more frail than I remembered, and older, like a woman in her seventies instead of her early fifties. I watched her hands—trying not to stare—and they were trembling uncontrollably. Both of them. It had been just the left one before. It seemed difficult for her to stand from the couch when she hugged me, and even more difficult to sit back down. She held on to my arm—not as a sign of affection, but for balance. I felt the weight of her, little that there was, leaning into me. I gave her a smile, an it's-okay, I-got-you smile, and she tried to reciprocate, but her face didn't seem to cooperate.

Drew was at the stove, donning his chef's hat and apron.

"Whatcha making?" I said, wrapping my arms around him from the back. I always loved how my head fell just on his shoulder, without having to stand on my tiptoes.

"Shrimp scampi," he said. "I opened a bottle of white. You want some?"

"That's a ridiculous question," I said, reaching for one of the wineglasses that were permanent fixtures on our kitchen counter. He poured for me, like a fancy waiter, one hand behind his back and all. One of his culinary schoolteachers made his own wine and gave Drew free bottles. This had become our routine every night—gourmet meals and homemade wine. His cooking had really improved. When he first started out, every night felt like an experiment with a strong probability of failure. I'd even have a snack on my last leg of the L Line, worried about going hungry. I hadn't done that in months, though.

"I'll set the table," I said, referring to the round wood table we'd inherited from his mom. We covered it with a white tablecloth because it still showed evidence of when he'd drawn on it with markers as a kid.

"So Drew was telling us about his taco shop idea," my mom

said, emphasis on the word "idea," as if it were fantastical, as if it would never be a reality. She had her feet up on our coffee table, wine in her hand. I guessed she was on her second or third glass.

"Pretty exciting, huh?" I said, laying out the silverware. We didn't have cloth napkins, so I just folded paper towels in half.

"Restaurants fail all the time, you know," my mom said. I hated her for saying that, then remembered I'd said the same thing to Marni.

"I'm sure it'll be successful," Drew's mom snapped, with as much force in her voice as she could muster. Whatever it was that was making her hands shake and disrupting her balance and disabling her facial expressions was slowly taking her voice, too.

"It's a big venture for a kid," my mom said.

I looked over to Drew, expecting him to refute her, but he just tended to the scampi, pretending not to hear.

"We're not kids, Mom," I said.

Drew dished out the scampi into four bowls and brought them to the table, along with a salad.

"Dinner's on," he said.

"It's just good he's finishing with that school," my mom said, unwilling to let it go. She never liked the idea of Drew going to cooking school. She thought he should get what she called a "regular job," like the one I had. She said that was a man's responsibility to his wife. I tried to explain that times were different, that men and women were partners now, but she just shook her head and said, "It's just not right." I reminded her that she didn't need a man to take care of her. She said, "But I sure as hell wanted one."

"I think you'll realize I'll be successful when you try this," Drew said, indicating the meal on the table. My mom took her seat and I walked Drew's mom to hers, my hand on her lower back. She slouched against her chair and groaned like she was exhausted by the trek from the couch to the table. My mom poured herself another glass, finishing off the bottle.

His mom took the first bite. "It's delicious, honey," she said.

"There's no such thing as shrimp scampi tacos, though," my mom said, still blowing cooling breaths on her first bite.

"Mom, please," I said. "Drew makes amazing tacos."

"We're going to have a great menu," Drew said, maintaining his smile, per usual. Nothing rattled him. "We'll have carnitas tacos, chicken tacos, portabello mushroom tacos for the vegetarians."

"Well, I hope it all works out," my mom said. She took a long gulp of wine, like it was juice on a hot day.

"And then grandkids," Drew's mom chimed in.

She was focused intently on her meal, concentrating on stopping her hands from shaking so she could control her fork. They wouldn't stop, though. It took her a few minutes to take a proper bite. More often than not, the food fell off the fork before she could get it to her mouth.

"Grandkids?" my mom said, like someone had just suggested we all take a spaceship to the moon. "They're still kids themselves!"

"Mom," I said, "stop."

"It's okay," Drew said, ever the pacifier. "I think we have a few years before kids."

"Maybe not *that* long," I said.

He looked at me with furrowed brows, asking me with the creases in his forehead what I meant. We hadn't discussed kids much, with the exception of far-off fantasies presented whimsically in moments of romance: "I bet our kids get your eyes," and "I can't wait to tell bedtime stories."

Drew looked down, resumed eating.

"How have you been doing, Mom?" he asked, changing the subject.

"Fine," she said, eyes on her fork, just a few inches away from making it into her mouth. Her bowl was still mostly full and the rest of us were halfway done.

"Did you see that new doctor?" he asked her. Drew was on her case about this frequently. He called her a few times a week, checking in, asking her about the shaking hands and what the doctors said. She always claimed they didn't know what they were talking about. She doctor-hopped, saying she needed to find someone she trusted. I told Drew, "She doesn't like what the doctors are telling her. She wants to find someone who will lie to her." He said it wasn't that. I didn't know who was in stronger denial—Drew or his mother.

"I saw him," she said. She scrunched up her nose. "No good."

"Does he think it's Parkinson's, too?"

That's what all the doctors were diagnosing—Parkinson's. She didn't want to believe it because there's not a damn thing out there to cure it.

"That's what they all say," she said. She paused in her eating, put her hands in her lap so we couldn't see them. It was like she was trying to hide the evidence of her errors in judgment. "But I found a new doctor who has a different theory."

Her eyes were wide with hope and excitement. They seemed even bigger since her face had become so gaunt.

"He thinks it's a complex bacterial infection. He suggested doing this thing called chelation therapy to remove toxins from my blood."

"Sounds like a quack," my mom said. I gave her a hard stare.

"What's his specialty?" I asked, trying to be respectful.

"He's a chiropractor," she said, avoiding our eye contact, "but he has so much experience with these strange illnesses."

"I don't care what he does, as long as you get better," Drew said. He reached under the table to take her hands in his. I wondered if they stopped shaking when he held them.

We finished our meals—all of us except his mom. It was no wonder she was losing weight at such an alarming rate. When alone, in her own home, she probably didn't even bother. A bowl of cereal could take an hour.

I cleared the table and started washing the dishes—my usual duty—while Drew offered our moms little ramekins of tiramisu he'd made earlier that day.

"I'm going to take them home," he said, when the ramekins were licked clean. "Don't wait up for me."

He thought he was being sweet by saying that. *Don't wait up for me.* But I wanted to wait up for him. I wanted his command to be, *Be naked when I get home.*

After I put the dishes away, I got into bed, naked, except for black lacy underwear I'd found at the back of my drawer. I stared at the ceiling and waited to hear Drew's steps on the stairs. It would take him a while. He had to drop off his mom in Newark, then my mom in Irvington. Bruce jumped up in bed next to me and I just lay there, flat on my back, one arm at my side, the other draped over the dog, and waited.

He put his key in the door around eleven o' clock. I could tell he was tiptoeing through the apartment, trying not to wake me. He was considerate that way even though I rarely was. The wood floors creaked despite his conscientiousness. He turned the knob on the bedroom door slowly, but that creaked, too. He peered in at Bruce, who started wagging his tail. Drew shushed him.

"I'm awake," I said.

"I thought you'd be dead tired after this week."

"I am. I can't sleep. I'm antsy."

He sat on the edge of the bed and took off his shoes and socks, then stood up to pull off his jeans and unbutton his flannel shirt.

"Antsy about what?"

"I don't know. Something."

When he was down to just his boxers—blue-and-gray-checkered, worn thin in the crotch from too many wears and too many washes—he climbed into bed next to me. Bruce followed him.

"I'm sorry about my mom," I said.

"Nah, she's fine."

"No, she's not. She's rude. She's always been rude."

He was lying flat on his back, like me. I rolled onto my side, facing him, bending my elbow so I could prop up my head on my hand.

"Then I'm sorry about *your* mom," I said.

"What about her?" he said, looking at me, his eyes innocent and concerned with nothing.

"She's getting worse, Drew," I said. Then: "It's pretty obvious."

He turned to Bruce, nuzzled into him. He needed the dog in these situations, for the distraction.

I touched Drew's stomach, grazed his sides with my fingertips in the way that gave him goose bumps all over. He continued giving his affections to the dog. I tried harder: kissed his cheek, sucked on his earlobe. He always liked when I sucked on his earlobe.

"It's been a while," I whispered.

He knew what I was referring to. "I've had so much on my mind," he said. He picked me up with an ease I appreciated and put me on top of him, one thigh on each side.

"I should be one of those things on your mind."

"You are."

"Prove it."

We had sex the way people do when it's forbidden, when there's not much time, when niceties are excluded. There were no soft whispers, no slow stroking of each other's naked bodies, no finesse. It was fast and furious and over in five minutes.

I rolled off him and looked at his face—shiny with sweat, afterglow. I caught my breath.

"I've never seen those black panties before," he said, as I pulled them back on.

"I forgot I had them."

"You shouldn't forget something like that."

We laughed. I pulled the sheets up to my chin. They were cool. I'd shove them off at some point in the night.

"Do you think we're complacent?" I asked him.

He looked at me, perplexed.

I clarified: "Doesn't it feel like one day just kind of rolls into the next?"

"Sure," he said, like it was a good thing. Maybe it was.

"But are we kind of . . . blah?"

He leaned over and kissed me.

"I'm not. You are," he teased. "I'm going to make breakfast tacos in the morning. Eggs, salsa, black beans. They won't be blah. You can tell me if they're good enough for the restaurant."

"Sounds good," I said, forcing a yawn, not because I was tired, but because I was trying to put my body through the motions of being tired, to trick it.

He turned out the light. We didn't have room for nightstands, so we kept a standing lamp near his side of the bed. We lay in the darkness, both still awake after ten minutes or so, as evidenced by the rustling of the sheets.

"You really want to wait a few years to have kids?" I asked.

"I don't know," he said.

"Yes, you do."

"You want to have kids *now*?"

"I asked you first," I said.

"I don't know. We're young still. I don't even have a career yet."

"You will."

"There's too much we have to do first."

"Like?"

"I don't know. Things."

We shuffled around the sheets uncomfortably.

"It would be cool to be young parents," I said.

"Em," he said, his tone asking me for permission or forgiveness or something, "I'm not ready."

There wasn't much I could say to argue with that.

"Is it selfish that I want you all to myself for a while?" he asked, pressing his nose into my cheek, giving me a kiss. In the darkness, he only got half my mouth.

"Yes, you're a selfish jackass," I teased, using one finger to press his nose and push him away.

"You know what we should do?" he said, with the excitement I always loved about him. "Finally go on our honeymoon."

See, Marni was wrong. I was wrong. We weren't complacent.

"Yes!" I said.

"Where do you want to go?"

Most people, when asked this question, name Paris or Tahiti—somewhere exotic and far, somewhere once-in-a-lifetime, somewhere with a different language and different food, somewhere magical.

But, ever-practical, taking into consideration my hectic job and the tentative taco shop opening, I said:

"How about California?"

"California it is," he said.

He gave me his good-night kiss and I tried to let the thought of our honeymoon soothe me to sleep, like a nursery rhyme. We'd run from ride to ride through Disneyland, as giddy as the little kids around us. We'd sleep late in fancy hotel rooms, roll around naked in bed, order ice cream for breakfast, tell the cleaning service, *Come back later.* We'd walk hand in hand on the Hollywood Walk of Fame, see a movie at the Chinese Theatre. We'd eat at all the famous chefs' restaurants and daydream aloud about Drew being the next Wolfgang Puck. We'd sunbathe on wide stretches of beach, reading books. It'd been so long since we'd made time to read. In college, we'd said we couldn't imagine a life without books, and here we were.

I counted the attractions like sheep. But it didn't help. I was still antsy. I looked over to Drew, wanting to talk more, ask when we would go to California, but he was asleep. A moment later, he started snoring—a common occurrence after too much wine. Even if he was awake, I didn't know what I wanted to say. Something was still bothering me, gnawing at me, but I couldn't say what. It was that feeling of having a sought-after word on the tip of your tongue and not being able to articulate it. Neurons fire in search of it, unable to rest until the answer is plucked from a mass of useless knowledge. I got no answers, no resolution, just a bunch of neurons firing until dawn.

EIGHT

When I first moved to California, I had horrible insomnia. Some nights, I worried that I would be found and taken back to New York. Some nights, I worried that I wouldn't. I didn't know what I was doing in California, pregnant, alone. In weak moments, I imagined relief at seeing Drew's face at the door, saying, *The jig's up*. Now, all these years later, that thought gives me goose bumps.

There was this one time when past and present collided, when the jig could have been up. Claire was eight. It was a Saturday and I took her to a craft fair in Topanga Canyon. I'd seen signs for it. I had the day off. I needed an activity for my daughter. There's this pressure as a parent to entertain your child. It still weighs on me.

We were looking at beaded necklaces when I saw a woman approaching out of the corner of my eye. She was making a beeline straight for me. Nobody made beelines straight for me because I didn't know anyone well. I had acquaintances, mostly mothers of Claire's friends or regulars from the bar, but they wouldn't approach me with such intent.

"Emily Morris?" the voice boomed.

It was as if someone in the crowd of people had yelled, *Bomb!*

It was all I could do not to duck under the table. Claire, of course, just kept looking at the necklaces. The name Emily Morris meant—and still means—nothing to her.

The woman stopped right next to me, put her hand on my forearm.

"It is you," she said.

I looked up tentatively. "Excuse me?" I said, trying my best to look perplexed instead of petrified.

"It's Jade," she said, "from Mathers and James."

Despite the years that had passed, she looked exactly the same, except that her hair was now dyed auburn red. She must have been in her sixties, but her skin was still porcelain-white and relatively wrinkle-free. I stared at the hand that was still clasping my forearm. Each of her fingernails was painted a different color, just like back then.

"I'm sorry?" I said.

Claire was listening to us now, watching this strange woman attempt to convince me of who I was.

"I was your boss! In New York! *Eons* ago!"

She was so excited about this fateful meeting. I felt bad letting her down. It was the first time in California that I kind of wanted to be Emily Morris, for just a second.

"I don't know—"

"You never lived in New York?" She was genuinely baffled.

I shook my head. "Sorry," I said.

"It's just incredible," she said. "The hair is different, but the face. I remember faces. And auras. I remember auras."

It made bizarre sense that she would be here, in hippie Topanga Canyon, looking at homemade jewelry.

"Maybe I have a twin," I said. I attempted a laugh. It came out choked, false.

She looked at Claire, long and hard, then back at me. Her smile suggested that she knew I was lying, but that she'd accepted it, moved on already. Jade, seeker of peace.

"Well," she said, "maybe you do."

She finally released my arm and said, "Sorry to bother you. Have a beautiful day."

I said, "You, too," and turned back to the jewelry, fiddling with pieces, pretending that this encounter hadn't completely unnerved me.

"That was weird," Claire said, picking up a bracelet and turning it over in her hand.

"Really weird," I said. I helped her with the clasp. "You want it?" I would have bought her anything in that moment.

"Can I?" she said. I nodded.

We walked to the cashier and she looked up at me and said, "You don't even look like an Emily."

That night, I did not sleep.

The night before the biopsy, my old friend insomnia returns. I make the mistake of going online, researching inflammatory breast cancer. *Rare. Very aggressive. Invasive. Progresses rapidly, often within a matter of weeks or months. Poor prognosis.* Then there is this fact, confirmed by many sources: Women with stage three have a forty percent survival rate at five years, and women with stage four have an eleven percent survival rate at five years.

It's that eleven percent that keeps me up until sunrise.

Only eleven percent of people survive five years.

That means eighty-nine percent of people die.

That means by the time Claire is eighteen, she no longer has a mom.

Eighteen. Technically a grown-up. This might comfort some mothers with cancer, but not me. In my life, all the truly difficult and important things happened well after I crossed the threshold to adulthood.

Claire says I look like I need a cup of a coffee, then proceeds to pour me one. She drinks the milk in her cereal bowl, turned pink by her Froot Loops, and tells me she'll meet me in the car. She's ready for this day that I dread.

I drop her off at school, wish her luck on her math test, and watch her walk away, a hop in her step. Claire gets excited for math tests—for any test, actually. She's an overachiever who has somehow dodged the title of "nerd." I don't know how she does it. I was never smart or popular. "You're very average, hon, flying under the radar," my mom once told me, as a compliment. The other kids like Claire. One of them—a boy—runs up to her. Maybe that's Tyler. She's mentioned him—"just a friend," she insisted, though her blush indicated otherwise. They walk side by side. They're both lanky. She's slightly taller than him. He says something that makes her throw her head back and laugh. Despite my nine A.M. appointment, I smile.

The biopsy is, in a word, unpleasant. The needle is the size of a pencil. I leave knowing that they have a chunk of my breast tissue—and my fate—in their lab. They tell me the results should be back Monday morning. On my way out, they say, "Have a good weekend," as if that's possible.

On Saturday, Claire and I go to the Melrose flea market. She is on the hunt for a pair of vintage cowboy boots. We buy pink lemonade and a big salted pretzel, passing it back and forth between us, pulling off pieces until it's gone. She tries on a pair of boots that are three sizes too big and asks if she should stuff the toes with toilet paper. I ask her why she wants cowboy boots so badly and she can't say anything besides, "I just do." Instead, she buys a miniature succulent in a tiny clay pot, clutching it in her palm like it's a living pet.

On Saturday night, I take her to Heather's house for a sleepover, exchange a few forgettable pleasantries with Heather's mom, whose name I can never remember—Melissa? Carissa? Something with an "issa." Then I work my shift at the bar. I make the usual small talk with the usual customers. Bill's in construction and comes in every Friday and Saturday night because "those are the best days to meet ladies." It is a very rare occurrence for a female to set foot in Al's Place, but Bill never seems to realize this. Arnie is a sixty-something alcoholic who's at the bar at least four times a week, for several hours at a time. He doesn't get sloppy, so we don't cut him off. The only way I can tell he's actually drunk is when he starts talking about his daughter, who, incidentally, died of breast cancer a couple years ago. It's not clear if he was an alcoholic before that.

At the end of my shift, nearing two A.M., as Al is shuffling out Bill and Arnie, who, somehow, have a track record of getting home safely, I fill a frosted glass with Budweiser from the tap and take a sip.

"You okay there, Con?" Al says.

See, I never drink at work. Or, hardly ever. Al knows me well enough to know that I only drink at work when I'm celebrating something or when I'm very upset. The last time I drank at work was when Claire got first place in a science fair. I came in bragging, one of those annoying parents everyone despises, and Al said, "Well, we gotta drink to that," and we did. Before that, there was the time JT had a heart attack and I got shit-faced on gin and tonics. I thought he was going to die. My despondence surprised me. I'd grown rather fond of JT, I guess. It's not that we're particularly close, but he's always checked in on Claire and me at least once a week. He cares. He never gives me a hard time about being late on rent. Whenever something goes wrong with the water heater or the air conditioner or whatever else at the cottage, he deals with it. Claire doles out hugs whenever he stops by. I heard her refer to him as "like a grandpa" once when she was talking to Heather. The heart attack didn't kill him, though, didn't even come close. "The Big Man in the Sky doesn't want anything to do with me," he said. And then he made fun of me for fretting.

"I'm okay," I say. "Just got some things on my mind."

It's tempting to tell Al everything. I know he'd wrap his big, tattooed arm around me and tell me everything will be fine, and it would be tough to doubt him. He'd tell me to take some time off. He'd send me home with a bottle of his finest whiskey. I can't tell him, though, not yet. I don't even have the results yet. Maybe it's nothing. It has to be nothing.

"If you say so, little lady," he says, wiping down the counter and then throwing the damp towel around his neck.

I tell him I'll lock up, which is my way of saying I want to drink alone.

I'm hungover on Sunday, but Claire and I do our usual beach walk anyway. She once asked me, around the same time she asked who her father was, why we didn't go to church. I didn't want to explain what an atheist was, or that I was one, so I told her the beach was our church. That began a Sunday tradition of running through the waves before any of the sunbathers show up, when dedicated surfers dot the horizon.

"I am so looking forward to this week," she says, rolling up the legs of her jeans so she can let the waves crash into her.

"Why's that?" I ask, trying to share her enthusiasm for this upcoming week, this week when I find out if I have cancer. I vacillate—back and forth, back and forth—between thinking it's truly impossible I have cancer to thinking I have a few weeks to live. I've decided it's best to prepare for the worst and be nicely surprised if it turns out okay. That must be what the professionals—these mammogram-takers, these biopsy-readers—do. No sense getting hopes up, implying all alarms are false. If they do that and the news turns out bad, the shock could kill someone faster than cancer itself.

"I forgot, I didn't tell you, I'm going to submit my name to run for class president."

"Really?" I say.

"Really," she says. "Wouldn't that be the best thing ever?"

I miss the overused superlatives of youth.

"I'm so proud of you, sweetie," I say, reaching for her and pulling her into my chest with so much force that we almost fall backward onto the sand.

"God, Mom, what's wrong with you?" she says, worming her way out of my embrace.

"I can help you make posters and stuff."

She shrugs. "Sure, if you want." She doesn't really need me to help, that much is clear.

She does a spontaneous cartwheel. Her enthusiasm, this high she's on, scares me. If I have to tell her I'm sick, the comedown could be crushing.

"Just know I'll be proud whether you win or lose," I say, doing my best to temper her excitement.

She looks at me like I'm growing a second head. "Why are you acting so weird?"

"I'm not acting weird," I say. "I just want you to be realistic."

But, see, kids her age aren't that interested in reality.

She does another cartwheel and says, "What's the fun in that?"

The call comes around noon on Monday. I know it's the doctor's office because the number is blocked. I'm working a shift at the bar. It's quiet. Mondays get busy, but not until after six. I abandon my post and go into the back office. Even though there's nobody else in the bar, I still feel the need to hole up somewhere.

After three rings: "Hello?"

"Connie?" a voice says, in lieu of the expected, *May I please speak to Connie Prynne?*

"Yes?"

"It's Dr. Tan."

I sit down in Al's leather chair, with its ornately curved wood arms. It's meant for a lawyer's office, absolutely absurd for a bar.

She takes a deep breath, which is not good.

"They got your biopsy report back. I wanted to call you myself," she says.

So we can grab a drink and cheers to good test results?

"I'm afraid it's cancer."

I wait a beat and then say, "I'm afraid, too," an uneasy attempt at humor.

She is silent.

And then she launches into a three-minute description of the much-feared-but-needed next steps. She says we'll need to see if it's spread to the lymph nodes, determine the stage of it. There will be tests. She rattles off some of them—ultrasound, CT scan, bone scan, breast MRI. She says the oncologist will likely recommend six cycles of chemotherapy. She doesn't explain what a cycle is and I don't ask because I'm not ready to know. I'm still stuck on "I'm afraid it's cancer." After the chemotherapy, she says they'll likely do a mastectomy, then radiation to target the "residual cancer." She ends her diatribe with, "This is an aggressive cancer, Connie, but people beat it."

Eleven percent of people, I want to say. But I don't. Because I don't want her to confirm that.

"I've asked my colleagues for some great recommendations of oncologists in the area. Do you have a pen?"

I say I do, and then I dig through Al's drawer to find one. He's got more packets of Skittles than he does pens. He gives them to Claire when she comes.

On the back of an electricity bill, I scribble down the names and phone numbers of strangers who may be responsible for saving my life.

"I'm sorry to have to tell you this," she says.

"I'm sorry, too."

"If there's anything I can—"

"Do I have to tell Claire?" I ask.

"Claire?"

She delivered my daughter, but she doesn't know her name offhand. She has so many patients besides me. Suddenly I feel very alone.

"My daughter," I say.

She takes another ominous deep breath.

"Connie," she says, "the treatment is tough. You'll feel ill. You're going to lose your hair."

And for some reason, that's the news of this phone call that makes me cry. I cover the phone with one hand, my mouth with the other.

"Claire will understand," she says, in a stiff doctor's attempt at consolation. Doctors are trained in medicine, not kindness. They can't be blamed for their missteps.

"That's the problem," I say. "She'll understand."

NINE

Drew's restaurant, the Modern Taco, opened on November 9, 1997, and closed on October 3, 1998. It didn't even make it a year. It should have shut down in summer, but Drew wanted to give it a chance and I couldn't bring myself to discourage him.

We knew starting the restaurant would demand large up-front costs. Domingo, Drew's partner, knew that, too. He was the one with most of the funds to invest. We contributed the twenty grand in savings we'd accumulated in the years I'd been at Mathers and James. I told Drew that was all we had, which was a lie. I'd put five thousand in a separate account. A secret account. A just-in-case account I didn't tell him about because he would have said preparing for failure would jinx any success. Who knows, maybe that was true.

Domingo should have known better. He was older—in his late thirties—and claimed to have grown up in the restaurant business. His father, he said, owned a very successful Cuban restaurant in Queens. He'd been saving up for his own taco shop for years. He had eighty grand to prove it, so we took him seriously. We trusted him.

It wasn't the food that was the problem. Drew developed the

menu—a variety of tacos, from the usual to the exotic. There were short rib tacos and pork belly tacos and wild mushroom tacos and lobster tacos and black bean tacos. Every day he offered a special: fried chicken tacos or rabbit tacos or plain ol' ground beef tacos. He went to different markets around Brooklyn, seeking ingredients that called out to him. It made him feel alive, he said. He spent fourteen hours a day at the restaurant—cooking, mingling with the customers. They loved his food. Some became regulars, stopping in for a couple tacos on lunch break. So, no, the food wasn't the problem.

The problem was Domingo. Domingo was in charge of running the day-to-day business. Maybe because most of the up-front money was his, he took to spending it without consulting Drew. Not that Drew would have helped. Drew wasn't a businessman; he was a chef. "An artist," he liked to say.

Domingo insisted on top-of-the-line equipment, better advertising, new décor. They bought heavy rustic tables from a designer furniture store when they could have scoured the classifieds or yard sales for better deals. Domingo hired three servers when they really only needed two—and he paid them ten bucks an hour when they should have made eight, at most. His rationale was that he wanted to attract top-notch employees. That was the thing with Domingo—his ideas were good in theory, but only in theory. For the first two months, he didn't even use a bookkeeping system. It wasn't until February that he realized they were way too far in the red.

There were other issues, too. It cost a thousand dollars to fix a plumbing problem that caused the drains in the kitchen to back up. During the dinner rush, customers said they couldn't find anywhere to park on the street. A few complained about the cost of the tacos—three or four bucks a pop. Street-cart tacos were a dollar each, after all. These were gourmet. They knew that. They appreciated the special ingredients, the sophistication. But a four-dollar taco was a four-dollar taco.

Drew was convinced it would get better. Sure, they had kinks to work out, but that was just part of opening a restaurant. He maintained his enthusiasm, his almost manic energy, for months. It wasn't until July that he came to me, in bed, just before midnight, smelling of sweat and food, and said, "I think we're in trouble." He fell onto the mattress, flat on his stomach, his head turned to one side, not facing me. I put my hand on his back—hot and sticky. All I said was, "I know, babe."

After the "Closed" sign went up in the front window, I let Drew wallow in self-pity. There's a certain equilibrium in all relationships and I knew I had to counteract his sadness for us to maintain some kind of normalcy. I perked up for his benefit. I assured him we'd be fine, even though I had doubts. It was usually his role to be optimistic—to a nearly delusional degree, at times—but he abandoned that post and I felt compelled to occupy it. The restaurant was separate from us; it could fail, but we wouldn't. Yes, we lost our investment, but we would be okay. I told him about the five thousand dollars, hoping that would raise his spirits, but the fact that I'd had the secret account depressed him more.

The thing is, I'd always known Drew was a dreamer; I just never knew what would happen when the dreams fell apart.

He'd never been much of a drinker. We had wine with dinner most nights, and there was always a six-pack of beer in the fridge, but he was never the type who needed a drink. In fact, he was downright cautious about becoming that type. His mom had told him that his father had had a drinking problem, and whether that was true or a lie constructed by a woman bitter about her husband leaving, Drew lived in fear of the power of genetics. But about a week after the restaurant closed up, I came home from work to find him on the couch with a bottle of Jack Daniel's next to him—a cliché scene if I ever saw one. I had to restrain myself from rolling my eyes. I'd asked Marni, over drinks after work, "When can I tell him to start looking for another job?" and she said, "Why should you have to *tell* him? He should know." She was right. But I understood Drew. I knew what the taco shop meant to him.

"We need to get you out of this," I said, sitting with him on the couch, reaching my hand into his bag of chips, as if to say, *I will join you in this misery because I love you*. Bruce jumped up on the couch with us, climbing over our laps, tail wagging.

"Bruce agrees with me," I said.

Drew just sighed his defeated sigh.

"I have an idea," I said. "Let's do our California trip."

We'd never actually planned it. We kept putting it off, saying, "Let's buy tickets after the restaurant opens," then, "Let's buy tickets after the restaurant gets a bit more stable," then nothing.

Drew took a sip of his whiskey.

"What?" he said, his tone already discounting whatever visions I had in my head.

"Our honeymoon. We should do it. Finally." I put my hand on his leg. I was trying, so hard.

"I don't think it's the best time to be going on a trip. We just lost all our money and I have no job."

"Right—you have no job. So you have free time. And I haven't taken a vacation since I started at Mathers and James. We've got to do it while we can."

I'd always resented the cheerleaders in high school. Now I had become one.

"It can be part honeymoon, part twenty-seventh birthday celebration."

"What's so special about turning twenty-seven?" he said.

"We're going to find out really soon."

I played with the little hairs on the back of his neck. He fidgeted.

"I don't know," he said, leaning his head back until it banged against the wall.

"Drew, it's all going to be okay," I said. "We'll look back on this and see it as a brief hard time when we were young. We have time to make back the money we lost. We have all kinds of opportunities."

As soon as I said that, I worried he'd ask me to specify those opportunities. Thankfully, he didn't.

"If you want to go to California, if that will make you happy, then we'll go. But I can't guarantee it'll make me happy."

I kissed him on the lips, expecting no reciprocation of affection and getting none.

"You don't have to guarantee anything."

I booked the tickets the next day, leaving five days later, on October 16. I would have preferred to go in summertime, but everyone at work said there were no seasons in California anyway, that fall was as good a time as any, maybe even better because there would be fewer tourists. The Saturday before, I found an antique ivory suitcase—one of those hard-sided ones—at a secondhand store in Williamsburg. It had rusted buckles and read, in black lettering, "Going to California" next to a peeling-off palm tree decal. I bought it, even though it wasn't the most practical luggage choice. Not much would fit in it, but that was okay. We were only going for five days. I just needed one swimsuit, a few pairs of shorts, T-shirts, a couple nice dresses for hoped-for fancy dinners.

"Can you help me with this thing?" I said to Drew. I'd managed to stuff everything into the suitcase, but was having trouble closing it and fastening the buckles. We were flying out of JFK the next morning.

"Sure can," he said. His attitude had improved since I'd booked the trip. He'd distracted himself with looking up activities for us to do while we were there. He wanted to see a taping of *The Price Is Right*. He wanted to go to Universal Studios. He wanted to get a map of where the celebrities live. It would have been fair to remind him that we only had five days, but I didn't want to dampen his spirits, so I said nothing, let him think we could do it all.

He sat on the suitcase, his weight closing it enough for me to snap the buckles shut. We high-fived.

"Did you get Bruce's food ready?"

The plan was to drop off Bruce at Marni's place, bring her dinner as a thank-you for taking care of him while we were gone.

"All set. I've got his leash and some toys in a bag."

It was this, these preparations, that were getting Drew out of his funk. He was a person in need of a new daydream and this trip was it.

"All right, get him in the car and I'll meet you downstairs," I said.

He called to Bruce and teased him cruelly by saying, "Wanna go for a walk?" Whenever Bruce got really excited, he pranced all over the wood floors, his nails click-clacking with unbridled zeal. Drew closed the door behind them and I did a check of everything on my mental packing list. I went into the kitchen to grab a Ziploc bag for my toothbrush and that's when the phone rang.

"Hello," an old woman said, her voice shaky with age. "My name is Gladys."

Drew's grandmothers had passed away before I met him; my mom insisted I never meet my grandmother (for reasons never divulged to me). I had no idea who this Gladys woman was. I walked the phone into the kitchen with me, stretching the cord as far as it would go, and grabbed a plastic baggie out of a drawer. All I had to do was put my toothbrush in it, throw it in my carry-on, and I'd be done packing, ready to go.

"I think you have the wrong number," I said.

"Wait," she said. "Is Andrew there?"

"He's not here at the moment. Can I ask who this is?"

"I'm Janet's neighbor."

Janet. Drew's mother. I didn't want to ask the next question because I feared where it would lead: "Is everything okay?"

"I'm afraid she's taken a fall," the woman said. "I saw it. She was going out to get her mail and she fell right there on the cement."

I sat on the couch, feeling my excitement fizzle.

"Is she all right?"

"I couldn't say, dear," she said. "Hit her head pretty bad—got a goose egg on it. And it seems she broke her wrist. She's asking for Andrew. I found the number on the bulletin board in her kitchen."

At that moment, I heard Drew in the stairwell, taking the steps two at a time, still possessing the enthusiasm I'd lost so suddenly. He opened the door and, not realizing I was on the phone, said, "Bruce's in the car. Ready to go!" Then he saw the look on my face and he knew.

"Gladys," I said into the phone. "We'll be right there."

We didn't speak until we turned onto the 280 West.

"What time does our flight leave in the morning?" Drew asked.

"Eight o'clock," I said. "We should be at the airport no later than seven."

It felt good to talk like this, as if we were still going. It also felt pointless.

Drew's mom still lived in the same house where Drew grew up—a three-bed, one-bath in a bad enough neighborhood that the front door and all the windows had wrought-iron bars on them. When we got close enough, we saw his mom sitting on the front lawn—or what used to be the lawn. The grass had gone brown and straw-like. The last time we saw it—in spring—it was still green. Summer had taken a toll.

She was holding her arm close to her, cradling it against her chest, her face contorted into a look of perplexing pain. The goose egg Gladys mentioned was, in fact, there, right smack in the middle of her forehead. An old woman—Gladys, most likely—was sitting beside her, looking up and down the street for help to arrive. My heart palpitated when I realized it was us, Drew and me, who were the help.

Drew parked in front and we got out hurriedly. He went right to his mom.

"What happened?" He squatted down and made a motion to

take her arm in his hands for inspection. She held her arm closer to her, like a feral animal protecting its offspring.

I didn't know my role in all this, so I thanked Gladys for calling us. She reached at me with her wrinkly hand, asking me for help up. She was as frail as any old person, but her weight was heavy. I almost fell backward pulling her to her feet. She took a moment to balance herself, then began a slow walk back to her house, shaking her head and muttering, "Someone's got to look out for people in this neighborhood."

When I turned back to Drew and his mom, he was still trying to coax her into showing him her arm. I crouched down next to them.

"It's the stupid cracks in the cement that made me fall," she said bitterly. Her voice was faint. I could only hear her if I was within a one-foot radius. "They haven't repaired the sidewalks in *decades*."

I glanced out toward the mailbox, along the path she would take from her front door to retrieve her mail, trying to find the alleged cracks. I didn't see any capable of tripping up someone.

"Ma, I've got to take a look," Drew said, with the authority and sternness of a professional. I fancied him a doctor in that moment, wanting the diagnosis to be a bad bruise, requiring ice and nothing more.

Reluctantly, she released the tense hold on her arm and let Drew look at it. The moment he touched it, she clenched her teeth fiercely and a tear started a diagonal journey from her eye to the crease of her nose. It wasn't just a bruise. Drew looked at me, regret and apology in his eyes.

"Ma, it's broken. It's definitely broken," he said. "We've got to get you to the hospital."

She said something neither of us heard. We both leaned closer.

"I don't have health insurance," she said. She bit her lip—either a response to the pain or an attempt to hold back tears. She seemed ashamed, embarrassed. She couldn't look at us directly.

"Don't worry about that now," I said, though I was worried about it. I could see the bills in the mail, having to pay them.

"Come on," Drew said, taking her good arm, her right arm, trying to pull her up. In the excruciating time it took him to help her stand, I realized how incapacitated she was. Drew's biceps were flexing, straining to lift her. She had no strength left. Neither did Gladys, really, but Gladys must have been close to ninety. Drew's mom was fifty-three. Her body had gone flaccid. When she was upright, I saw her for all she was—emaciated, sick.

"Emmy, can you get my purse?" she said in a whisper. I imagined her vocal cords had gone limp just like her muscles. Whatever was plaguing her was siphoning all her strength, one day at a time.

"Of course," I said, relieved to have a task.

I slid past them, went to the front door, undid the latch. What I found inside was astonishing. I gasped, audibly. We hadn't visited in a while and that was even more apparent when I was inside, in a living room that contradicted its name. It smelled like death: gone-bad food, mold, layers of damp dust, mouse droppings. And, if I wasn't mistaken, there was the faint, slightly sweet smell of urine. How often was she not making it to the bathroom in time?

The coffee table was covered with mail—some opened, some unopened—and protein bar wrappers. That must have been what she was subsisting on; cooking anything would require too much effort. A fallen stack of newspapers occupied half the couch. It was like she hadn't had time to clean, but she had all the time in the world; she'd been on disability from work for months. Time wasn't the issue. She couldn't take care of herself, plain and simple. That realization, in that moment, changed me, changed what I'd assumed for the future, our future. I grabbed her purse off the kitchen table and disregarded the mess—figurative and literal—knowing it would be waiting for me later.

When I came outside, Drew was helping her into the passenger's seat. He strapped her in, closed the door, and jogged to the other side of the car. On his way, he gave me another look, this one terrified, telling me, *I didn't know it was this bad*. I took a breath deep enough for him to see my chest rise and twisted my mouth to one side. I didn't know it was that bad, either. It wasn't just the broken wrist, but all of it, the totality of her life, a life that had led to this broken wrist. We just didn't know.

The ten-minute drive to East Orange General was another mostly silent one. I sat in the back, but I could see his mom in the side mirror. Her lip was trembling. She was terrified, too. It was like even though she'd been living this, even though it was her body, and her life, under siege, she didn't know it was that bad, either.

The ER was crowded for a Wednesday night. Drew went up to the registration desk while I walked his mom to one of the few available plastic chairs in the waiting area. There were all types: a feverish Hispanic woman with sweat beads on her forehead; a tired-looking white woman with a toddler sprawled out next to her, taking up two seats; a college student holding a bloody washcloth around one finger; an Indian family, the women in saris, with so much calm in their faces that I didn't know if any of them had an actual emergency.

"It shouldn't be too long," Drew said, coming back and sitting beside his mom. I was on her other side. He put his arm around the back of her seat, reaching over to massage my shoulder. I gave him a small smile to show my appreciation, but I didn't want to look at him. I knew he'd want to start the conversation about canceling our trip and I wanted nothing to do with that conversation.

The nurse didn't call us back until ten o' clock, two hours after we'd arrived. Drew's mom was rocking back and forth slowly in her chair, still clutching her arm. It had swollen up noticeably. We didn't need an X-ray to confirm anything.

The nurse showed us to one of the examination areas. She pulled the curtain shut for an illusion of privacy, though we were well within earshot of all the other patients and their ailments. She took his mom's vitals, needing the child-sized cuff to get the blood pressure reading. She said a doctor would be right with us and then disappeared beyond the curtain.

The doctor looked younger than Drew and me. He was an Indian man, small-boned, with receding hair. He could have been one of those unfortunates whose hair started disappearing in high school. That tragedy probably drove him to his books and success in academia. He mentioned his name quickly, but I didn't catch it. His accent was still heavy. He couldn't have been in America more than a few years.

"Let's see what we have here," he said, sitting on a stool with wheels and rolling up to Drew's mom. He was gentle and compassionate, confirming his newness to the profession. In time, he was sure to become the prototypical seasoned doctor—gruff, blunt, tired of people and their injuries. He peeked at her arm, careful not to hurt her any more than she already was.

"I'm going to have someone take you to get an X-ray, okay?" he said, talking to Drew's mom like she was a child, which she was, essentially.

She nodded sheepishly.

"This is what happens when you try to shoot the basketball too much," he said. He laughed at his own terrible joke and we smiled politely.

An X-ray tech with tattoos visible underneath the sleeves of his scrubs and earrings in both ears came to escort Janet. She looked scared to go with him, and I didn't blame her. The three of us—the doctor, Drew, and I—watched her walk away. It was a shuffle more than a walk. She couldn't risk raising a foot completely, so she just slid across the floor.

After she disappeared around a corner, the doctor said, "How long has she had Parkinson's?"

He was looking at his clipboard, making notes. It was like he thought he was talking to colleagues, not family members.

Drew cleared his throat. "We're not totally sure that's what it is."

That got the doctor's attention. He looked up, confused.

"Well," he said, squinting his eyes, thinking, giving his words careful thought, "whatever it is, she is having a great deal of difficulty walking. She has fairly extreme rigidity. She can barely stand without aid."

Drew nodded. I could feel the guilt emanating off of him. We should have known it had gotten so bad.

"I'm guessing she's struggling with day-to-day tasks," the doctor said cautiously. "Is that correct?"

"She fell getting the mail, so . . ." Drew trailed off. He looked away and, as he did, I could see the glassiness of his welled-up eyes in the fluorescent overhead lights.

"I'm sure she takes falls on a daily basis," the doctor said. "You should be grateful that she only broke her wrist this time. It could have been her hip, which would require a surgery that would be very hard on her body."

I resented this little Indian man for telling us what we should and shouldn't be grateful for. I wanted to tell him about our vacation, about how we just wanted him to lie to us and tell us she would be fine and we could go.

"The tremors—the shaking in her hands—that's gotten better, though," Drew said. His tone was defensive.

"That can happen in later stages of Parkinson's."

We nodded as if we understood, but we didn't.

"Stages?" I asked, my voice quiet. I wasn't sure I wanted to be heard or answered.

"There are five stages," the doctor said. "She is probably stage four."

"What happens at stage five?" I asked, still quiet.

"Increased difficulty with movement—standing, walking. Most stage five patients have nursing care."

He was too direct, too much to the point. We wanted to dance—twirl and spin—around the point, for at least a little while longer.

"It's not terminal," he said. He blurted it, like it was the one piece of good news he had to give us and he couldn't wait to share it. I knew, even then, well before I'd see the worst of it, that it might not be good news that Parkinson's wasn't terminal. In the support group I'd join months later, the other relatives and caretakers would all admit that, in the darkest hours, they wished it was terminal, that it would all end. As it was, it could go on for years, decades even.

"What do we do?" Drew asked, with a helplessness that made me grab his hand and squeeze it.

The doctor reached in his pocket for his pager. Whatever it said startled him.

"You should start talking to her about caregiving options," he said. Then he excused himself, said he would be right back. And we stood there, clueless as to what was ahead, but knowing that we wouldn't have "options." She didn't have insurance and we didn't have a stash of money for a live-in nurse. We were the option.

It was after midnight by the time we got out of the hospital. Drew's mom chose a hot pink cast, a rather pathetic attempt to keep the situation humorous and lighthearted. We walked her into the house and Drew got his first look at the disaster it had become. His shoulders slumped in defeat. He sat her on the couch and moved some of the newspapers so he could make a seat for himself. As I made my way to the kitchen, I heard him say:

"Ma, we gotta talk about this."

Drew and I had divvied up responsibilities while waiting in the hospital: he would talk to his mom; I would cancel the trip. I left a message with Jade, telling her I'd be in the office the rest of the week. Then I called Marni. I was hoping she wouldn't pick up so I could just leave a message, but she did pick up and I had to explain the situation to her. She said, "Oh, Em." The sadness in her voice made my throat constrict and my eyes water. I told her I had to go and hung up quickly. I recomposed myself and then called the airline's twenty-four-hour help line. I told the woman on the line that we'd had a family medical emergency. She didn't say she was sorry for us. She just asked for our confirmation number and the last name on the reservation.

"So our credit card will be refunded?" I asked.

"No, ma'am, we can't give you a refund. But we can give you a credit so you can go to California on a future date."

I hated her, the twang of her Texas accent, the fake graciousness of her voice. She was probably playing a game of solitaire on her computer while talking to me.

"Okay, then, a credit," I said.

"You'll just need to send in proof of your medical emergency."

"Proof?"

"A doctor's bill—anything with the date on it."

"Fine, we'll do that," I said. "We'll send in the bill."

It turned out there wasn't one bill; there were many. I never made copies of them to mail in. It wasn't that I forgot. I remembered. But it became gravely apparent that California—or any vacation, for that matter—wouldn't be part of our lives as long as Drew's mother was part of our lives. On especially bad days, I considered getting the airline credit and taking the trip alone, even envisioned myself on a chaise lounge with a book and a fruity cocktail at my side. But I declared my own idea crazy before Drew had the chance to. I mean, what kind of wife leaves her husband and his ailing mother to sunbathe in paradise? A shitty one, I told myself. A shitty one.

TEN

Drew and I had this ritual: Friday nights, after a long week of work, we'd make calzones. It was our thing. He was in charge of the dough and I was in charge of the fillings. We tried to make them a little different every week—different meats, different cheeses, different vegetables. Sometimes we used a cream sauce, sometimes marinara.

On the day of the last calzone night I remember, he called me on my lunch break and said, "Babe, I was thinking pesto tonight."

When was that? It must have been in that period of time after Drew's mom broke her wrist, after we canceled our trip, but before our lives changed completely.

"Pesto?" I said.

"As the sauce, as the base. It's genius."

I couldn't help but smile. "Genius," I said. "I'll pick up some tomatoes and mozzarella."

When I came home that night, the house had that smell that I always looked forward to after excessively stressful weeks full of client presentations and unrealistic deadlines. Drew danced with me in the kitchen. A Goo Goo Dolls song was on the radio. He was in one of his good moods.

"My love," he said, kissing my cheek, "tonight's calzone just may be the very best yet."

I put my groceries on the counter and let him twirl me until I got dizzy. We ended up sitting on the linoleum floor, in hysterics, and I thought, for a second, *We can always be this happy.* I hadn't even had a sip of wine yet. I was just drunk on optimism.

Drew started visiting his mom regularly after her fall. At first it was just during the days, which were free for him because he didn't have a job. Slowly, caring for her became his job; or, Marni said, caring for her became the excuse he had for not finding a job. Sometime after the holidays, he decided to make her dinner a few nights a week, meaning I was on my own, eating takeout in front of the TV. When that became a norm, he started calling around eight o'clock saying, "I think I'm just going to stay the night here." His voice was slurred; he'd had too much to drink. I wasn't about to insist he get on the road and come back to me.

By April, he was at his mom's house more often than he was at home with me. He had a duty, he said. He owed it to her, he said. The loyalty that I used to consider a strength began to reveal itself as a weakness. I tried to understand, but I was angry—especially on calzone nights.

On this particular Friday, I was determined to be the one who had too much to drink. I came home to the dark, quiet apartment, not as sad about his absence as I was about my acclimation to it. I fed Bruce, washed my dishes from that morning's breakfast, sorted through a stack of mail—bills, mostly, enough bills to drain the paycheck I'd just gotten that day. I took the cork out of a bottle of Merlot with at least two glasses left in it and poured the wine into one of those large plastic cups they give away as promotional items at fast-food restaurants. This one was from Wendy's.

I took a sip, then sat myself down at the kitchen table, pondering what to do for dinner. I decided on the Mexican place Drew didn't like. Even though he wasn't there to disapprove, I enjoyed the rebellion. I decided I'd been too agreeable with him, generally. I'd never pushed to get my way—for Mexican food and other matters—and look where it had gotten me. Alone on a Friday night.

As I called in my order to a woman who spoke very broken English, I took big gulps of wine, and started opening the bills, checkbook at my side. I was in charge of the finances in our marriage. It was a role I accepted early on, after Drew forgot to pay the electricity bill and our apartment went dark. He admitted money management wasn't his strong suit. Remembering this, I muttered to myself, "What *is* your strong suit?" while tearing open an envelope containing the credit card statement. I reviewed the charges, using a pencil to make checkmarks next to the ones I recognized. Drew used to tease me about my attention to detail with the bills. I'd told him he'd thank me one day, though that day never came.

There were some unusual charges, but I knew exactly what they were—a Newark grocery store, a Newark pharmacy, a PSEG gas and electricity bill. My face got hot and I imagined steam shooting from my ears like in cartoons. I yanked my purse by the strap, pulling it across the table toward me so hard that my compact mirror and a tube of ChapStick came sliding out along with my phone. I dialed his number.

"Hey," he said. I could tell just from that one word—*hey*—that he was already drunk. I hoped I sounded the same. I hoped he'd feel guilty.

"Do you think we're made of money?" I said, raising my voice enough to startle myself. I sounded like some actor playing me in a TV movie.

"Huh?" Drew said.

"You're buying your mom's groceries? Paying her bills?"

I never wanted to be that kind of wife, the nagging kind. I used to see women scolding their husbands in public and cringe in embarrassment of them. I'd tell Drew, "They're giving all women a bad name." I wanted to be the cool wife, the envy of his friends. It took me a few years of marriage to realize that no woman starts as a nag, no woman becomes a nag willingly; a man makes her that way.

"Em, we're waiting on some Medicare payments," he said. I used to be the other half of the "we" in his life. Now his mother was that person.

"Okay, let me ask again: Do you think we're made of money?"

He sighed loudly. "Try to be patient. It won't be this way forever."

"Really?" I asked, genuinely wanting to know.

"Have some compassion, Em."

He had the upper hand. He was caring for a disabled person. It was a sob story that earned the sympathy of anyone who listened. That's what I hated most—on the rare occasions I told people about the situation with his mom, they said, "God, that's awful. Poor Drew." I'd want to shout, while pulling fistfuls of hair from my head, *What about me?* Marni was the only person who understood. When I told her the arrangement, she said, "Jesus. How are you staying sane?" and I said, "I'm not."

"She can't take care of herself, Em," he said.

"Stop saying my name like that."

"Like what?"

"Like you're explaining quantum physics to me. I understand the situation, *Drew.*"

He got quiet, or maybe he was just taking a drink. That's what I did—sip wine from my large plastic cup.

"I don't know if you understand how bad it is," he said.

And I didn't, frankly. I avoided visiting. When I was away from her, I could hate her. I could blame her for making me resent my husband. When I saw her—with the skeletal body and blank stare of a concentration camp victim, unable to walk or stand without aid—I was overcome with a whole different kind of hate. Hate for myself, for the coldhearted bitch I'd become.

"Sometimes, pieces of poop fall out of her pant legs while I'm walking her to the bathroom," he said, whispering, as if she might be in earshot and he didn't want to destroy whatever dignity she had left.

There was nothing I could say to this. Any protests would sound selfish and uncaring. In the competition to see which one of us had it harder, he would always win. He was spending his days doling out nutritional supplements because she'd ditched conventional medicine in favor of holistic promises. He was cleaning the dirt from under her nails, shaving her armpits, cleaning out her ears with Q-tips, cutting up her food into tiny pieces like moms do for toddlers. He said just wiping up her drool was a full-time job. She was always drooling. The week before, she was sitting on a footstool, just a couple feet off the floor, and fell forward, busting open her nose because she didn't have the dexterity or strength in her arms to stop the face-plant. Drew said, "It's a good thing she didn't break her nose," but I thought maybe it would have been a good thing if she *had* broken her nose. Maybe a doctor in the emergency room would have talked sense into everyone this time, insisted on professional care. I'd told Drew that's what she needed—a professional. He'd said, "Do you know how much that costs?" and I didn't, so I'd shut up.

"I know it's bad," I said.

"Do you?" he said, angrier now. The whiskey, or whatever it was he was drinking, was giving him a tone.

"I mean, I don't know firsthand." I was defeated, I knew that.

"Right, exactly."

"It's hard on me, too, though," I said. My voice had become small, weak, the type of voice I'd criticize other women for using in intimidating situations with men. If I used that voice at work, Jade would have insisted I attend a hippie self-empowerment retreat in the Catskills.

"Babe, you gotta just hang in there. For me."

There was a knock at the door—the Mexican food delivery. I told Drew to hold on. When I stood, I realized just how drunk

I was. My legs felt wobbly. The boy delivering the food couldn't have been more than twelve years old. I gave him a twenty and closed the door. By the time I got back to the phone, I wasn't even angry anymore. I was tired.

"You just miss me, don't you?" Drew said, attempting to bring our fight to a sweet conclusion.

I wasn't even sure that was it, though. I didn't miss him as much as I missed the time of our life, our marriage, when everything seemed so simple and we had nothing but hope for our years ahead.

"I guess," I said.

"How can I make it better?"

It would be easier, I thought, if he was an asshole. Being nice made it worse, just replaced my anger with guilt.

"I don't know," I said. "She owns her house, right? What if she took out a mortgage on it? Wouldn't that pay for someone to help so you could come home?"

"She already has a mortgage on her house. And now she's on Medicare. She's not working. It's not like a bank is going to give her another loan."

I don't know why I even tried to offer suggestions. He shot them down every time.

"Even if they did give her a loan," he said, "it's unlikely that would be enough to pay for someone, long-term."

Long-term, I thought.

Then he said: "I've thought about her living with us, so we could be together . . ."

Visions of this possibility flashed before my drunken eyes: coming home to her on the couch, drooling, leaving wet spots on the cushions; forcing polite small talk, straining to hear her, while staring into her sad eyes, large and petrifying because of the deep, sunken eye sockets and eyelid skin so papery thin that the little blood vessels underneath were visible; making all her meals, which included mostly pureed foods like mashed potatoes and soups—foods babies could eat; waking up multiple times a night to walk her to the bathroom so she wouldn't wet the bed and ruin another mattress—she'd already ruined one. I got visible chills, goose bumps all up and down my arms.

"She can't live with us," I said.

He was quiet again.

"Ever," I clarified. "If she does, I won't be living with us."

"Wow, Em," he said, with a condescending grunt, like he was in utter disbelief of my cruelty.

"Stop using my name like that," I yelled. I'd never been a yeller. I put my hand over my mouth.

"You sound like your mother." It was the worst thing he could say to me, a button he'd neglected to push in all the years we'd been together. *You sound like your mother.* In that one statement, he was calling me a crazy, selfish, irrational bitch.

"You're an asshole," I said, glad he couldn't see my lip quivering, the tears coming.

"Em, calm down," he said, patronizing. "I just want you to have some compassion."

I slammed my almost-emptied cup of wine on the table, so hard that drops splashed out the top.

"Stop making yourself the saint!"

"I'm not a saint. I'm just doing what has to be done," he said, which was exactly what a modest, humble saint would say. Somehow, during these arguments of ours, I always ended up apologizing. I had no choice.

"Look, I—" I began.

He shushed me. "I think I hear her calling for me." We were both quiet while he listened. He said she'd call for him from her position on the couch for help to the bathroom or for a glass of water. Her voice was so faint that sometimes he wasn't sure if he heard her or not. Maybe it was just in his head. It was making him crazy, Jack-Nicholson-in-*The-Shining* crazy, he said. Worst of all was when she called for him and he went and all she wanted to do was comment on the weather or show him something funny on TV. She'd become a burden in just her attempts to make conversation.

"False alarm," he said after a moment.

I wanted to tell him the whiskey probably didn't help sharpen his senses, but I refrained.

"Will I even see you this weekend?"

"Well, I was hoping you'd come out on Sunday," he said. "For Mother's Day."

I'd forgotten about Mother's Day completely, but I pretended I hadn't: "I have my own mother, if you recall. I have a day planned with her." In truth, I'd never celebrated Mother's Day with my mom. The Hallmark cards that said things like, "Thank you for always being there for me," didn't ring true. I hadn't even talked to my mom since Drew's restaurant closed. I hated that she was right about its failure. I didn't want to hear her say, *I told you so.*

"Oh, okay," he said. I'd made him feel bad. It was my only victory of the phone call.

"I'll just see you when I see you."

"You know what? I'll come home tonight," he said. "She's ready for bed anyway. I'll just come back tomorrow in time for breakfast." That was the main concern—her eating. He'd bought a scale at the drugstore and made her get on it weekly. She was only ninety pounds.

"You don't have to do that," I said.

"I know I don't have to," he said. "I want to."

"Okay." He'd completely diffused my anger, leaving me empty.

"I'll be home in a couple hours."

I looked at the clock—almost eight o'clock. I didn't see the point in him coming home, just to go to sleep together. I was too tired to argue, though. If I did, he'd say, *So you don't want to spend the night with me? What* do *you want?* There really was no winning for me. In this drama, I was cast as the bad guy.

"Just drive safe," I said.

When I got off the phone, I moved to the couch and ate enough to absorb the wine and stop my head from spinning. I fell asleep at some point and when I woke up, it was almost midnight. I was supposed to be worried. A good wife—or just a good, conscientious person—would have been worried. I wasn't, though. I rolled my eyes, assuming he'd changed his mind or fallen asleep, and got into bed.

At eight o'clock in the morning, Bruce jumped off the bed and ran to the front door, the fur on his back standing straight up. He huffed—he was never much of a barker—and turned in circles nervously. I heard keys jingling and knew it was Drew. Bruce knew, too. He stopped turning in circles and huffing, the fur on his back fell flat, and he started wagging his tail.

"Hey, buddy," I heard Drew say.

I lowered down in bed, pretending to be asleep. I didn't want to talk to him.

When he came into the bedroom, I peeked at him through a sliver of open eye. The room was still dark. It was a gloomy, rainy May day, the sun choosing not to make an appearance. Were shadows playing tricks on me? Half of his face looked to be bloodied. I opened both eyes, watched him as he crossed the bedroom, undressing as he walked. It wasn't shadows—his face was scraped up, badly.

"What happened?" I asked.

He seemed surprised that I was awake and coherent.

"Did you get in a fight?"

"No," he said, "I wish that was it."

I turned on the lamp to get a better look at him. It was as if he'd taken a carefree dive into the sidewalk, reminiscent of the dives I'd taken as a kid onto the Slip 'N Slide during summer.

"I got in a car accident," he said. "Looks worse than it is. The window broke when the car hit the pole—cut up my face a little."

He was totally composed about the whole thing. My ears rang.

"The car *hit a pole?*"

"It was stupid. I was almost home. Ran a light, like an idiot. There was another car coming. I swerved hard to miss it. Hit a pole."

His level of calm was eerie. He must have been in shock. He grabbed onto the back of his neck.

"May be hurting later," he said.

"Is the other person okay?"

"He's fine. Like I said, I swerved to miss him."

"Well, that's good," I said. "Did you go to the hospital?"

"Nah," he said. "I'm fine."

I'd heard stories of people bleeding internally without even knowing it, or having concussions that made them forget their names a day later.

"We have to go to the hospital," I said.

He got into bed defiantly. "I'm fine," he said. He closed his eyes and I watched him, wide-eyed, convinced he'd fall into a coma if I blinked.

"The car is totaled," he said, eyes still closed.

I swallowed hard. I had so many questions about this—*How are we going to afford a new car? Will our car insurance payments go up? If you can't drive to your mom's house, are you going to bring her here?*—but it wasn't the appropriate time to ask them.

"Did the police come?" I asked.

"Yeah," he said. "The other guy stopped, called them."

I swallowed hard again.

"Were you drunk?" I asked, my voice weak and small again.

He groaned. "I was over the legal limit. Barely. It's bullshit. I was fine to drive. It was just a stupid accident. I hadn't had a drink in over an hour when it happened. I would have gotten into the accident if I was sober."

"Did they take you to jail?"

"Yeah, Em. That's procedure. That's what happens."

"Okay," I said, nodding, trying to tell myself it would be all right. But, again, I had so many questions—*How much was bail? Do we have to hire a lawyer? How much does that cost? Will they take away your license? Will this be on your record? Will it affect you getting a job?*

"I need to get some sleep," he said. "Can we talk about this later?"

"I guess."

I kept vigil over him while he slept, watching his chest move up and down, confirming he was alive. I did love him, immensely—a realization that shocked me more than it should have. The thing is, I wasn't sure love was enough.

ELEVEN

When Claire was six years old, I was in an accident on the 405 freeway. It was a multiple-car situation. Mine was the least involved car, an innocent bystander sideswiped by a truck after it plowed into a little two-door sedan. The driver of the sedan then plowed into the center divider and died. After talking to the police and calming my nerves, I was able to drive away from the scene. There was some damage to my side door, but I didn't have a scratch on me. I went straight to the bar. I didn't have to work that day, but I had to talk to someone. And considering I had a limited number of someones, Al would do.

"I don't even want to think about if Claire had been in the car," I said, still reeling.

She was at school, thank God.

"Then don't think about it," he said.

"What if I had been the one in the sedan?" I said to him.

He popped the cap off two Blue Moons—one for him, one for me. It wasn't even noon yet.

"You can't think shit like that, Con," Al said.

I had a feeling he relied pretty heavily on this not-thinking-about-shit policy in his life.

"What would happen to Claire?"

That was more distressing to consider than my own death. Up to that point, I hadn't really thought about what would happen to Claire if I was gone. Just another example of my stupidity, I suppose.

"I'm telling you Con, you can't go there," he said.

"It's a practical matter. I should have someone to look after her, in case something happens to me."

"Ain't nothin' gonna happen to you," he said.

We each took sips from our beers.

"And if somethin' did, I'd watch after her," he said. He wasn't looking at me when he said it. He was using the towel that was usually affixed to his belt to wipe down the counter.

"You would?" I said.

Al had no experience raising children, but he loved Claire. Earlier that same year, he'd stepped in to fill the dad role for a Girl Scouts father-daughter dance. When I thanked him profusely and got teary-eyed watching him put the corsage on Claire's tiny wrist, he told me to shut the hell up.

"Damn it, Con, I said I would, so stop talkin' 'bout it."

I obeyed and tucked away his promise in the back of my mind for safekeeping.

Usually, on the anniversary of 9/11, I make sure I'm working at the bar, for the distraction. The first few years after I moved to California, people talked about the anniversary. The event was still fresh in their minds. Then, after the five-year mark, the date kind of passed without much attention. People posted things on Facebook with the "Never forget" message. I always found that appalling. *Never forget?* As if that directive is necessary, as if some people have a choice to remember or not. I don't.

This year, the anniversary of 9/11 is the day I meet with my oncologist. And even though my mind spins with the what-ifs of my cancer, I still think of those buildings falling. Some hippie in Topanga would say this is poetic.

My oncologist is a woman named Dr. Richter. She's in her fifties, her graying hair pulled into a peppy ponytail on top of her head. It bobs when she nods, which she does a lot when listening to me ask my seemingly never-ending questions. There is a picture of two girls—her daughters, I presume—on the bookcase behind her desk, facing patients like me who sit in the chair, listening to our fates. The girls are around Claire's age, their smiles as big and life-loving as hers.

"The good news is it's stage three," she says. I must look pleased, because she feels the need to temper my relief by adding, "For now."

Forty percent survival rate after five years. Sixty percent of people die.

"It seems to be isolated to your right breast and lymph nodes."

"The bad news is I still need chemo?" I say.

"Oh, no, that's not bad news. At least there's something we can do. At least you're not a lost cause."

Chemotherapy is good news. This is the beginning of how cancer changes perspective on everything.

"You should think about getting tested for HER2," she says.

I've read about this online—the infamous cancer gene.

"About one in three of my breast cancer patients have it."

"Oh," I say. You would expect my mind to be racing, but it's frozen still.

"The regimen I'm prescribing for you would be the same whether you have the gene or not. But some patients want to know for the sake of their children."

The sake of their children.

I stare at the girls in her picture frame. They smile back at me, totally oblivious to all this.

"You have a daughter, right?" she says, glancing at my chart.

"Yes," I say, my voice shaky. "Claire."

I still haven't said a word to Claire about the cancer. She's been abuzz with her presidential campaign at school. The election is in

November, "just like the real one." Her campaign starts in October. Four other kids are running. She is working on her "platform."

"I was thinking some of the vending machine profits should go toward feeding the homeless," she told me.

I don't know where she gets these ideas.

"You have a good heart, Claire."

My eyes got a little watery and she said, annoyed with my sappiness, "Geez, Mom, what's wrong with you?"

My first chemo treatment is a day away, so I have to tell her. That's all I think about on my morning run—probably the last run I'll be able to do for a while. Running has been my stress reliever, my sanity saver. Without it, I may go crazy. Time will tell.

Claire is one of those rare kids who doesn't need to be woken up for school. She's already in the kitchen, popping freezer waffles in the toaster, when I come back from my run. I have to tell her. Today. I'll be tired from the chemo. I might vomit. There's baldness in my future. Claire wants to feed the homeless with vending machine profits; she's not an idiot.

"How about you skip school today?" I say.

It's a Thursday.

"We'll go to the Santa Monica Pier. We've never done that."

She looks unenthusiastic. Claire hates to miss school. Like I said, she's one of those rare kids.

"Come on," I say. "It's just one day."

She considers this.

"I guess I don't have any tests or anything."

"Well, then, it's meant to be."

There's this ice-cream parlor—Soda Jerks—in the historic Carousel Building on the pier. It's a throwback to the thirties and forties, when things were supposedly simpler.

"Why's it called Soda Jerks?" Claire asks, reading the sign as we cross the threshold of the store. It smells like waffle cones. A few stereotypical tourists—cameras slung over their shoulders—sit at the counter. They have accents like Al's.

"That's what they used to call the people who worked at the soda fountains—because they had to jerk the lever for the soda to come out," I say, pointing to one of the guys behind the counter doing just that. He's dressed in all white, with a white hat and black bow tie.

"Like a bartender for ice-cream drinks."

"Exactly."

We sit at the counter. She orders the Will Rogers Hot Fudge Brownie Sundae and I choose the Route 66 Banana Split, convincing myself that a banana is a fruit and fruit is cancer-friendly.

There's a little sign on the counter, featuring a cartoon character from the 1950s. It reads LIFE IS UNCERTAIN, SO EAT DESSERT FIRST.

"I want to talk to you about something," I say.

She's only just dipped her spoon into her sundae. When she lifts it to her mouth, the chocolate sauce drips off in a thick stream. She gets chocolate in the corners of her mouth and I can tell by the way she looks at me—with seriousness—that she doesn't know it's there.

"What?" she asks. She puts down her spoon.

"You have a little chocolate," I say, indicating on my own mouth where it is on hers. I miss the days when she was really little, when I'd use my thumb to wipe away her food mishaps.

She licks off the chocolate.

"You got it."

"What do you want to talk about?" She knows I'm stalling. She's worried. I don't usually take this tone with her.

I've thought up different ways to tell her—from the inappropriately jokey (*Hey, guess who has cancer?*) to the boringly clinical (*The doctors have discovered cancerous tissue in my breast and lymph nodes*) to the morosely serious (*I've been diagnosed with a possibly terminal cancer*). Nothing sounds right. And, when it comes to telling your daughter that you—her mother, her everything—has cancer, nothing will ever sound right.

"I have cancer," I say.

My ears start ringing immediately. I see the guy behind the counter, the soda jerk, out of the corner of my eye. Is he eavesdropping?

She puts her spoon on the counter deliberately, stares into her sundae.

"You should have at least waited for me to finish my ice cream," she says.

My ears stop ringing.

"Sorry," I say, for ruining the ice cream, for the cancer.

"What kind?" she asks, cool and collected.

"Breast."

She nods—once, slowly.

"This girl at school, her mom had breast cancer," she says. "She's okay now."

It's likely her mom didn't have the kind of breast cancer I have, but now is not the time for details.

"Lots of women get breast cancer," I say. The least I can do is contribute to her comforting storyline.

I wish the chairs swiveled so I could face her more directly. As it is, our bodies are twisted awkwardly toward each other.

"Are you going to be okay?" she asks.

"Yes, honey, I'll be okay." Dr. Richter's parting words were, "Think positive." All those years of med school boiled down to one corny motivational phrase.

The ice cream is already melting, leaving behind a syrupy soup. Claire makes circles through hers with her spoon.

"What's going to happen?" she asks.

I share the same question. That's the most terrifying part of being a mother—the expectation of having all the answers.

"My doctor has a treatment plan. I'll start chemotherapy tomorrow."

"Wow," she says. "Tomorrow."

"I'll have that for about six months and we'll see if that gets the cancer," I say, noticing that I'm talking to her like she's five and cancer is the bogeyman. I clear my throat.

"Then what?"

"They'll remove my breast, just to be safe," I say.

This makes her eyes go big.

"It's not scary. It's the best thing to do," I tell her.

"Then what?"

"There's radiation to get the last of the cancer," I say, wrapping it all up in a bow. "I think that's a month or two."

"So, by summer you'll be fine again," she says.

"Right," I say, withholding so many caveats—*if everything goes as planned, if the cancer responds to the chemo, if the cancer doesn't spread before we get it.*

She sits up straight, like she's been electrocuted by some lightbulb going off in her head.

"Is there a cancer charity?" she asks.

"Many, I'm sure."

"That's what the vending machine profits should go to."

She's a far better person than I ever was or will be.

"I liked your original idea, too," I say. Because I don't want this, my cancer, to become her life.

She shrugs. "I like this one."

She slurps a spoonful of her melted ice cream.

"And we should plan something fun for summer, when you're back to normal."

Normal. I'm not sure I'll define that the same way ever again.

"Whatever you want."

"Road trip. We'll see the Grand Canyon, the Statue of Liberty, everything."

My heart skips a beat when she says "the Statue of Liberty." I swore to myself, when I got in that cab fourteen years ago, that I would never go back.

"Whatever you want," I say again, because, really, what else is there to say?

We push our ice cream bowls aside and walk out to the pier. There's a line for the Ferris wheel. We wait patiently behind a group of older teenagers talking way too loudly, the way teenagers do. Two of them are passing a cigarette back and forth between each other, taking puffs. If I die, if I'm not here to see Claire all the way through adolescence, I fear she will be one of them, taking puffs.

"I had a feeling something was wrong," she says, staring up at the gondolas. There are twenty of them. I've counted as we wait.

"I know," I say.

"You're no good at keeping things from me."

But, see, I am. There's so much she doesn't know.

We get to the front of the line.

"Together or separate?" the Ferris wheel operator asks us. Greasy hair hangs in his face. He smacks gum with an alarming amount of apathy.

"Together," Claire says, before I can answer. And when we shuffle into our gondola and take our seats, she reaches over and holds my hand tight, out of love or fear or both.

TWELVE

Drew's mom moved in with us a week after the car accident. We made our modest living space into her bedroom, filled our already-full closet with her clothes, covered our kitchen counter with the pills she hoped were magical.

"It'll be temporary," he said, "just until I get my license back."

His license was suspended for six months. He could no longer drive to her house to care for her. During this time, I had dreams of dominoes falling, one after another, in a seemingly endless line.

"Trust me, she doesn't want to be out of her house any more than we want her in our house."

I got lost at the part where he said, "Trust me."

I started staying late at the office or going out with Marni after work. I wanted to come home to find Drew's mom already asleep. I wanted to close my eyes on the short walk from the front door to the bedroom and pretend she wasn't there, curled up on the couch, drooling on my throw pillows.

"I really don't know how you and Drew are handling all this," Marni said. We had just finished dinner at a Thai restaurant in the

Village and were walking arm in arm to the subway station. It was one of those summer nights that had a hint of fall in the air—a brief chill, a preview.

"We're not. Or I'm not. Drew drinks whiskey to handle it. He's become something of a connoisseur."

"Well, you're going to have to escape in your own way."

"You're my escape, silly."

"You're gonna get sick of me," she said.

"Never."

We hugged at the station. She kissed me on the cheek and I got sad as I watched her disappear down the corridor to the train that would take her home.

A few days later, Jade insisted I leave the office before six since I'd been doing so much overtime. Marni couldn't meet for dinner—she had a date. So I was home by seven. Drew and his mom were watching *Jeopardy!*, sitting so close on the couch that an unknowing visitor might think them an odd couple. My favorite blanket was draped over the armrest, a blanket I'd had since I was a kid. There were nights my mom left me alone and I covered myself in that blanket and waited for sunrise. Now there was a large damp stain on it.

"What happened?" I asked. I pulled it to my face to smell and I knew the answer before Drew had to say anything. His mom wet her pants on an almost daily basis. We had started putting trash bags over the couch cushions.

"She had an accident," he said. "She didn't realize she was sitting on it."

She looked at me with regret. "Sorry," she whispered.

Drew must have seen my eyes enlarge with rage, because he said, "Don't worry, I'm taking it to the Laundromat tomorrow."

That didn't help, though. I didn't want the blanket washed. It was delicate. It had never been washed—not in the two decades I'd had it. I liked that it smelled like the passage of years.

"Why don't you go for a walk?" he said, standing and guiding me to the front door like a bouncer attempting to divert a threat in a crowded club. He opened the door for me, practically pushed me out, told me with his eyes to come back when I was calmer, less likely to kill someone.

I walked down the steps to the sidewalk and when I rounded the corner of our block, I quickened my pace until I was running, until I was sprinting, until I was so exhausted that I was physically incapable of screaming even if I wanted to.

I was wearing my work shoes—loafers.

That escape Marni said I'd need? I found it. I started running nightly, until I was so exhausted that I could return to the apartment without anger. I got so good at it, started running so many miles, that I returned to the apartment with complete apathy. I didn't listen to music; I just listened to the rhythm of my feet and the cycle of my inhales and exhales.

Within a week, I was running before work and in the evening. I ran three times a day on weekends. I ran with the gusto of Forrest Gump. Over a midweek lunch with Marni—we didn't meet for after-work happy hours that often anymore because I didn't want to miss my evening runs—she said she was worried about me.

"Whenever women run, they're running away from something," she said. "Every time I see a woman jogging, I pity her. I want to stop her and have a heart-to-heart and ask, *What the hell are you running from?*"

"But it's okay for men to run?" I asked, flexing a feminist muscle that I knew Marni would appreciate.

"Men have, like, a primordial need to run. It goes back to their days as hunters sprinting across the Great Plains to kill mammals."

She stabbed a tomato in her salad as if it were one of those just-mentioned mammals.

"Marni, that's bullshit and you know it," I said.

She used her finger to wipe up the dressing left in her bowl, then licked her finger shamelessly. "I just think you're running from something," she said. "Which is fine. I would run, too, if I was in your situation—metaphorically, I mean. I'd never actually run unless some rapist was chasing me."

"I guess I won't ask you to come along sometime," I said, though I wouldn't have asked anyway. I didn't want a companion.

"Look, just don't get hit by a car or pass out from exhaustion or lose every ounce of body fat."

She reached across the table and pinched my upper arm.

"Apparently I'm too late with the body fat thing."

One day, at work, I was looking up information about Parkinson's online and saw a list of support groups. There was one for caretakers—in Brooklyn Heights. So, that Thursday night, I ran four miles, in the dark, to a church on Jay Street. I didn't tell Drew I was going.

There were seven of us total, including the group leader—a sixty-something woman named Pam whose credentials were twofold: she was a retired social worker and her brother had Parkinson's. The newcomers had to introduce themselves to the group, AA-style.

"Hi, I'm Emily. My husband's mother has stage five Parkinson's and she's been living with us since May."

That was all I said. I didn't tell them that I made Drew get out of bed first in the morning because I didn't want to greet his mom. I didn't tell them that every time she started to topple over, like a diseased tree falling in a forest, I thought about whether to steady her or let her fall. I didn't tell them that I considered calling Social Services on myself, claiming to be a neighbor witnessing elder abuse, so that they would take her away. I didn't tell them these things because I thought they would tell me the same thing Drew did—to have a little compassion.

Everyone welcomed me, then moved along to the two other newcomers. I was the youngest there by about twenty years, which made me feel sorrier for myself. This wasn't supposed to be happening to me—to us—now. When his mother first moved in, I said to Drew, like a toddler throwing a tantrum about a time-out, "It isn't fair." He told me it would be helpful if I'd complain only about things that had a solution. I didn't talk to him for two days.

The woman sitting across from me was also there for her first meeting. She had wild gray hair, long and wavy. She tapped one foot on the floor impatiently, like she couldn't wait for her turn to talk. When it came, she said:

"I'm Nancy. My seventy-two-year-old mother just moved in with me. Stage five. I'm about to lose my fucking mind."

Everyone just stared at her. I tried not to laugh. She must have felt the need to explain, because she went on:

"I have siblings—three of them. None of them want to take in my mother. She was crazy before Parkinson's and she's even crazier now."

She spoke fast, like she was on uppers, hands flailing all over the place. I liked her immediately. When she saw my amused smile, she winked at me.

Most of the meeting involved trading tips. It was like a Parkinson's advice swap meet. The group spent twenty minutes discussing adult diapers. "There's this new one that isn't as poufy as most of them. My mom doesn't fight me as much about wearing it at night," this lady named Alice said. The others looked at her like she was the messiah and jotted down the name. They all had notepads readily accessible.

Then Pam spent a half hour explaining "circle theory." I wasn't sure it was a real thing or something she made up. She instructed us to draw a circle on a paper and put the name of the Parkinson's patient in that circle. Then we drew a circle around that and put the name of the primary caregiver in that ring, then another circle with the name of the next-closest person, and so on. Pam said, "Comfort in, complaints out," meaning we were supposed to offer comfort to people in circles more inward than our own, and complain only to people in circles farther out than our own. In my life, this meant Drew's mom could bitch and moan as much as she wanted, to anyone at any time. And Drew could bitch and moan to me as much as he wanted. I had to offer the two of them comfort. I was in the third ring. I could only bitch and moan to people farther out from the situation than me—Marni, mostly. Unloading my frustrations on Drew was a no-no.

After the meeting, Nancy tapped me on the shoulder at the snack table, which featured a sad-looking bag of Pepperidge Farm cookies.

"Is it just me, or is that circle theory a crock of shit?" she whispered. I scanned my immediate surroundings to see if anyone else was listening in on us. They all seemed preoccupied with others. There was lots of slow nodding and hugging going on.

"Yes," I said. It felt like I'd just confessed a sin.

She asked if I wanted to go somewhere for a real snack and a real talk. I said, "Sure," and we walked to a coffee shop down the street that displayed carrot cake muffins in the window.

Even though we'd left the meeting, we still whispered our confessions across the little round bistro table, clutching steaming mugs in our hands. I told her how overwhelming it was that Parkinson's wasn't terminal. I asked her if it made me an awful person that I wished it was, that I wanted nothing more than an end point.

She scoffed. "Honey, sometimes I hope my mom will catch a flu that turns into pneumonia."

We both knew that was how most people with advanced Parkinson's end up dying—that or infected bedsores or a bad fall that leads to necessary surgery that the body just can't handle. I wasn't at all shocked by her revelation. I'd had the same thought drift into my mind when all the defenses of propriety were down. I was relieved, and she was relieved that I was relieved. We were fast friends—by necessity, really. We had no one else.

"You know what bugs me more than anything?" Nancy asked.

"Hmm?" I said, taking an exploratory nibble of my muffin, confirming it was edible. The girl at the counter had given it to me for free because she thought it might be stale. She couldn't remember when they were made. She looked high.

"When people say that God only gives us what we can handle."

"Or when they say we learn from things like this."

"All I've learned is that God must not know me at all," she said.

I realized why I liked Nancy. She threw one hell of a pity party and I was happy to attend. After all, Drew wouldn't let me throw my own.

"Thing is, you're way too young for all this shit," she said.

"I know," I said. "Though I don't think anyone is ever at an age to deal with this."

"True. But you're supposed to be planning your own life, not helping someone else survive the end of theirs."

It felt good to hear the thoughts in my head verbalized, validated.

"Drew always says, 'These are just the cards we were dealt,'" I said. "If he uses that line one more time . . ."

She took a long sip of her coffee. I asked how she could sleep after drinking a mug of coffee late at night. She said, "I don't sleep anyway. May as well have the energy to make the sleepless hours productive."

"Sometimes I think about what we'd be doing if we didn't have to deal with his mom," I said.

"And what would that be?"

I stared at the muffin, picked out the raisins, and put them on my plate. It wasn't that I disliked raisins; I just wanted some kind of project to distract from my current thought process.

"We'd probably have a baby by now," I said.

A baby—the ultimate project to distract myself. I'd contemplated this hypothetical child a lot, mourned it as if I'd miscarried. This baby was a girl, in my head. Her name was Lila. Or Claire—sweet and simple Claire. Or maybe Winnie. I'd always loved Winnie in *The Wonder Years*.

"How old are you?"

"Twenty-eight in a few weeks," I said.

She said, simply, "Guess it's about that time."

It was that time. I'd always thought I wanted two kids, at least. I was an only child and wouldn't wish that loneliness on anyone. I'd done the math—even if I got pregnant that night, I'd have my first baby just a couple months before turning twenty-nine. After a year of adjustment—physically and emotionally—we would try for a second. I'd have that baby when I was thirty. That seemed old to me. I'd envisioned myself as a younger mom. When my own mother was thirty, I was already eight.

"It doesn't even seem in the realm of possibility now—having a child," I said. "I mean, Drew's mom could go on like this for years."

Nancy nodded. She understood. Like me, she'd read the online message boards with frustrated posts from people who had been doing their caretaking for a decade or more.

"She's your child," she said, making no attempts to spare me the harshness of this reality. "You make her food, wipe her ass, put her to bed."

"For the record, I don't wipe her ass," I said. "Drew does. He knows better than to ask me to do that."

"At least he'll be good at changing diapers when that time comes."

"*If*," I said, "*if* that time comes."

I ate my discarded raisins, one at a time. It was just before ten o'clock. The high girl was starting to wipe down the counters.

"Do you have kids?" I asked Nancy.

I felt like I knew her so well already, and yet not at all.

"Nope," she said. "I have a slew of nieces and nephews, though."

"Drew and I don't have any sisters or brothers, so I won't even have those."

I was crashing her pity party, making it my own.

"I was married once," she said. She leaned back in her chair, so far that the front legs came off the floor. I remember when kids used to do that in school and the teachers would scold them, say, "One day you'll fall on your head, then you'll see."

"I think I was too selfish for the whole institution," she said. She pulled at a huge turquoise ring on her left middle finger. She wore rings on all her fingers, as if compensating for what society deemed the all-important ring.

"Selfish?" I asked, interested.

"I wasn't good at it—caring for someone else, being a team with someone. I just wanted to do my own thing, live life my way," she said. "I wanted to take trips when and where I wanted. I wanted to have a bowl of cereal for dinner some nights. I wanted to sleep without someone kicking me or snoring. I know, it's crazy."

"It's not crazy," I said.

"I guess the universe is teaching me a lesson by giving me my completely debilitated mother to care for round-the-clock. So much for selfishness."

"How old were you? When you got divorced?"

"Just about your age. Got married when I was twenty-four because it was what I was supposed to do. Gave it a try—probably not my best try, but *a* try."

"Any regrets?"

She put a chunk of muffin in her mouth and, while chewing, said, "Nope."

With that, she looked at her watch and said she had to get home. She had a neighbor watching over her mother and was already going to be late. We left the coffee shop and she asked where I'd parked. I told her that I didn't come in a car, that I had run, and she looked at me like I was stark-raving mad.

"I'm giving you a ride home," she said. There didn't seem to be a way to object to this.

She pulled up in front of my apartment building, reached over across the center console, and gave my hand a squeeze.

"Will I see you next week?" I asked, as nervous as a girl being dropped off after a first date.

"Unless I kill my mother first and go to prison," she said.

"You mean go to a different kind of prison," I said.

She pointed a you-got-it index finger at me and winked.

"Know what? How about you and me do our own meeting?" she said. "At the coffee shop? Same time?"

"I'd love that," I said.

She reached down by her feet for a balled-up piece of paper, a windshield flyer advertising dry cleaning. She smoothed it out, wrote down her number, and gave it to me.

"Hang in there, kiddo," she said, then drove away.

Drew's mom was still awake when I walked into the apartment. She was sitting up straight against the back of the couch, two pillows stacked on each side of her so she wouldn't tip over. The TV was on, its glow highlighting her catatonic stare.

"Hi," I said. It hadn't become any less awkward to communicate—or attempt to communicate—with her in the months we'd shared a home. She couldn't manage to reciprocate my greetings and I couldn't manage not to take it personally.

Drew walked in from the bedroom, a glass of water in his hand.

"You're home late," he said, taking the water to his mom, tipping it into her mouth slowly. It had become more difficult for her to clutch a glass. We switched to plastic cups, but then decided it was time to just spare her the embarrassment of spilling.

"Yeah," I said. It hadn't become any less awkward to communicate with Drew, either. He set the glass on the end table and came to me, put his arms around my waist, kissed my neck. I never knew how to feel when he did this, when he tried to act as if everything were normal, as if his mom weren't right there watching his desperate attempts to win my affections.

I pushed him away gently. "I'm pretty tired," I said.

I gave his mom my good-night wave and escaped to the bedroom. I heard Drew wish his mom sweet dreams. He used a booming voice with her, as if he assumed she couldn't hear, just because she couldn't speak.

"You okay?" he asked, closing the bedroom door behind him.

"Long day," I said. There was no point in sharing my unhappiness with him. He would just say there was nothing he could do about it and we would be left standing there, at an impasse neither of us knew how to circumvent.

"She seemed stronger today," he said. "She was lying down on the couch and I saw her push herself up to a seated position."

Nancy was right—Drew's mom was our baby. We cheered for even the smallest physical achievements.

"That's good," I said, less than halfheartedly. Quarter-heartedly.

"Her voice seemed to have a little more oomph today, too."

I didn't know if Drew was in enough denial to really think she was going to get better, or if he just wanted me to think that.

I went to our bathroom across the hall. He followed me, stood behind me as I washed my face, brushed my teeth.

"I can give you a massage," he said.

I didn't want a massage, though. I didn't want any of these attempts to make it better, to make it something it wasn't.

I spit into the sink. "Maybe tomorrow. I just want to go to sleep."

"You sure you're okay?" he asked, following me to the bed.

"Uh-huh," I said. He didn't probe more. He knew that was dangerous.

I gave him a kiss on the cheek, the kind grandmothers give their grown children. Then he got into bed on his side, and stayed there. Neither of us would sleep well, anticipating his mom calling out to him around two o'clock in the morning, needing to use the bathroom. If I wasn't awakened by Drew getting out of bed, I was awakened by the light flashing on and the bathroom fan whirring away.

THIRTEEN

Drew got his driver's license back right before Thanksgiving. I thought that would coincide with an immediate plan to move his mom back home. When a week passed without that plan, I couldn't restrain myself anymore.

"How much longer is she staying with us?" I said to him. We were in our bedroom. That was the only place the two of us were ever alone. We spoke in whispers regularly, taking on his mother's voice, as if in a show of strange solidarity.

"Just give me time to figure something out," he said. He was noticeably agitated, impatient with my question even though it was the first time I'd asked. It must have been bouncing around in his head for a while, like a pinball in a machine.

"You see how much worse she's gotten in the last six months," he said.

With just that one statement, I understood: she wasn't going anywhere.

Nancy and I continued our Thursday night meetings at the coffee shop. Bitching sessions, we called them. We didn't meet on

Thanksgiving, of course. We were both busy preparing turkeys and pretending life was normal for the sake of our loved ones. When we met the Thursday after Thanksgiving, we hugged like we hadn't seen each other in months.

"I missed you," I said. She'd come to be the only person in my life besides Drew, his mom, and coworkers. Marni had found herself a boyfriend and effectively disappeared from the planet. My mother had a new boyfriend, too. It was one of her chaotic on-and-off-again situations that consumed every minute of our few-and-far-between phone calls. She asked how I was, but it was obligatory, not curious. And that was fine with me. I didn't want to tell her about my life. She would just make me feel worse about it.

"How was your Turkey Day?" Nancy asked.

We draped our coats over our usual chairs, at our usual table in the back corner. The girl behind the counter had come to know us, and we'd come to decide that she wasn't always high; she was just a little dumb. She remembered our orders, though—cinnamon herbal tea for me, black coffee for Nancy. And she always brought us one of the baked goods they were going to throw away at the end of the night, like we were homeless people, charity cases.

"Drew's mom briefly choked on my mashed potatoes. So that was exciting."

She laughed. These were the things that humored us.

"You don't have my full sympathy until you've done the Heimlich," she said.

"You have?"

"Oh, yes. That's the incident that drove me to that stupid caretaker group," she said. "It was a piece of toffee, of all things." She simulated the trajectory of the toffee, drawing an arc in the air from her mouth to my side of the table.

"Jesus," I said.

"Nah, he wasn't there. I don't know where the fuck he's been."

We giggled like schoolgirls.

"So when's she leaving?" Nancy asked, blowing on her coffee. Her lips had deep lines in them, like she'd spent years in the sun or smoked thousands of cigarettes. I rarely asked about her past. Our presents were much too consuming.

"It's become a question of *if*," I said.

"Tell me you're kidding."

Last we'd talked, I'd been hopeful. I'd picked out the new couch we'd get to replace the one she'd slept on all those months. I'd told Nancy maybe Drew and I would talk about having a baby.

"He said he needs time to figure something out."

"What's there to figure out? He can go back to taking care of her *in her own home*. Or hire someone to do it. That would be the smartest idea. I'm hiring someone."

"You are?"

"I've had it," she said, with a quick jerk of her head that sent the tail end of her braided hair flying over her shoulder. "I figure my mom can't live for more than a year or two like this. She's already choked, broken her hip, and had stage three bedsores. I can afford two years of care, max. If she's still going after that, I'll have to kill her."

This was just how Nancy spoke. She wasn't serious. She loved her mom. I could tell by the way she checked her cell phone every five minutes to see if she'd missed a call, if there was a new emergency.

"Drew says we can't afford to hire someone."

"Well, yeah, that's probably true."

The words slapped me in the face. It was devastating to hear someone besides Drew telling me there was no other option.

"If he got a good job, it might be an option," she said. Then: "Maybe."

"He says the pay from a restaurant job wouldn't cover the cost of hiring someone," I said.

Oh, how I wanted her to dispute him, say he was wrong.

"Well, yeah, that's probably true, too."

My shoulders slumped.

"You might just have to wait it out," she added.

"It" being Drew's mother's life.

"That's what I'm doing," she said, "waiting it out."

It occurred to me right then that maybe Nancy wanted me to be miserable, like her. She wanted the company.

I sipped my tea. She sipped her coffee. I waited for the burst of anger I felt to dissipate. I couldn't hate Nancy. She was just the messenger of truths I needed to face.

"You're going to have to do Christmas with her," she said. I'd already confronted this particular truth, shook its hand, agreed to be civil.

"I know. I'm going to have Drew go get her boxes of Christmas decorations tomorrow," I said. "We'll put them up. She's obsessed with Christmas."

"Look at you—Saint Emily."

I shrugged. "I have to balance out all my complaining with some goodwill."

Drew and I had just had a big fight a couple days before in which he'd said he never knew I could be such a bitter person. It hurt to hear. I felt guilty, like I'd become this person he didn't marry, like I'd duped him.

"You're a better person than me," Nancy said.

I didn't believe that was true, but it was good to hear it anyway. At home, I saw myself as callous, cruel, because that's how Drew saw me.

Nancy checked her phone and said she had to get home. On our way out, I asked if she'd show me the Heimlich maneuver, just in case I needed to use it. And there we were, on the sidewalk outside a Brooklyn coffee shop, Nancy grabbing me and hoisting me upward. To drivers passing by, we must have looked insane.

Drew's mom had thirteen boxes of Christmas decorations. Five boxes of just Santas: fat Santas, thin Santas, stuffed Santas, wood Santas, glass Santas. A set of reindeer and a sleigh meant to occupy a grand mantel. Snow globes, a village of ceramic houses with snow-covered roofs, garlands, wreaths, and three boxes of ornaments. And she had a six-foot-tall fake Douglas fir that we propped up to the left of the TV. It was too big for our small space. I told Drew that just looking at it gave me heart palpitations. He said, "You're so dramatic." I said, "No, I'm so claustrophobic."

We set aside Saturday night to put up all the decorations. It was hard to tell if Drew's mom was happy—she didn't have enough strength in her face to form a smile—but Drew said she was. He could tell, he said.

"I'm going to pick up some food. You two get started," he said, kissing me on the nose before heading out the door with Bruce. I would have rather been the one to pick up the food. He had to know that.

I started unpacking the boxes slowly. I put everything out on display on the hardwood floors. It looked like a Christmas-themed yard sale in our tiny apartment. Drew's mom surveyed it all and pointed one mostly bent finger in the direction of the sleigh and reindeer.

I went to her side, leaned in so close to her that my cheek grazed hers. This was the only way to hear her.

"Shhh—" she said.

"What?" I said.

The first "What?" was always patient, kind, understanding. The second was embarrassed. The third was frustrated.

By the fourth attempt, I understood that she was saying, "Shelf," that she wanted me to clear the books we had and replace them with the reindeer and sleigh. I obliged because, really, what other choice is there with a sick person?

I transported the books to our bedroom closet, stacked them beside a pile of her shoes. When I came back, she was pointing at the fattest of the Santas.

I spent an hour like that—being directed around my own home by a woman who couldn't speak. There was no need for it to be an hour. Drew was taking his sweet time. I knew that because it was exactly what I would have done. It was why I wanted to be the one to pick up the food. I eyed my running shoes by the door. The second Drew walked in, I would be gone, around the block before he could ask if I wanted him to put the pizza box in the oven to keep it warm.

She bent forward toward the coffee table, as slow as the Tin Man in need of a squirt of oil. Her destination was obvious: a plate of sugar cookies with red and green sprinkles on them. Drew had bought them yesterday. His mom's favorite, he said. We were constantly trying to fatten her up, to no avail.

I set the plate on her lap to save us both the agonizing time it would have taken for her to obtain a cookie on her own. While she nibbled on one, I went to my running shoes, sat on the floor, laced them up. I was ready.

When I turned around, she was blue. That fast. Her eyes were big and frightened, her hands slowly moving to grasp her neck. In a ridiculous display of irony, she was choking.

Before I was sure I knew what I was doing, I was behind her, my fists pulling into her stomach, right below her ribs. She was so thin that I feared breaking her completely.

Then, just as Nancy had promised, a partially dissolved piece of cookie flew out of her mouth and she gasped for air the way people do when they've been underwater too long. The blue left her face and the pink returned. She told me *Thank you* with her eyes, though she wouldn't manage the actual words for several minutes.

And I hugged her. I was either relieved she hadn't died, plain and simple, or I was relieved that I wasn't the reason she died.

Just then, Drew walked in. It was as if he'd been waiting outside the door for this situation to resolve itself.

"Where the hell were you?" I asked. I pushed him in the chest, like teenage boys do when they start fights.

He looked dumbfounded. "What happened?"

"She fucking choked," I said. The adrenaline was still pulsing through me. I'd never before been so aware of the size of my veins, of their capacity.

He went to his mom, knelt down on one knee, met her eyes with his.

"Are you okay?" he asked her.

She nodded weakly.

"She's okay because Nancy happened to show me the fucking Heimlich maneuver the other day."

"Who's Nancy?" he asked.

In that instant, we both realized there were secrets we were keeping from each other. Things had changed between us.

"A friend," I said. "It doesn't matter."

He brought his mom's ever-present water glass to her lips. She sipped carefully.

"She can't eat food on her own anymore," I said. I was yelling still, the adrenaline making it impossible to lower my voice.

He got up, came to me, put his hands on my shoulders, like a fireman calming the owner of a burning house.

"You're just scared, okay?" he said.

"Calm down," he said.

"Deep breaths," he said.

I wanted to punch him in the face. I could feel my nostrils flaring, the way boxers' do in those fights you have to pay to watch on TV. He gripped my shoulders harder.

"She needs to move out," I said.

"You need to hire someone to take care of her," I said.

"We need our life back," I said.

I'd said these things before, but always in the confines of our bedroom, our situation room, our war room; never in front of her. He looked away from me, to her. Her feelings mattered more than mine. It was a truth I'd known for a while, now proven.

His mom curled her finger, beckoning him. He went to her, leaned in to hear whatever she said. It took him two attempts—"What?" "What?"—before he understood.

"She's sorry," he said.

He looked at me like I was the enemy, like I had lodged the cookie in her throat.

"She's just scared, Ma," he told her.

I grabbed Bruce's leash off its hook, the leather in my hand an immediate relaxer, the way a stuffed animal is for a toddler afraid of the dark.

"I'm going for a run."

Bruce and I ran to Knickerbocker, where the taco shop used to be. A brightly lit Go-Go Juice was in its place. I lingered outside, watched people come and go with their tall Styrofoam cups. Most of them were in gym clothes—spandex, sweats. I needed to call Nancy. The only other time I'd called her was before our first official coffee shop meeting, to confirm it was actually happening. There was an unspoken understanding that we weren't that kind of friends. We went about our lives during the week and confided in each other like soul mates on Thursdays. That was it. I went to the pay phone at the end of the block anyway, and dialed. It rang three times before she picked up.

"I had to use the Heimlich," I said.

There was a long pause.

"Oh, crap," she said finally.

"He doesn't understand. I can't do this anymore."

"I know," she said, instead of something motivational like, *Yes, you can.*

I lowered my chin to my chest, stared at the cement with old pieces of gum melted into it, part of it now.

"Do you want to come over?" she asked. "I have my own choking hazard, of course, but we can talk it out. You can sleep on the couch. My ex used to say it was very comfortable."

"No, no," I said. That wasn't why I had called. I didn't really know why I had called.

"Em," she said, "you're going to have to make a choice. You're going to have to wait it out or leave."

Wait it out. I wished she would stop fucking saying that. My face was hot. Why did those have to be my only options—wait it out or leave?

"I'm sorry," she said, as if reading my mind, "this isn't the time. Look, come over if you want."

"No, really, it's fine," I said. "I don't know why I called."

Bruce licked my leg, wagged his tail.

"I know it sucks," she said. "You okay?"

"Yep," I said. It was a blatant lie, but neither of us was willing or able to poke at it.

"Okay, well, see you Thursday?"

"Sure," I said, though I didn't think I would. I wasn't sure if Nancy and I having this horrible situation in common was a comfort anymore. For some reason, I'd thought the two of us would come up with some way to make it all better. That was proving to be a childish fantasy. Nancy was older, but not wiser. She was just as helpless as I was.

"Call if you need to," she said.

"Okay," I said, knowing I wouldn't.

I knelt down to Bruce and kissed his wet nose. I envied his ignorance. We walked back past the Go-Go Juice and then I broke into a sprint all the way home.

FOURTEEN

Chemo isn't as bad as I feared. I go to an infusion center, where about twenty other cancer-stricken people sit in chairs, hooked up to poison that is supposed to make them well. Most occupy themselves with their phones and iPads. Some go old school and read actual books or knit. Nurses bring juice and blankets to us with the pleasant politeness of flight attendants: *Can I offer you a warm towel?* There are even call buttons on the arms of our chairs.

They've got me on a regimen of Adriamycin and Cytoxan—AC, Dr. Richter calls it. She says only about fifteen percent of people with my type of cancer—my rare, brutal, obnoxious kind of cancer—have a complete response to this regimen, but there are other things we can try if I'm not in that fifteen percent. They implanted this thing called a port under my skin, up near my collarbone, so I can easily be "plugged in" to the tube that delivers the chemo. Actually, before the chemo comes rushing into my veins, they give me a bag of Zofran to keep me from puking. I guess it works because I haven't actually puked yet. I just feel like I'm going to—very similar to how I felt when I was pregnant and how I felt the time Claire and I took a boat across the channel to Catalina.

The Adriamycin comes first. It's bright red like Hawaiian Punch. Then comes the Cytoxan, clear. It doesn't hurt when it's happening. The problems all start when I go home.

The fatigue is heavy-feeling, like I'm walking around with a sack of rocks on my shoulders. The nausea comes and goes. There are sores in my mouth. I tongue them when I'm anxious. They kill whatever appetite survives the nausea. I've lost five pounds off my already slim frame. Some days, I take a couple handfuls of pills just to function. There's Zofran for the nausea, then laxatives and stool softeners for the constipation caused by Zofran. Oh, and I have to take Neupogen to keep my white blood cell count high so I don't get an infection that my body is too tired to fight. Neupogen causes bone pain—a pain I'd never known before, like an ache deep below the muscles. I take Vicodin for the bone pain. Vicodin makes me sick to my stomach. You see how it goes.

I've put off telling Al. I've gone to work like normal. Sometimes, if I stand too long, I get dizzy and the I'm-going-to-barf feeling intensifies, so I sit on a stool behind the counter. I don't want to call in sick. It's only here, at the bar, when I can be in complete denial that this cancer thing is happening to me. But I'm in my second month of chemo now and my hair is starting to fall out. I wake up in the morning and find sections of it on my pillow, arranged as neatly as Claire's first hair clipping in her baby book. I have to tell Al.

"Can I talk to you?" I say. It's a Thursday, toward the end of my shift. The bar is quiet. Arnie is on his way to drunk, mumbling to himself in the corner.

"What's up?" Al says. He's bent down, counting beer bottles in the mini-fridge.

"Well, I just wanted to warn you that I'll be bald soon," I say.

He stands up, slow and creaky. I can tell he already knows what I mean.

"No," he says, flatly and decidedly, as if he is God and he has determined that this is not real.

I nod.

"That's bullshit," he says. As if cancer is a speeding ticket when you're only going five miles per hour over the limit.

"That's what I've been telling myself, too, but it doesn't seem to make it go away."

I smile, for his benefit. If I'm not mistaken, his eyes look a little watery.

"I plan to keep working. I'm doing chemo and it's going fine so far, and—"

"You can take time off if you need to," he says. "Paid leave or whatever the hell."

I want to hug him, but his upper lip is stiff and it's obvious he wants to keep it that way.

"You don't need to do that," I say. "I want to come in."

"Fine, then," he says. There's edge in his voice. A bar patron listening in would think he's mad at me.

"You wouldn't know how to do the accounting if I left," I say, trying to be jokey. I've come to manage the books for the bar. I'm good at it, thanks to my last professional years as Emily Morris. Al says every year that he wants to retire and he expects me to take over. He keeps working, though.

"Insurance's taking care of everything?" he asks.

"Yes," I say. "I don't know what I'd do without it. Thank you."

As promised, Al got a health plan through the bar after I'd worked a year. He takes a nominal fee out of my paycheck for it. The one time I asked how much he has to pay for the plan, he waved me off and said, "It's a write-off for the bar, doesn't matter." Al, the businessman. The plan can't be cheap because it does, in fact, cover my chemo.

"I'm going to be okay," I say. It's a possible lie that I keep telling.

"Of course you are, damn it."

When I clog the shower with enough hair to require extra-strength Drano, I tell Claire it's time. We've talked about this in advance, planned that she will shave my head for me. The idea isn't an original one: make yourself bald before cancer does. You have to exert control when you can.

Claire takes out her phone, snaps my requested "before" photo. I want to be able to remember who I was with hair.

"What if I cut you?" she asks.

I'm sitting on the deck in our backyard, the almost-rotted-through deck that JT has never bothered to replace. She's standing over me, razor in hand. My head is covered with way too much shaving cream.

"You won't cut me," I say. "We got the fancy razors, remember?"

Claire doesn't even shave her legs yet, a fact she reminded me of when we went to the pharmacy to buy the razors. The hair on her legs is still light and sparse. I should show her how, just so she knows. There's so much I have to teach her.

"Are you sure?"

"I'm sure," I say. "You want to practice on my arm?"

She nods and we cover my arm in a similarly overabundant amount of shaving cream. She approaches it tentatively, carefully, and starts making a path through the cream with the razor.

"You're not even touching my arm," I say with a laugh.

It's sweet, this gentleness. I guide her hand with mine, show her how much pressure to use. After five minutes, my arm is bare and shiny. I wipe the leftover shaving cream on my shirt.

"Now hurry up before I have shaving cream running down my face."

"Okay, okay," she says.

I close my eyes, relax. This is the closest I'll come to the meditation recommended by the hippie-dippie holistic medicine people. I've researched it all, clicked through hundreds of websites and blogs. I read myself to sleep with online message boards, other patients sharing their treatment regimens, their supplements, their yoga routines, their chemo time-passers. Chemo takes hours. I don't know how people tolerated it before smartphones. Claire and I play Scrabble. She wins and I'm not even letting her. I used to scroll through Facebook, looking at the vacations other people were taking, the birthdays they were celebrating, the family time they were "cherishing." That started to piss me off so I just play Scrabble now.

"I think I'm done," she says.

"You think?" I say. "It should be pretty obvious if you're done."

She wipes off my head with a towel, walks a circle around me to inspect her work.

"Then I'm done. You're bald as can be."

I watch as she takes in the new me, this alien life-form that is her mother.

"Do I look weird?" I ask.

"Yes."

This is one of many reasons I love my daughter. She's smart enough not to say something cheesy like, *It works for you because you have such a pretty face.* Is anybody's face really *that* pretty? Pretty enough to distract from a shiny, bald skull? I don't think so.

I touch my hands to my head. The skin is thinner than I expect, pulled tight around bones that bear the responsibility of protecting my brain. It all seems very vulnerable.

Claire takes out her phone again and snaps the "after" photos—one of just me, and one of me and her, her arm stretched out long to get both of us in the frame.

I take the towel, shaving cream, and razor inside, preparing myself for what I'll see in the hallway mirror. Claire follows on my heels—anxious, antsy, ready to counteract all the criticisms that come out of my mouth.

There are no criticisms, though. I stand there, before the mirror, and I laugh—loudly. Because I look ridiculous.

"It wouldn't be so bad if I still had eyebrows and eyelashes," I say.

I laugh so hard that I start to cry, tears rolling out of their ducts easily—no eyelashes to stop them. And then I collapse to my knees.

"Mom," Claire says. "Are you okay?"

"I don't know," I say, because I really don't. I'm hysterical.

Claire rubs my back with her palm, saying, "It's okay," over and over again until I catch my breath.

"Sorry," I say. "More emotional than I thought it would be, I guess."

I give her a weak smile, the same weak smile I give her when I come home from chemo and she asks how it went. I always say, "Fine," even though I feel like shit. It does no good to give her insight into my pain. She'll just want to dedicate her existence to taking it away. And she can't. She has a life. She's running for class president. She's playing soccer. She's hanging out with Heather and Riley and Tyler and whoever else.

"Mom," she says, as I make my way to the bedroom, completely done with today even though the sun hasn't set. I remember that I need to make her dinner and change my direction to the kitchen.

"Yeah?"

"Can you do me now?"

"Do what?"

"Me. My head."

She runs her fingers through her long, wavy hair to show what she means.

"Oh, no, Claire. Absolutely not."

"Why?"

"Your hair is beautiful, sweetie," I say. "This isn't your battle. It's mine."

"I'm pretty involved," she says, hands on hips with mock sass.

"How are you going to feel at school as the kid with no hair?" I ask her, convinced this will change her mind. It would have changed my mind when I was her age. Ostracism was my primary fear between the ages of ten and twenty-five.

"I suppose I'll feel cold sometimes. I might have to wear a beanie," she says, deadpan.

"If you want to do it, you'll have to get someone else to help you. I can't be responsible for removing all that hair from your head," I say.

She breaks into a smile. "I'll consider that permission."

Before I can counter her, she takes the shaving cream and razor from the floor, where I dropped them mid-breakdown, and marches to the bathroom.

"Claire!"

When she doesn't turn around, I follow her. She already has the faucet running, rinsing the razor like a shaving pro.

"I should probably just chop it off first, huh?" she says.

She doesn't wait for an answer. She goes to the kitchen, rifles through the junk drawer, and comes back to the bathroom with a pair of rusty old scissors. She doesn't hesitate—she just starts cutting. Chunks of her gorgeous hair fall to the floor. I find myself straining to catch all of them, like they're hundred-dollar bills flying out the back of an armored bank truck. There is no point in telling her to stop now.

She stops cutting when the hair is up to her ears, jagged and haphazard. She looks like a crazy person, someone in an insane asylum.

"Okay," she says. "Here goes nothin'."

I sit on the toilet, looking down at my feet because I can't bear to see her do this. She's finished in twenty minutes. I know she's done before she says so. I can tell by her sigh.

"I could get used to this," she says.

I dare to look up. She is turning her head from one side to the other, analyzing the angles. In that moment, I realize that, yes, it is possible that a face is pretty enough to distract from a shiny, bald skull. And that realization brings tears to my eyes.

She reaches out to me, takes my hands in hers as I stand up off the toilet. She grabs a few squares of toilet paper and jams them into my fist.

"Mom, seriously, stop with the tears," she says. "You're killing me."

I'm startled by the bald person in the kitchen. It takes me a second to remember that's my daughter. She's beating eggs in a bowl, making breakfast, making me feel guilty. She's taken on the responsibility of preparing meals on the days I have chemo treatments. She keeps track of those days by writing *Kill Cancer* on the appropriate calendar squares. She's got her pink Converse sneakers on, specially ordered online when she took on this breast cancer campaign in my honor. She pins a pink ribbon to her shirt every day she goes to school. She says other kids are doing it, too. She sends me pictures of them, huddled together, puffing their chests out like proud pigeons to display their support of me, this woman they don't even know.

"You know, I don't need a hot breakfast. I'm more than capable of putting cereal in a bowl."

"I know," she says, pouring the beaten eggs into a pan. "The protein is good for you."

My fear is that she'll get burnt out on this. Or she'll convince herself that doing all these things will contribute to the "Kill Cancer" goal. If the chemo doesn't work, if I die, I don't want her to feel like she failed.

I expect her to wear a hat or something, but she doesn't. I drop her off at the curb, as usual, and she marches into school, the sun reflecting off her bald head. Kids stare. A few of them, when they recognize it's her, come up and talk to her, mouths agape. Without hair, her smile takes on even bigger proportions.

"I like the new 'do," the infusion center nurse says in reference to my baldness.

When I started coming for chemo, I didn't make eye contact with anyone. I wasn't there to make friends. But after several weeks of seeing the same people over and over again, I can't help but smile or give a nod of recognition. I still don't talk to them, despite there being just a few feet between us. I don't want to know their stories.

I do talk to my nurse, though. I figure I should get on her good side, be one of her favorites. It's childish, really. She administers the drugs, but she has no control over my cancer. I want her to. I want someone to.

"Thanks, my daughter styled it herself," I say.

Her name is Amy, the nurse. She goes through the usual motions, taking off the bag of Adriamycin, putting on the bag of Cytoxan.

"Impressive. How old is your daughter?"

Up to this point, we have shared basic facts about ourselves with each other. She's thirty-two. She has a cat—a fact she revealed when I inquired about the black pet hair on her white scrubs. She knows I'm forty-four, that I have "the weird kind of breast cancer," that I have no pets.

"She's thirteen going on forty-five."

"Oh, I know the type," she says with a knowing laugh. "Mine's six. Audrey."

There we are—two mothers just talking about our children, like mothers do, while a cancer battle is under way beneath my skin.

Once I'm all hooked up, she gives my hand a kind pat and says I should call her if I need to. I have a couple hours of sitting ahead of me. I have to pee, but I command my bladder to wait. I'm on wheels, I'm mobile, but it's a hassle to roll across the room, in front of everyone, my IV bag swinging from its hook.

Ten minutes into my two-hour wait, the empty seat next to me is occupied by a guy I haven't seen before. He looks to be about my age, mid-forties, maybe a little younger. He doesn't have eyebrows, either. He's a regular.

"I've never seen you here before," he says. I can tell immediately, by just the curiosity in his voice, that he's one of those overly chatty people. He befriends people at bars and on planes on a regular basis—or at least he used to until people got scared of his hairlessness, the obviousness of his disease. People with cancer, we're feared. We are walking reminders of what nobody wants to think about.

"That wasn't a pickup line," he says in response to my curt smile.

Who the hell is this guy?

"I should hope not."

"It could be. You're attractive. No wedding ring. Maybe your fingers are just swollen, though. From the chemo."

I'm flattered and confused and annoyed all at once.

"I'm not married," is all I say.

Nurse Amy hooks him up to whatever drug regimen his doctor swears by. The bag is bulging. He'll be here for hours.

"Name's Paul," he says. "Prostate cancer. Six weeks into chemo."

"Connie," I say. I don't offer any more details. Amy looks amused at this interaction of ours.

"I used to come in the mornings. That's probably why I've never seen you."

"Probably."

"With work, afternoons are better."

I nod. He probably wants me to ask about his work, his life, but I have no interest. Thankfully, he goes radio silent for the rest of my time there. I say good-bye to him on the way out, to be polite. And then I say good-bye to Amy. She takes me by the forearm and pulls me close to her.

"Don't mind Paul," she says. "He's lonely. That's all."

"Aren't we all?"

"Well, he's harmless, just so you know," she says. "This place sucks. It wouldn't be the worst thing to make a friend."

FIFTEEN

Less than a month after Drew's mom's choking incident, on the eve of the year 2000, everyone was talking about Y2K. Extremists said the world was going to end. I kind of wished it would.

But life went on as usual. Drew's mother continued to live with us. We—or Drew, rather—started supervising all of her feedings. I kept running, stopped meeting up with Nancy. I spent as much time at work as I could. Until, one day, even that was taken away from me.

This is going to change everything. That's what I was thinking as I packed up my desk at Mathers and James. I didn't know how everything would be changed, but I knew it was inevitable, as ominous as dark gray clouds in early February.

Everything fit in one box. My personal belongings were few. Most of my desk was occupied with work folders: one for each project, older drafts at the back of each folder, most recent at the front. I'd become obsessively organized since Drew's mom moved in with us. A shrink would say something like, *You're creating neat piles at work because home life feels so messy. You're struggling to maintain a sense of control.* I didn't see a shrink because I already knew that.

I had a lame motivational calendar with majestic photos of mountain ranges paired with quotes like, *Aspire to climb as high as you can dream.* I threw that away. I had a *Seinfeld* coffee mug someone gave me—I can't even remember who—that read, *Top of the muffin to you.* I threw that away, too. There was an empty vase on the windowsill behind my desk. Drew had sent roses for Valentine's Day, and when they died I saved the vase they came in, harboring aspirations of filling it with fresh flowers every week. I never did that. I tossed the vase at the trash can. It hit the edge and shattered, the noise alerting my work neighbor to rush in and say, "You okay?"

I had one framed photo—of Drew and me on the day we got married. We looked so young and, frankly, dumb. I was staring at the camera straight-on, holding the bouquet of carnations his mom had brought for me. My smile was big and cheesy, the kind kids give for ice cream cake or Disneyland or puppies. Drew wasn't looking at the camera; he was looking at me, as if he was so enamored that he couldn't turn away, even just for a second.

I put the picture in my purse, pushed it down as far as it would go, irritated with the corners of the plastic frame sticking out the top. Then I took out my phone and dialed Marni's number.

"I need to meet you for a drink," I said as soon as she answered.

"Now?"

It was four o'clock on a Friday—close to the end of a work week for many people, but about five hours from the end of Friday for her. There is no end to the week in the advertising world of New York.

"Yes. Can you?"

She hesitated, so I blurted it out:

"I just got laid off."

We met up at the Dive. For once, she was already there when I arrived, sitting at the bar, a drink in front of her. When I came in, she stood reverentially, the way people do for brides walking down the aisle.

"I'm so sorry, honey," she said, putting her arms around me. She smelled like a women's magazine. I wanted to hug her for longer than would be socially appropriate. I hadn't hugged or been hugged in months.

"It's okay," I lied, hopping up on a stool next to hers.

"What the hell happened?"

She took a long suck on her straw. She was halfway through some kind of brown liquor, on the rocks.

According to rumor, the partners—Mathers and James themselves, whom I'd never met—got a deal they couldn't refuse from a giant conglomerate who wanted to buy them out.

"Was it ICP?" Marni asked.

"Hm?" I didn't know the advertising world as well as she did.

"International Creative Partners. They're preying on every small agency in Manhattan right now."

"Yeah, maybe it was them. I don't know," I said. "They brought in their own people. They said there were 'redundancies.' "

"How very British of them," Marni said with a look of disgust.

"What am I going to do?" I asked. The bartender came by to ask if I wanted a drink and I waved him off. My stomach had been upset since I'd gotten the news. All I wanted to drink was Pepto-Bismol.

"Well, first you're going to be rightfully pissed off," Marni said. "These companies don't care about people like you and me. I was hoping not to be jaded until my late thirties, but that's becoming a seriously unrealistic goal."

"I'm not even mad," I said. This seemed to disappoint her. She was ready to yell and scream and organize some kind of revolt.

"I swear you've gotten way too good at suppressing every emotion you have."

"I don't have time to be mad," I said. "I'm just worried."

"You'll be fine. I'll investigate any job openings at my agency, though they haven't been hiring for a while. We lost a few big clients after the holidays. My entire life has been pitching new business lately and I'm just so sick of—"

She stopped abruptly, as if she remembered that I was the only one allowed to have problems. "Go on," I said, trying to be a friend.

She said, "It doesn't matter. Let's just focus on getting you a job."

"I don't even know where to start," I said. "I haven't even looked at my résumé since I started at Mathers and James."

"So that will be task number one," she said. She took a pen out of her purse—a purple, sparkly pen with no cap. She drew inkless circles on a cocktail napkin until the purple showed itself, then wrote down, *1. Résumé.*

"You know what else you should do?" she asked. "Contact a recruiter. They'll do the hard work for you—find leads, that kind of thing."

She wrote that on the napkin: *2. Recruiter.*

She finished her drink and then pushed the empty glass out of her way like its presence was bothering her. She put the end of the pen in her mouth, gnawing on it, eyes rolled up to the right, deep in thought.

Suddenly she took the pen out of her mouth and tapped it on her temple. "Duh," she muttered to herself. She pulled the napkin close to her and wrote on it, not letting me see what she was writing. After she was done, she pushed the napkin to me.

3. Tell Drew to get off his ass.

I wanted to crumple the napkin and throw it over the bar, into the overfilling trash can by the cash register. Instead, though, I folded it politely and put it in my purse.

"You can't be mad at me for bringing it up," she said. "This would be the perfect time to lovingly encourage him to win some bread for a while."

"You're forgetting his sick mother," I said. "Which, hey, I understand. I'd love to forget her, too, but that's pretty impossible with her living in our apartment."

The last time Marni saw me, I was doing a much better job of keeping my composure. She looked startled.

"Sorry," I said, quickly. "I've become a total bitch."

"Thank God. That just means we have more in common." She leaned over and gave me a little kiss on the cheek.

"We'll figure something out," she said. I appreciated the "we," the insinuation that I wasn't alone in this even though I knew I was. I'd lost every sense of "we" in my life lately. Drew and I no longer felt like a "we." He was "him" and I was "me."

Marni looked at her watch. "I hate to do this," she said, "but I have to get back to the office." Her face was twisted into a look of sincere apology.

"No, go. We'd be in real trouble if you lost your job, too," I said, using the "we" she'd offered.

She pulled a ten out of her bag and put it on the counter, along with a few quarters dug up from the depths of her purse. We walked out of the bar together, her arm around me, holding me close to her body. She was warm.

Outside, she faced me and put a hand on each of my shoulders, like a coach does with a pitcher before he takes the mound in a World Series game.

"You'll be okay," she said. "Please believe me."

"I'll try," I said.

" 'Try' is a weak man's word." When both of us worked together at Mathers and James, this was something one of the account guys used to say on a way-too-regular basis.

"I *will* be okay." I tried to sound confident, but felt like I was making a false promise.

"I'll call you tomorrow, 'kay? I'll have some names of recruiters. You work on your résumé tonight," she said. "And talk to Drew."

During my walk from the DeKalb subway station to the apartment, I thought about how I'd announce my joblessness to Drew . . . and to his mother. I wanted her to know, too. I wanted her to understand that she was about to become an even greater burden on us than she already was. The announcement would be dramatic. For once, I would be the center circle, the most important according to support-group-Pam's stupid theory.

They were sitting at the kitchen table, with a man I didn't know. Drew looked up at me with a look of surprise and guilt, like I'd caught him cheating on me.

"You're home early," he said. He cleared his throat.

"Yeah," I said, keeping my eyes on the man I didn't know. He was in his early forties. His hair was gelled back and he was wearing a suit. He had papers spread in front of him on the table. He looked from me to Drew and back again, then took it upon himself to stand and stick out his hand.

"Greg," he said. "You must be Drew's wife."

"Right," I said, not sharing my name. I shifted my glance to Drew. He wouldn't meet my eye.

"We were just discussing some comps near Ms. Morris's home in Newark," he said, waving his hand over the papers on the table.

"Comps?" I said, taking a few steps closer to examine the papers. They were real estate listings.

"Comparables," he clarified. "Properties comparable to hers that have recently sold in her area."

"Why?" I said, already figuring out the answer for myself while the question hung in the air.

"We're just exploring some options," Drew said, trying to make it all seem casual. It wasn't casual, though. It was gelled-back-hair-and-a-suit serious.

"You're selling her house?" I said.

"Just exploring options," this Greg said, understanding where his alliances lay.

"Right," I said.

Drew's mom whispered something into Drew's ear. He nodded and said to me, on her behalf, "It's just an idea. If we sell her house, we'll have some money for the three of us."

"The three of us," I repeated back.

There was a time when I thought of the three of us as Drew, Bruce the dog, and me. I looked at Bruce, stretched out on the floor in front of the couch. I wanted him to cry with me. I swallowed back what tears I did have, gave a polite, "Excuse me," to Greg, and walked to the bedroom as fast as I could. I changed out of my pants suit and into sweats, grabbed my Nikes, laced them up, and left, slamming the door behind me. In my head, I could hear Drew apologizing for me to Greg, as if I were the problem: *Sorry, she's been a little emotional lately.*

I ran until my stomach growled with hunger for dinner. Two hours had passed. I knew Greg would be gone, so I ran home. When I got there, breathing fast and heavy, Drew was standing out front, chatting with neighbor Jim, this old guy who lived alone with two parakeets. Drew was smiling, making small talk. He was always better with people than I ever was. I waved to Jim with as friendly a demeanor as I could muster. When you're fighting with your spouse, you want anyone and everyone to realize it's not you who's the crazy one. Jim waved back, then stuffed his hands into the pockets of the same windbreaker he always wore and headed upstairs.

"Good run?" Drew asked.

"Yep," I said. I bent at the waist, grabbed the front of my shoes, stretching out my legs. I didn't want to look at him.

"I didn't mean to ambush you like that," he said.

"Oh, I know," I said, still bent over. The blood rushed to my head with urgency. "You meant to meet with him while I wasn't here so I'd never know."

"Em," he said, with his let's-talk-about-this-like-adults tone.

I rose up. "Yes?"

"Look, I'm sorry."

He'd started doing this a lot—delivering these blanket apologies, covering me with them, wrapping me with them.

I lifted my leg up to the building wall, letting the heel of my shoe rest in the grout between two bricks. I bent at the side, stretching out over my leg like a ballerina. My eyes were closed, my forehead resting on my shin. That's when I started crying, into my pant leg.

"Em?" he said. "Are you okay?"

He came to me, put his hand on my back. I could feel the boniness of my spine under his fingers.

I looked up at him, finally ready for him to see the reality.

"I can't do this anymore," I said.

His jaw hung a little, making him seem more pathetic than I'd ever wanted him to seem.

I'd never said this, specifically, before—not to him at least. I'd said it to Nancy. Marni had said it to me: *You can't do this anymore.*

"I can't come home to this every night," I said.

"The Realtor?"

He was dumb sometimes. This fact caused a small pain in my chest that could only be my heart breaking.

"No. Your mom. You. The whole thing. I can't do it."

"What do you want me to do?" he said. He asked this frequently, knowing deep down that I wouldn't be able to come up with any solution; or that I wouldn't be cruel enough to suggest what he'd consider impossible. This time, though, I made my need known.

"Take her home," I said. It was a relief to state it, out loud. I'd finally done it—requested that impossible thing.

"Em, she needs twenty-four-hour care."

I arched my neck back. The sky was black, but I couldn't see any stars—a con of city life.

"I can't even tell you how many times you've told me that," I said.

He threw his arms up toward the black sky. "It's a fact. I don't know what you want me to do. Perform a miracle?"

That's how he saw it, this caring for his mother—a duty that only a miracle could remove.

"Go live with her, then," I said. "I'll stay here."

He thought I was calling his bluff. He exhaled something between a laugh and a gasp. I took my leg off the wall and stood there staring at him. He expected me to say, *I don't mean that,* which was a lie I wasn't willing to tell.

"Are you serious?" he said.

"I don't see another option. She needs twenty-four-hour care." There was satisfaction in using his words against him.

"We're *married,* Em," he said.

"That's exactly my point—we're a married couple, not nurses."

He took a deep breath and walked in a circle, just like Bruce did when he was nervous.

"You can take care of her there until you figure out something else," I said.

He stopped his circle-turning and put his hands on his hips like a defiant teenager protesting a curfew violation.

"You're serious," he said. "This is what you want?"

He wasn't angry. He was surprised, worried.

"I think we're months past considering what I want."

I wasn't angry, either. I was tired. I crossed my arms across my chest, strummed my ribs with my fingers.

"Oh," I said, "and I lost my job."

With that, I went up to the apartment, ignoring his pleas that I come back to talk more. His mom was watching TV. I sat close to her and made the effort to ask how she was feeling. I never did this, but the prospect of her leaving filled me with the compassion Drew always insisted I try to have.

He took her home the next day. I wondered if she hated me until I saw her sad attempt to smile as they said good-bye, her bags slung over Drew's shoulders. She understood, better than Drew did. He wouldn't look at me.

I washed every sheet and towel and cleaned every dish in the apartment. This was for the best, I told myself. We'd settle into a routine of not seeing each other at all during the week. That was the plan. On Saturday mornings, he'd come home, with her in tow. They'd stay the night, then leave again after an early Sunday dinner. Drew and I would talk on the phone every day. Absence would make our hearts grow fonder. We'd say, *I miss you,* and mean it. We'd fall in love again.

At least, that was the plan.

SIXTEEN

I spent the first few days of my unemployment as a stereotype—sitting around in pajamas, sleeping late, watching terrible TV. The apartment was quiet in a way it had never been, even when it was just Drew and me. To compensate, I played loud music—Tori Amos and Joni Mitchell and Janis Joplin and anything else that made me feel like the strong, independent, empowered woman I wanted to be. I didn't go running; I didn't feel the need. I just took Bruce out for long walks.

Marni said I should call a recruiter named Patricia Wilson. She charged a fee—a hundred bucks per session. I hedged at that and Marni argued, "She's the best of the best. She's, like, epic in New York. She's a career fairy godmother." So I called. I didn't get to talk to the woman herself; her assistant made an appointment for me. I took note of her address in the city and promised to bring a pristine résumé. That's what the assistant requested—pristine.

I got a haircut for the first time in years, chopped off three inches. At the salon, I flipped through a women's magazine with an article that said making even the smallest changes in your life can be the start of a "personal revolution." I'd kicked out my husband, essentially; the revolution was under way.

Patricia Wilson's office was in a high-rise on Fifth Avenue, nine floors above an art gallery and a Baskin-Robbins. I told myself I'd get an ice-cream cone if the appointment went well, and I'd get a different flavor than my usual cookies and cream, in accordance with the "personal revolution." I wore my best business suit—charcoal-gray pants with a matching blazer, and an emerald-green shirt underneath. The green shirt was my good-luck shirt at Mathers and James. Whenever a big client presentation made me so nervous that I couldn't sleep the night before, I wore that shirt. And never once did my greatest fear—suddenly forgetting how to speak English—become a reality.

The elevator stopped at the ninth floor and I stepped out. An etched metal plaque on the door of suite 900 read THE WILSON GROUP. Patricia didn't just work at a recruiting agency; she owned it. She managed a group.

Beyond the double wooden doors was a grand reception desk, manned by a beautiful, dark-haired twenty-something. She could have been temping between modeling gigs.

"You must be Emily Morris," she said, making the kind of eye contact that's unnerving, the kind of eye contact that makes you paranoid there's food on your face.

"I am," I said. I approached the desk and shook her hand. She had a clipboard ready for me, my name already typed at the top of the form affixed to it.

"Would you mind filling out your information? Patricia will be right out."

I took a seat in one of only two chairs in the waiting room. They were armchairs that you'd usually see in front of a large fireplace, upholstered with some kind of satiny material that I was almost afraid to touch.

The form asked questions about my past work experience and future goals. I checked a box saying that I would be interested in personality assessments to match me with the best possible employer. I wondered what my assessment would say: That I was bossy or passive? Obedient or rebellious? Easygoing or stubborn? I wasn't sure who I was anymore.

I heard Patricia before I saw her. The click of her high heels was slow and steady, like she was in absolutely no rush to get anywhere. Her strides were long, so I figured her legs would be. She was one of those women men stared at on the street, pausing in the midst of eating a street-vendor hot dog to admire.

"Emily?" she said, emerging from the hallway. She was even prettier than I'd imagined. She must have been in her forties, but her skin was as milky smooth as that of her young receptionist. She had blond hair, in loose curls halfway down her back. She wore an expensive-looking black dress, belted at the waist, and red high heels. Her lipstick matched her heels perfectly.

"It's nice to meet you," I said, standing, my legs shaky as if I were rising to greet royalty.

"Come back to my office," she said.

I followed her down the hallway, kept pace with her relaxed gait. I watched the sway of her hips and felt convinced this woman could get me anything—a job, a million dollars, anything.

Her office was huge and looked even bigger because there was hardly anything in it. She had a glass coffee table with an antique pink fabric couch, the kind with only one armrest that you picture in a shrink's office. Her desk was glass like the coffee table, with a chair that matched the couch. She had no filing cabinets, no bookcases, no photos of pets or babies or a husband. There wasn't even an errant Post-it lying around. It was as if she wanted no distractions and expected her clients not to have any, either.

"Sit," she said, motioning to the couch. I obeyed. She pulled her desk chair over and placed it beside the couch, then retrieved a hardcover notebook and a pen—like a calligraphy pen—from her desk drawer and took her seat.

"So," she began. "Let me tell you a little bit about what I do."

Maybe this was a joke Marni was playing on me. Maybe this

woman was one of New York's famed madams and she thought I was a prospective escort.

"I consider myself a matchmaker of sorts," she said.

I wouldn't put it past Marni.

"I want to create relationships that last," she said.

I held my breath.

"When I place you in a job, I want you to feel like it's the perfect fit for you."

I exhaled.

"That sounds great," I said.

"First of all, I think it's very important to perfect your interviewing skills."

She talked slowly, like she had all the time in the world, like she used to be a hypnotist or a sex line operator.

"I've gone ahead and made a list of companies that I know have openings," she said. She pulled a paper out of her notebook and handed it to me.

"Now, these positions are mostly administrative. They wouldn't be in your exact field. But I want you to go and interview just to practice building your confidence."

"Like fake interviews?"

"Well, if you decide the position sounds appealing, I suppose you could consider it a real interview," she said with a sly smile.

She must have seen my confusion because she said, "It's unorthodox, I know, but it's the best way to practice."

I nodded like I agreed, though I wasn't sure I did. I glanced at the list. I didn't recognize any of the companies.

And then:

"I know this guy," I said, pointing to a name toward the bottom of the page.

It was Gabriel—Gabe—Walters. From college. His name was listed under a company called Berringer. His title was vice president, domestic sales.

"How funny," Patricia said, with just the smallest of smiles, no hint of a laugh.

"I went to college with him."

"Well, Berringer is a great company," she said.

"What do they do?" I asked.

"Investment management." She said it quickly, like she wanted to move on. I didn't want to, though.

I hadn't thought about Gabe Walters in years. He was everyone's crush in college—and would have been my date if I hadn't decided to spend that fateful night with Drew instead. I'd never been one to revisit the past, but the present was begging me to.

"I could do my practice interview with him," I said.

She uncrossed her legs, her two feet side by side just so, and smoothed out her skirt.

"I would prefer you practice with employers you don't know in order to simulate a real-life interview situation," she said.

"Of course," I said, feeling stupid.

Within a few minutes, she had penned stars next to two other companies on the list and said she would set up interviews with them.

"But don't they know it's not real? The interview?"

She looked at me like she knew so much more than I ever would.

"We don't tell them that, no. That would defeat our purposes. We choose large corporations, corporations that have money and time to waste, companies with protocols in place saying they have to interview a certain number of candidates to be considered fair. It works out fine for all involved."

She stood and I did the same. On my way out, she gave me a lengthy questionnaire that she said would help her determine the best work environment for "someone like you." She said to fill it out that night and send it back to the office. At my next appointment, I'd report on how the interviews went and she would have my questionnaire analysis complete. Before I could even say thank you, she was greeting another girl in the waiting room—a girl who looked just as clueless and hopeful as me.

I opted for a strawberry ice-cream cone because it sounded right for a humid day just shy of the official start of summer. I crossed Forty-second Street to Bryant Park. All my years in the city and I'd never spent a leisurely afternoon in the park. I'd seen other people do it—sitting in chairs, at tiny round tables, on the expansive lawn. It all seemed very Parisian. Drew and I had come here once, for an outdoor fall film festival. I couldn't remember for the life of me what had been showing. It had been right at the beginning of us, in that small and precious window of time between the night we met and the first time we had sex, when it wouldn't have mattered what we were watching because our minds were otherwise occupied with anticipation of each other's touch at the end of the night. I do remember that I'd brought my black cardigan, the one I always wore, and ended up tying it around my waist because it was so warm outside—still summer in early October, Indian summer, as they say.

There were several untaken chairs. They were probably occupied a few hours earlier, during the midtown lunch rush. I sat, licked my ice cream until I got to my favorite part—the soggy cone. I nibbled at it in a circle, like a neurotic woodland creature. When I finished, I balled up the napkin in my hand and leaned back in the chair, closing my eyes and turning my face toward the sun. It was one of those New York days that made me forget completely what winters were like. Selective amnesia, Marni always said. Days like this keep New Yorkers in New York.

I took out my phone and dialed Marni. No answer . . . just her voice telling me to leave a message. I didn't. I'd thank her later for suggesting Patricia. I was bored enough to consider calling my mom, but I knew if I talked to her she'd just confirm that my life was a mess. I hadn't told her I was jobless. I still hadn't told her how bad things had gotten with Drew's mom. It was better that way.

I looked at my watch, realized how little time had passed. I could go home, spend the rest of the day with Bruce, but I was in the city. It felt like a waste of an opportunity—to do what, I didn't know.

I wandered up Sixth Avenue. When I was a kid, my elementary school class did a double-decker-bus tour of the city. The guide told us how Sixth Avenue became Avenue of the Americas in 1945, as requested by the mayor. Stubbornly, real New Yorkers persisted in calling it "Sixth Ave."

I remembered there was a bar nearby, a place I'd gone to with former coworkers for a happy hour. I took a right on Forty-fourth Street and, sure enough, there was O'Malley's. It was just what the name implied—a dirty Irish pub.

I'd never been the type to visit a bar before sundown. We'd taken clients to nice restaurants with fancy wine bars for three-hour lunches, but never to a pub like O'Malley's. The stools at the bar were mostly empty. A big-bellied man sat by himself, his hands so large they made the tankard of beer he was clutching look miniature. He didn't even look up when I walked in. Two guys, with ties swung over their shoulders, sat in one of the booths. Their faces were red with drunkenness. It was likely they'd had their own three-hour client lunch and then decided to ditch out on the rest of the workday. I'd done that sometimes, but I always went straight home to Drew.

The bartender gave me a lazy nod. This wasn't the type of place that welcomed you. The booths were on raised platforms. I stepped up into one and looked at the beer list. I wanted something strong, something that would make me not care that I had an entire empty afternoon before me. I chose the darkest Guinness stout they had. I'd never liked stouts.

A few sips in, I took out the questionnaire Patricia had given me, along with the paper with the starred companies she wanted me to use for interview practice. I was intent on completing my questionnaire and sending it back to her so she'd realize I was a serious overachiever worth her time. But I kept looking at that name—Gabriel Walters. I wondered: *Would it be so crazy to call him?* I imagined him answering and me starting the conversation with, *So, funny thing today* . . . I imagined us laughing like the adults we weren't in college.

I started filling out the questionnaire:

Q: At a party, are you the type to socialize with many people, 1 or 2 people, or no one?

A: 1 or 2 people.

Q: How would you rate your confidence level with public speaking on a scale of 1 to 10 (1 = no confidence, 10 = completely confident)?

A: On a good day, 8. On a bad day, 1.

I put down my pen and finished my beer with one long gulp. There was no harm in calling Gabe. Patricia had said his company, Berringer, was a good one. I wasn't picky about the type of work I did. Any job would do. The worst that could happen was he'd say I wasn't a good fit. Or, maybe, the worst that could happen was he wouldn't remember who I was. *You know, Em. Emmy? Emily? Emily Used-to-be-Overton? You asked me out—several times. I canceled our date that one night because I'd met someone.*

I could always just hang up.

It was easy to get the main number for the Berringer corporate office. Before I knew it, a receptionist was putting me through to his extension. If it had been a couple years earlier and I didn't have a cell phone, I would have abandoned the idea to contact Gabe. I would have sobered up by the time I got home to my landline and decided I was being ridiculous. New technology allowed for impulsivity.

The phone rang once, twice, three times, then:

"This is Gabe." His voice was deep and strong. He spoke in public with level-ten confidence, I was sure.

"Gabe," I said. "This is Emmy. From college. Emily Overton."

The five seconds of silence that followed felt like five minutes. I squeezed my free hand so tightly that a couple of knuckles cracked.

"Emmy Overton?" He said it with the type of surprised enthusiasm I'd hoped for. I relaxed my hand. The bartender brought me another beer.

"It's me," I said. I wanted to blurt out a coherent explanation for why I was calling, but my throat was clenched shut by nervousness.

"Are you finally ready for that date I offered eight years ago?" he asked.

I laughed, thankful for the broken ice. He didn't only remember me, but he remembered wanting to date me. There was no pause in the calculation of how many years it had been; he knew.

"Sometimes a girl needs time to think about such a thing," I joked.

He laughed.

"It's good to hear from you," he said. "What the hell are you up to?"

"Well, at this moment, I'm just starting my second beer."

I took a sip.

"Sounds like a better Thursday than the one I'm having."

"Trust me," I said, "I'd much rather be behind a desk right now." This declaration wouldn't make sense to an employed person, so I explained: "I got laid off last week."

"I'm sorry to hear that."

"I worked at an ad agency. They're notorious for layoffs. Lots of client turnover, that kind of thing. It's amazing I lasted as long as I did. That was my first real job out of college, if you can believe it. So much for loyalty to employees."

He was quiet. I was saying too much.

"I've heard ad agencies can be brutal," he said, straining to contribute to the conversation I was dominating.

"Anyway," I said uncomfortably, "that's actually why I'm calling."

He was quiet again.

"I may have heard through the grapevine that you're hiring right now."

"Oh," he said. "Right." There was a subtle disappointment in his voice, like he'd wanted to believe I was calling for a reason other than hitting him up for a job. "What grapevine might this be?"

"I can't reveal that information," I said with false seriousness.

He coughed and said, in a suddenly professional tone, "It's an administrative assistant position in the international sales department. Coordinating travel arrangements, handling expense reports, scheduling appointments, receptionist duties."

He said it like he'd explained the position to a hundred other people. He may have already had someone in mind to hire. I just said, "Uh-huh."

"What did you do at the ad agency?" he asked. This was becoming an interview, which was what I thought I'd wanted. I felt a little let down, though, deflated. Maybe I wanted it to be something else.

"I was just a writer," I said, downplaying myself. Then: "I hear Berringer is a great company."

"It is."

With the help of the beer, I asked, "Do you think I could come in for an interview? Catch up?"

"Those are two different things—an interview and catching up."

"I suppose so," I said. My heart was beating fast. "We could just do drinks. Or something. Keep it casual."

"That sounds good," he said, his voice relaxing again. "Does tomorrow work for you?"

"Tomorrow. Friday. Sure," I said. "I don't see why not."

I waited for him to suggest a time. A lunch would mean one thing; a dinner, another.

"You know Mangiapane's? In the Village?"

"Heard of it," I lied.

"Pianist starts at seven. Meet you then?"

"Great," I said.

I heard someone's voice in the background and Gabe said he had to run. When I hung up, I felt dizzy—from the beer or something else entirely. I asked the bartender for water and sipped it until I could close my eyes without feeling the world spin around me.

SEVENTEEN

I would describe myself as a cynic, but there are times I think I'm a closet optimist. I'm just afraid of vocalizing my hopes and jinxing everything. I assume, for example, that the chemo is working. It must be. There are days when I feel like it is killing every cell in my body, and that must include the cancerous ones. There are lots of people in the infusion center who come in for treatments like they're just part of a regular routine, like going to the gym or getting a manicure. I eavesdrop and they all speak of end points—*When this is over, When I'm done,* that kind of thing. Maybe we're all just trapped in a bubble of denial.

"It's not working as well as I'd hoped," Dr. Richter says when I meet with her.

Bubble, popped.

I sit there, unblinking, staring at that picture of her girls.

"It doesn't look like the cancer is spreading, which is a good thing, but it's not retreating, either," she says.

"Not retreating," I echo.

The way my body reacts—a wave of nausea, clammy hands—tells me I wasn't ready for this news, not at all.

"I'm going to try Taxol," she says, writing down something on a pad of paper.

She looks up and her face softens when she sees my expression. I must look horrified.

"Most of my patients do the combo ACT regimen."

ACT—Adriamycin, Cytoxan, Taxol. Going through cancer is like working in corporate America—so many acronyms.

"And that's better?"

"The response rate with using Taxol after AC is as high as thirty-three percent."

So, sixty-seven percent of people are still shit out of luck.

"That's not very high," I say.

"In the world of cancer, it's high."

The world of cancer sucks.

"I've had successes," she says.

But the tightness of her smile tells me she's had failures, too.

The infusion center is decorated for the holidays, a half-assed attempt at merriment. There's a fake tree—frocked—in the corner, underneath the wall-mounted television. A few ornaments hang from it. Red, green, and silver tinsel is strung from one corner of the room to the other. The red strand has fallen from its taped-up spot. I keep waiting for someone to fix it.

"So they're switching you to Taxol," Nurse Amy says, hooking up a bag of the brand-new poison.

"Yeah, the other stuff wasn't working, apparently."

Nurse Amy does a little flip of the wrist to suggest this is no big deal.

"Lots of people do ACT," she says. She knows the acronyms.

The bag is attached, the poison is flowing.

"Most people seem to have fewer side effects with this one," she says.

"I sure hope that's true."

I want to believe her, I really do. I've been a crappy excuse for a mother lately because I'm just so exhausted. The chemo is bad, yes, but it's the attempts to show Claire that I'm okay, that our life doesn't have to be totally consumed by this, that really take it out of me. I don't know how I'm going to tell her the chemo isn't working. All this, and the cancer just sits there, unmovable. *Not retreating.* I resisted asking Dr. Richter what happens next, if the Taxol doesn't work. I will die, but when? A year? Three years? Five years? Will I get to teach Claire how to drive? Will I know her first boyfriend? Will I see her graduate high school? These are the important questions.

Paul comes in wearing his usual Cubs baseball cap. He's from Chicago, originally. Somehow, I have found myself in conversation with him almost every time we're here together. Amy says I have a kind face. Maybe that's why he keeps talking to me. I told her that my kind face is a disservice to the general public. It sets unrealistic expectations.

"Taxol," he says, squinting to read the bag.

"Trying something new," I say. Here in the infusion center, we speak of chemo drugs like they're different entrées at a popular restaurant.

"I was on Taxotere first," he says. "Similar name. Not sure if they're similar drugs."

"Didn't work?"

He shakes his head. I'm comforted by the failure of his chemo drug. It's sick, I know.

"The one I'm on now seems to be working, though. Jevtana. I told my doctor it sounds like the name of an airline with direct flights to Bali—Jevtana Airways."

"The not-so-friendly skies," I say.

He laughs way too loudly.

"You're funny." He's one of those people who laughs and then feels the need to comment on the laugh.

"Isn't she?" Amy says.

I just shake my head at both of them.

"Hey, how's Claire doing?" Amy asks me.

I hate when she does this—asks about my personal life right in front of Paul. As a result, Paul knows way more than I'd like him to.

"I haven't told her about the Taxol," I say. She hasn't asked me directly if the chemo is working, so it's not like I've actively lied to her. Like me, she seems to be operating on the assumption that everything is going swimmingly, that we will go through this treatment and then wrap this damn cancer experience with a big bow—pink, of course—and go on a cross-country road trip.

"She's class president," I say, unable to resist sharing this tidbit. She won by a landslide. Starting January first, twenty percent of the vending machine proceeds will go to the American Cancer Society. I cried when she told me.

"We know," Paul says.

"You told us last time," Amy says.

"I did?"

"Chemo brain," Paul says. "We're all victims."

It's comforting to know it's a thing, this mental fogginess. Just yesterday, I had to really think about what goes into a Bloody Mary, a drink I've been serving for years on an almost daily basis. And I couldn't remember the word for the slicer I was using to grate cheese for pasta the other night. "Mandolin," Claire said. "Mandolin."

"I forgot my wife's birthday last week," Paul says.

I didn't know he had a wife.

"Well, ex-wife, so I guess it doesn't really matter."

"You were married?" Amy says.

"Yep, sure was. Eight years. Things started going south, then I got diagnosed and she split."

"Jesus," I find myself saying.

"Yeah, well, what are you gonna do?" he says.

You're going to be fucking angry.

Amy says, "Aww, Paul."

"Oh, god, I thought cancer was bad enough. Now I've got the my-wife-left-me sympathy to deal with."

"Sorry, I didn't mean it like that," Amy says. She gives his hand the same pat she always gives mine. I may not be as special to her as I think I am.

When she walks away, back to her nurse station, I say to Paul, "You are entirely too upbeat about very depressing things." Then: "You remind me of my ex."

It's the first time I've referenced Drew, albeit vaguely, in years.

"That's what every guy likes to hear," he says.

I've been thinking of him lately. Drew. The looming threat of dying makes you take stock of who you are (or were), the choices you've made. You ask yourself if you could have been a better, kinder person. It's a pointless, masochistic question because, no matter who you are, the answer is always yes.

"I just don't know how you do it," I say.

He shrugs.

"It's partially denial," he says.

"Oh, denial," I say. "I'm a fan."

"And I don't like to be pitied. I can't fucking stand it."

Yes, the pity might be worse than the hours spent in the chemo chair, harder than any of the side effects. I tell Claire and Al and JT and whoever asks that I feel great because I don't want it, the pity.

"The second I get down about things, they give me *that look*."

I know what look he's talking about—the one that makes you feel like a hopeless invalid. And I know the "they"—the healthy people who fear not that you'll die, but that they will, someday.

"So I just smile and try to stay up."

"They probably think you're delusional."

"Probably," he says. "I'd rather be the 'crazy cancer guy' than just the 'cancer guy.' "

"Fair enough."

He says he's tired, that he's going to try to sleep through his treatment. I wish him luck with that endeavor. I can never seem to sleep through mine. He pulls his hat forward so the bill is covering his eyes and rests his hands in his lap. Within a few minutes, he's out. And, though I've spent many lonely, conversation-free hours in this chair before meeting Paul, I'm acutely bored.

Claire and I have been having breakfast and dinner in the backyard almost every day. In California, you can do that year-round. There's something about facing mortality that makes you want to be in fresh air more, create moments like those in *Sunset* magazine.

"I think I'm getting tired of the bald look," Claire says.

She shaves her head once a week because the hair keeps growing back. Her cells are healthy, a fact that keeps me from thinking life is a total bitch. I knew she would want her hair back. She's a thirteen-year-old girl. It still makes me sad, though. The solidarity's been nice.

"It won't take long to grow it back," I say.

"No, no, no, that's not what I mean," she says quickly. "I have an idea."

An hour later, we are in the car on our way to an address on Hollywood Boulevard.

"Where are we going?" I ask.

"You'll see."

I slow the car, watching the numbers on the buildings come closer and closer to the number Claire has written down on the neon-green Post-it. And then we are there.

"That's it!" Claire says, pointing.

"It" is a small shop called Wigged Out. I sigh because I'm not really in the mood for this, but I want to make Claire happy. It's like this cancer thing is a bonding experience for her, something we are surmounting together. How will she feel when she knows we are not surmounting it?

I have to circle the block a few times to find a spot, the usual Los Angeles routine. After we park, Claire takes me by the hand

and pulls me down the sidewalk to a store filled with aisles and aisles of fake hair.

Claire gravitates immediately to a long blond wig, tries it on.

"Whatcha think?" she asks, twirling the synthetic strands around her finger playfully.

"It's very . . . *Brady Bunch,*" I say, but she doesn't know the reference.

A twenty-something girl asks if she can help us and Claire overrides my standard "Just looking" response to inquire about the different wig options. She tells the girl I have cancer, and though that's probably obvious, I'm still embarrassed. She also clarifies that she does *not* have cancer, though that's probably obvious, too. She has color in her cheeks, eyebrows, enviably long eyelashes.

"We have some great wigs made from real hair," the girl says. She is as pale as a cancer patient, with long black, probably fake hair.

"*Real* hair?" Claire says.

"People donate it," the girl says. Claire seems impressed.

The salesgirl guides us to the real-hair wig section. It creeps me out. All I can think of is the heads the hair came from, the people walking around in the world with short bobs in the name of charity. Claire seems unbothered. She tries on a black one—silky and straight. Asian, I'm sure.

"Mom?" she says, looking for my opinion. It's clear to me, standing beneath the abusive fluorescent lights, that Claire is not going to let us leave without buying wigs.

"It's pretty," I say. "But you should try something more fun."

Against my will, I am playing along. I go back to the fake-hair aisles and select a couple dark red wigs for her to try on.

"The red brings out the blue in your eyes," I say, as she analyzes what she sees in the mirror. The girl who works there is still lingering, agreeing with everything I say. Plus she adds that Claire looks like Emma Stone, which makes her smile. I don't know who Emma Stone is and I despise this salesgirl for making me feel left out.

"Okay, then red it is," Claire says, choosing the shorter of the two. The hair curls right beneath her chin, frames her face.

"It's good for the holidays, too," the girl says.

Claire confirms that she loves it. Then it's my turn. I try on a very short, pixie-cut blond wig. I look like that lady with the TV show that exploits her eight children. "Oh, Kate Gosselin," says the girl who works there and who seems to know every celebrity. Claire selects a slightly longer blond wig. The salesgirl calls it "the Reese Witherspoon."

"I'm so pale. The blond washes me out," I say.

"Let's try brown," Claire says. "You've never had brown hair."

I've never had brown hair during her lifetime.

Claire stands on her tippy-toes to place a medium-length brown wig on top of my head. She pulls it to one side and then the other. When she's satisfied, she turns me around to face the mirror. I gasp.

There she is—that someone I used to be—staring back at me. Even without eyebrows and eyelashes, I get a flash of Emily Morris. The wig hair is parted down the side, a few strands sweeping across my forehead, exactly how I used to arrange my own hair. *You look like you've seen a ghost*. That's the expression. My breathing is shallow, panicked. I feel like I did when Jade called out, "Emily Morris," at that hippie craft fair in Topanga Canyon.

"You don't like it?" Claire says. She looks disappointed. "I think it looks good."

"Agreed," the salesgirl says.

I shake my head no. Vigorously.

"It's itchy," I say. "On my scalp."

I yank it off. My face is flush. I'm sweating.

"We have wig caps," the girl says. She's examining her cuticles, completely unaware of the breakdown I'm having in her store. "It's like a nylon thing that goes under the wig, and—"

"No," I say.

They both look at me like I've lost it.

"Maybe this was a bad idea," Claire says. She takes the wig

from me, puts it back in its place. She thinks this, my freak-out, is about the cancer. But the cancer is nothing compared to seeing Emily Morris in the mirror.

"You don't have to wear a wig, Mom," Claire says. "I just thought it would be fun."

I've let her down. I wish I could explain, but I can't.

"Some people do scarves," the girl says.

Claire holds my hand to calm me down. "What do you think, Mom? A scarf could be pretty."

I'm still thinking about Emily Morris as I follow them to a wall display of scarves. Sadness overcomes me. I miss her. That's what it is. I miss her.

"Mom, these are so pretty," Claire says.

I force myself to focus. I stare at the scarves—solid colors, floral patterns, polka dots, stripes, plaid. The salesgirl selects a linen navy one and demonstrates how to wrap it around my head so it will stay in place.

"There," she says, standing back to evaluate me. When she moves out of the way, I see myself in the mirror. Emily Morris is gone. I feel my blood pressure start to drop, slowly.

"I look like I'm in a cult," I say.

"No, you don't," Claire says. "You just look like someone who is prettying up her cancer."

In my haze, Claire convinces me to buy a few different scarves—a pale pink one with a paisley pattern, a solid-color turquoise one, and a mint-green one with little white flowers on it. "Wear this one now," she says, handing me the turquoise one. I don't hate it, actually. It makes me feel less exposed, less vulnerable, more protected.

Claire's hungry, so we stop at a sidewalk café for an early lunch. I watch her peruse the menu. I wonder, if I had stayed in New York, if Emily Morris had raised her—what would be different? I hate that I can never know.

"Mom, this salad looks awesome," Claire says, pointing to something on the menu called the Antioxidant Powerhouse.

There's no way I can't order this. Claire has done her research. She reminds me of the importance of antioxidants and protein and whole grains on a regular basis. I'm not sure any of that makes much of a difference, but I can't just ignore the advice of the medical community and, more important, my daughter. If I shun it all and eat nachos and french fries, and then I die, they will look for reasons and that will be one. I don't want Claire to blame me when all is said and done. I don't want her to hate me.

When the salad comes, I stab the spinach spitefully. I don't know how anyone truly enjoys salads. They seem incapable of hitting the proverbial spot. Claire has ordered a salad, too, because her solidarity efforts are not just limited to bald heads.

"So," she says, prefacing something that makes me nervous, "didn't you meet with the doctor the other day?"

She keeps track of my appointments, my chemo sessions, in addition to being class president and having friends and playing soccer twice a week. I told her she doesn't have to worry about my cancer stuff, and she said, "I don't *worry* about it." I think that's a lie, though.

"Dr. Richter, yes," I say.

"Is it working? The chemo?"

The dreaded question.

I puncture a pomegranate seed with my fork.

"Well," I say, pondering, "it's hard to say."

I figure that phrase—*it's hard to say*—isn't dishonest. It *is* hard to say. How do you tell your daughter that all the drugs that have been coursing through your body for months aren't doing anything?

"It's not working," she says matter-of-factly.

I skip confirmation of this fact and say, "They just started me on a new drug. This one will work." I struggle with the word "will."

She uses a finger to gather the leftover dressing in her bowl, then licks it.

"Could you die?"

The more dreaded question.

When Claire was five, at that age when she was oddly prolific with asking questions, she said, on her birthday, "How old am I going to get?" I told her that none of us really know for sure, but that she'd probably be more than a hundred years old one day. She said, "And then what?" and I said, "Well, when you've lived as much life as you want to, you die," framing death as some kind of well-I-guess-it's-about-time personal choice. "What does that mean?" she asked. "It means you don't live here on Earth anymore," I told her. She asked where she would go and all I could think to say was, "Nobody really knows. But somewhere better."

"I guess it's possible," I dare to say, then immediately deflect: "But Dr. Richter is hopeful. I'm hopeful."

She nods slowly, taking this in.

"Well, that sucks," she says.

She seems angry, at me or the cancer, I don't know.

The waitress comes by at this inopportune time to collect our plates. We give her matching tense smiles.

"I didn't know it was that serious," she says. "You didn't tell me it was that serious."

It's at me, the anger.

"Honey, I—"

She puts her hand up at me, like a crossing guard. It shocks me into silence.

"Have you even thought about who would take care of me?" she says. There's fear in her eyes, along with the anger.

I can't come up with words to comfort her fast enough.

"You are so selfish," she says, spittle flying from her mouth.

She stands from the table in a huff and turns to leave. I grab her by the arm. She whips her head back and stares at me with horror, as if I've just slapped her across the face. Reflexively, I let go.

"Claire, please," I say.

People in the café are looking at us now. I am the mother with the teenage daughter who hates her.

"No," is all she says, pulling her arm close to her, possessively, as she marches out of the restaurant.

I don't go after her. I let her have this dramatic exit. She's right, I need to talk to Al about watching over her if I'm gone. When I'm gone. No, if. *Think positive.* That's what Dr. Richter said. I flag down the waitress for the check, and while I'm waiting I think again about New York, about Emily Morris, about the people who knew me. Am I supposed to tell Claire about all that? Is it complete honesty she wants? All these years, I've been so much more comfortable with lies.

EIGHTEEN

Drew called about an hour before I was supposed to meet Gabe at the restaurant with the live piano. It was right as I was stepping into my new dress—a clingy black thing with a hem that hit mid-thigh. I looked around the apartment, paranoid that he had me on some kind of surveillance.

"What are you up to tonight?" he asked. The question was innocent enough, but I got defensive:

"Nothing, why?"

"It's Friday. Thought maybe you'd head out with Marni."

He'd taken a sudden interest in ensuring I had fun without him, desperate to compensate for what he called our unfortunate circumstances.

"Marni's got a boyfriend now, so . . ."

I'd told him this before. He liked to forget that most people in love spent Friday nights together.

"How's your mom?" I said, the obligatory question asked during every call.

"Oh, you know—same ol', same ol'."

I nodded and pictured him doing the same, both of us wondering how to fill the empty spaces of these talks. Each call started to feel more and more like the calls with my mom, driven only by a sense of duty. The thing is, absence doesn't make the heart grow fonder; absence makes the heart grow weary.

"I have a lead on a job," I said.

"Well, that was fast."

"We'll see if it pans out," I said. "Do you remember Gabe from college? Gabe Walters?"

If I made it seem like it was nothing, then maybe it was nothing. That's what I told myself.

"Sounds familiar," he said.

It comforted me that he didn't remember. If he would have said, *You mean the guy who asked you out?*, I would have felt his apprehension-verging-on-jealousy and my own guilt.

"This recruiter I met mentioned this big company. Berringer. He happens to work there. VP of something. Small world."

"See? Everything happens for a reason," he said.

"You think so?"

"Yeah, why?"

"Never mind," I said.

"Okay, I gotta make Ma dinner. See you tomorrow?"

"Yep."

And then we hung up.

I didn't—and still don't—think there's a reason for everything that happens. Humans are just desperate to make one up.

I got to the restaurant—Mangiapane's in the Village—purposefully early, so I could have a drink at the bar to calm myself before seeing Gabe. The place was small, with worn wood floors and black-and-white pictures of someone's family—the Mangiapanes, by anyone's best guess—on the wall. None of the furniture matched. No more than two chairs at any one table even matched. It was like they had acquired the leftover loners from numerous yard sales. Every strange table was occupied. Groups lingered outside, smoking and waiting hopefully for a seat. The bar was cozy—just a few stools, manned by an old man with one of those long mustaches with curly ends that require a special kind of wax. His stools were all occupied, but he saw me scanning the area and said, in a booming voice reserved for radio announcers, "*Amore mio*, can I get you a drink?"

I was leaning against the front wall, sipping the last drops of a vodka tonic through my tiny cocktail straw, when Gabe walked in. He didn't see me at first. He walked past me to the hostess stand. He looked both the same as I remembered and entirely different. In college, he was not a man; now he was a man. Somewhere along the way, he'd learned how to style his hair—perfectly shellacked. If I didn't know better, I would have thought he was a model, coming from a photo shoot for *Esquire* magazine. His suit was obviously tailored, every seam in the right place. If I worked for his company, it would probably take two or three paychecks to pay for shoes like his. They looked to be authentic alligator skin. Marni had taught me to notice such things.

He said something to the waitress and she checked the reservation book in front of him and gave him the kind of smile women only give good-looking men.

"Gabe," I said, with a small voice at first. Then, louder: "Gabe."

He turned around and spotted me, then approached with arms out for a hug.

"Emily Overton," he said, using my maiden name, the only name he knew me by. He held me close. In college, he was a thin guy, burning all the calories he consumed on the soccer field. He still had the muscles from those athletic days, but he'd filled out.

"You look just as I remember you," he said.

"Is that a good thing?" I asked, baiting him for a compliment.

He obliged: "You know I thought you were beautiful."

His skin was darker than I remembered, the color of caramel. His crystal-blue eyes betrayed his Latin descent.

The hostess showed us to our table and we sat.

"I can't believe how this place has taken off," he said. "I used to come here when they first opened—not a person in here."

"Must be good," I said.

"It is, promise."

The waiter came by and engaged Gabe in an in-depth conversation about the wine list. I told Gabe to choose. They settled on a Pinot Noir. Gabe swirled the tester sip in his glass, swallowed it, considered, then said, "This is great, man," like they were already friends. He could charm anyone.

As we each had our first glass, we took turns asking each other the usual questions. He said he started at Berringer right out of college, as some kind of junior associate, and worked his way up—with the help of that smile, I was sure.

"You married?" I said, though I already suspected he wasn't. There was no ring on his finger.

"Nope," he said. "I'm still a bit young for that, I think."

I forgot this often. I was still young, a few months from my twenty-ninth birthday. I felt so old sometimes, so tired.

"What about you?" he said.

He may have tried to catch a glimpse of my ring finger, but I had slipped my hands under my thighs, like I used to do at the bars with Marni.

"I am, but I barely see him," I said, purposefully vague.

He cocked his head to the side like a dog trying to decipher his owner's high-pitched baby talk.

"Remember that night I ditched the date with you because I met someone?"

He nodded. "You mean the night I lost all will to live?"

I laughed then said, "I married that guy."

His eyes widened. "Wow," he said. He took a long drink. Then again: "Wow."

He seemed genuinely shocked, like he found it unbelievable that I'd chosen someone so early on in life. He'd probably been with fifteen, twenty women in the years I'd been with one man.

"What if we had gone on that date? You could've married me," he said, humoring himself at the very notion.

"I get the feeling you're not the marrying kind."

"I'm insulted." He leaned back in his seat, away from me. His smile was playful. "I just haven't found the right person."

"Maybe there is no 'right' person," I said, putting cynical air quotes around the word "right."

He leaned in again, elbows on the table.

"Some of us choose to stay optimistic," he said.

I finished my glass. "Good luck with that."

"You're begging me to ask what's going on with your husband," he said.

He was right. I was begging. I took a deep breath. And then I told him everything—about Drew's mother, about how we'd decided not to live with each other most of the week, about doubting the ability of true love to surmount all, about work being my only escape besides running.

After all of it, he sighed heavily, then said, "Well, the job is yours. If you want it. I can at least cross that off your list of worries."

"Really?" I said.

"If you want it."

"I don't know anything about the company," I said, laughing at the absurdity of accepting a job so blindly.

"We're an investment company."

I nodded like I knew what that entailed.

"We have a heavy focus on research. All our investment strategies are very analyst-driven. We specialize in specific sectors. We really *know* all the companies we recommend to our clients."

I continued nodding.

"I'll take it," I said.

"Are you drunk after one glass?"

"I might be."

He poured another glass for me and one for himself.

"You don't even know the salary," he said.

"It's better than zero, which is my current salary."

Our entrées came—spaghetti and meatballs for me, lobster ravioli for him. He transported a ravioli across the table from his plate to mine, and I transported a meatball from my plate to his. It felt intimate, this sharing of food. We took our first bites with closed eyes.

"So," he said. "Do you love him?" Then: "Your husband?"

His eyes were glossy, the effects of drinking his second glass too quickly.

"I don't know what that means anymore," I said. I looked down at the table. It was rustic, seemingly made of wood from a ship that had been at sea for a decade. Someone had carved a game of tic-tac-toe in it.

Gabe waited for me to say more.

"I care about him," I said.

"Do you think about leaving him?" he asked. Questions get braver, more brazen, as bottles are emptied.

I'd had passing thoughts of what it would be like to get my own studio apartment in the city. I'd fantasized about starting over, on my own. I hadn't shared those fantasies with anyone—not even Marni or Nancy—which meant either the fantasies weren't serious or I was afraid they could be.

"I don't know," I said. "I guess I think about it the same way people think about moving to the country and owning a vineyard."

He was quiet.

"Meaning it's not realistic," I said.

"I see." He said it in a way that made me think he didn't see at all.

"It's not like I could leave him, with everything going on," I explained. "He has a sick mom, no job."

Drew and I always said we wanted what our mothers never had—a true, lasting love story. We'd look at elderly people holding hands and say, "That will be us one day." And maybe that could have been us if circumstances hadn't intervened. Maybe that could have been us if we had both remained those hopeful, romantic people. Maybe that could have been us if we weren't changed by what life had in store.

"I mean, really, what kind of person would I be to leave him?"

He shrugged. "A fed-up person," he said simply.

I bit my tongue, literally, so hard that I tasted sweet blood in my mouth. I took a sip of water. I was angry at him for assuming he knew anything about my marriage and the ease I'd have leaving it. What was his longest relationship anyway? A month?

"Sorry," Gabe said. "I think I've overstepped my bounds."

I put down my fork. My appetite had gone, though three meatballs remained, tangled up in a pile of noodles.

"Maybe you did, but I asked you to."

He took a last bite of his ravioli and asked for the check. I took out my wallet and, predictably, he told me to put it away.

"Do you need a ride home?" he asked.

"I can take the subway."

"Let me drive you," he said, starting to stand. "It's no fun to be drunk on the subway."

He offered his hand as I stood, in that gentlemanly way. His car was parked right out front, something I'd never experienced in the city. Most people didn't own cars. It was a black BMW, shiny from a recent wash-and-wax. The interior was tan leather. There was nothing in it—not an empty soda can in the cup holder or a wrapper on the floor. There was no just-in-case rain jacket or umbrella, no old parking payment stubs by the windshield.

"Is it new?" I asked.

"Few years," he said.

"And you don't have a woman in your life mandating this cleanliness? You do it on your own, *by choice*?"

"I don't like messes," he said, which made me wonder how he could possibly consider leaving a marriage no big deal.

The drive was fast, about a half hour. All the people who congested the roads during the week were tucked away in various suburbs.

"I think the job might bore you," he said as he turned right on Flushing, almost home.

"A job is a job, right?" I said. My mom always said that. She hadn't taught me to be discriminating when it came to paychecks.

"Well, come in on Monday and we'll talk about it more. Ten o'clock? I'll have my assistant put something on my calendar."

"You have an assistant," I said. "Fancy."

"That's what you would be—someone's assistant."

"As long as it keeps me busy," I said. I meant that. I didn't care if it was a pay cut. What I had been getting paid at Mathers and James hadn't been enough to cover the expense of having an unemployed husband with an ailing mother. I thought, maybe, if Drew and I fell even deeper into debt, he would take some action to get us out.

I pointed out my building and Gabe pulled in front.

"It was really great to see you," he said as I opened the car door.

"You, too. See you Monday?"

"Monday," he confirmed.

Drew came home with his mom for our one night together. After we put her to bed, we lay in our own bed and I told him about the job. He was happy for me, or for the income. I waited for him to ask about the salary, but he didn't. He never asked about our debt, either. He was in as much denial about our financial distress as he was about his mother's situation and what had become of our marriage.

"I miss you when I'm not here," he said.

"Then come back home."

"I thought you didn't want her here." There was some hope, some anticipation, in his voice.

"I don't," I said, letting him down.

I could have asked what his plan was, but I knew he didn't have one.

He rolled onto me, his face so close to mine that our noses grazed. I knew we would kiss. I knew we would have sex that would last two minutes, the result of his built-up frustration over the week. It felt like a conjugal visit. I just wasn't sure who was in prison—me or him.

When I closed my eyes and let the predictable happen, I thought of Gabe—his wide smile, the silkiness of his skin, the way his body filled his suit. And the two minutes it took for Drew to go from desiring to exhausted were enough for me, too.

"You finished?" he asked, pleasantly surprised and a little too proud of himself.

"I did," I said. I kept my eyes closed so I could continue deluding myself. I imagined what it would be like to be in Gabe's arms, to feel his bicep cradling my head.

"Things will get better, Em," Drew said, rolling back to his side of the bed. When he was away during the week, I'd dared to occupy his side—first with an ambitious, wandering leg, then with my whole body. On more than one occasion, I woke up in the middle of the night not sure where I was.

"I know they will," I said, though I didn't know this at all.

I watched him fall asleep and thought about what to wear on Monday.

I got to the World Trade Center just before ten. It was bustling with people: women in dresses and skirts and heels, men in suits with ties that had already been loosened due to early morning stress. I took the elevator in the north tower to the 101st floor, to the Berringer offices. Gabe was at the receptionist's desk and said, "There she is!" The receptionist, Cassie, scanned me up and down, assessing my worthiness, as all women do in the presence of a handsome man.

He showed me to his office. It was a corner office, with a cherrywood desk, two tall filing cabinets, and two studded leather chairs. Expansive windows looked down—far down—onto the traffic on West Street.

"Have a seat," he said. I did.

"This is an amazing office," I said. The walls were mostly bare, except for his framed college diploma and a large framed painting of a ship in stormy ocean waters.

"Thanks," he said. He leaned back in his chair; it creaked. "So, you still want to work here?"

"If you'll have me," I said, my cheeks reddening as I said it.

"I think you'd be a great fit. I mean, selfishly, I want you around."

I tucked my chin slightly so he couldn't see the little smile that crept up on my face.

"Doug Miller will be your boss—vice president of international sales. He's great. And he knows you'll want to move up in the company. He won't keep you as an assistant forever," he said. "Of course, I'll help you move up, too, but we'll have to play it cool. People will know we went to college together, I'm sure. I don't want them to think I'm playing favorites."

"Right," I said, feeling like we were already conspiring. "Of course."

"Okay, then, well, can you start tomorrow?"

"Sure can."

When he stood, I stood. As he approached me, I thought he was going to shake my hand in a congratulatory way, but he hugged me instead, pulled me close to him. I felt his inhale. Was he smelling my perfume? When he released me, our eyes met for a quick, but telling, second. It was like we had already been together, I had already cheated on Drew. And it was bound to happen again.

NINETEEN

It took three months for something to happen—three months of after-work drinks and casual dinners and a façade of innocent friendship. Then there was the day the façade cracked.

Janine, Gabe's assistant, had just left on maternity leave and I was tasked with continuing to do my administrative duties in international sales and also take over for Janine. "You're just that good," Gabe said. My new role meant I was in and out of Gabe's office throughout the day. Manila folders passed between our hands. Sometimes our fingers touched—meaningfully, in my mind.

"You better not be next," he said as we chatted about Janine and her coming child.

"A baby? Not me," I said. "Unless it's immaculate conception."

He waited for me to elaborate.

"Drew and I haven't had sex since June."

I knew when I said it that it was something I shouldn't say. Not to Gabe, at least. Confessions like these lead to affairs. Somehow I didn't care. I wanted to test the theory, prove it wrong. Or maybe I wanted to prove it right.

The last time I'd had sex with Drew was when I imagined he

was Gabe. Drew tried, his male needs overpowering the obviousness of my disinterest. I pushed him away, said I wasn't "in the mood"—a cliché excuse played out on every sitcom that ever aired. Eventually, he stopped trying. We didn't talk about it.

One Saturday night, I woke up to the sheets rustling. He was turned from me. I knew by the force and repetitiveness of his motions that he was masturbating. I pretended to sleep. I was embarrassed for him. The next morning, I snuggled up to him—out of pity or guilt or something else that closely resembled affection.

"Remember when we first met, how thrilling it was to just touch each other?" I said to him. I had some hope that we could just admit we'd changed, that it wasn't the same, that it wasn't good anymore.

But he said, "It's still thrilling to touch you."

I kissed him on the mouth, but felt nothing. I remembered that first night, in his dorm room, talking for hours. I remembered staring at his hands, imagining them touching me. I didn't even need to be naked; just his hand on my skirt sent a jolt through my body.

Then there were Gabe's hands—soft, like he moisturized them, but also tough, like those of a farmer who labors in the fields from sunrise to sunset. During the workday, I dreamed about them reaching up under my skirt to caress my thigh. My panties got wet enough that I had to go to the restroom and pat them dry with toilet paper. I hadn't lost the ability to desire; I'd just lost the ability to desire my husband.

The realist in me knew that if Gabe and I had a "beginning" and then went well past it—years past it—I wouldn't desire him, either. But that's the thing about lust—it silences the realist. It deceives you. It convinces you that what you're feeling will last forever.

After my sexless marriage confession, Gabe said, "Not since *June?*"

His shock made me think he'd never gone more than a week without sex. I shrugged.

"That's sad, Em," he said. I liked when he called me Em. Everyone who knew me well—and only those people—called me Em.

"It is what it is," I said.

His eyes diverted to his computer screen, in response to the ding of a new email. He scanned it, then looked back at me.

"It's been a long week," he said. "Drinks after work?"

We went to this Mexican place a few blocks from the office. One of the regional associates suggested it, touted its margaritas as the best in the city. The chances of us seeing him—or someone from Berringer who also took his recommendation—were reasonably high. We weren't doing anything wrong, though. If we were, we would have chosen somewhere farther away. Wouldn't everyone assume that? As it was, we were just friends. We'd made that clear from the day I started. In fact, that's how Gabe introduced me to the staff—"This is my old college friend, Emily." We waved off the imagined suspicions of others who warned us with their raised eyebrows of the complications, the risks involved with attempting a friendship with the opposite sex. There was a common understanding: if both parties are single, the claimed friendship is simply a preface to something more; if one or both parties are married, the claimed friendship is simply a preface to something disastrous.

We played like we were above all that.

We played dumb.

I'd started taking notice of a few love affairs in our building—north tower trysts, I called them. I could see it in their eyes in the lobby, in the elevators. It was an attentiveness to surroundings, a concern for who might see through their charade as they pretended to be consulting about business, using code words that, in a language only known to them, translated to, *I want to fuck you in a storage closet.* Because that's how these things go. They're sinful and impulsive and thrilling. They occur in the backseats of cars, on corporate-carpeted floors, in secret rooms that only janitors know exist. There are bruises and rug burns and pulled muscles and an urgency usually reserved for greedy, impulsive teenagers. They—these trysts—are exciting because they're dangerous. They can break up marriages, families. They can cause two people stupid enough to conduct their affair on the same floor of the same building to lose their jobs—and much, much more.

But Gabe and I were just friends.

The margaritas came in glasses the size of bowls. I licked the salt off the rim of mine and took a drink.

"This is pretty good," I said. "Peter was right."

I perused the menu, trying to decide between a combo platter involving a tamale and an enchilada, or a trio of tacos. I felt Gabe's eyes on me, perusing me instead of his own menu.

"Does Drew know about me?" he asked. It was out of nowhere; we never talked about Drew. I made a point of pretending that he didn't exist, effectively placing myself in two different worlds—the world with Gabe and the world with Drew (which was really a world without Drew).

"Of course he knows about you," I said.

Gabe looked to me for more information.

"He knows you're an old friend from college. I didn't remind him that you were the date I ditched for him all those years ago," I said. "Would you like me to tell him that?"

He rolled his eyes, annoyed.

"Come on, Em. We know I don't give a shit about that. And you know that's not what I'm talking about."

I released my shoulders from their tensed-up position by my ears and put down my menu.

"He knows you hired me at Berringer," I said, knowing this wasn't what he was talking about, either. That was really all I'd told Drew, though. I didn't mention the dinners out with Gabe, the drinks, the attraction. Some nights, while I was out with Gabe,

Drew called and left messages. The next day, he'd ask where I'd been. I claimed I'd made friends—girlfriends—at work and was out with them. He claimed he was happy for me, happy to hear I was having so much fun. We were both terrible liars.

"So he doesn't know much of anything that matters," Gabe said flatly.

I wanted to tell him there was nothing between us that mattered, but I knew that wasn't true. He would argue back with a truth that would only make it impossible for me to continue compartmentalizing my life, guilt-free.

"I don't know what you want me to say," I said.

"Look," he said sternly. "I like you, Em. I liked you way back then and I like you now."

I stared into my margarita, hoping to find some kind of resolution among the floating ice cubes.

"I like you, too," I said weakly.

"I don't like you in the way I like Doug at work," he said. "You must know what I mean."

I nodded because I couldn't bring myself to form the words that agreed with him. I didn't know if I was ready to make all this real. We hadn't kissed, nothing had happened. We could just keep going as we were, playing dumb.

He went on: "I'm not sure how much longer I can keep this up."

"This?" I asked softly.

"If you haven't noticed, I don't date anyone. I'm just waiting. For you. Maybe you should do me a favor and tell me to stop."

But I didn't want to tell him to stop.

He hadn't even taken a sip of his margarita. Everything he said was said sober, clearheaded.

"I don't know what you want me to say," I repeated.

He provided the words on my behalf: "I know you like me—in that way—too," he said. Then: "What I don't know is if you would like me if you didn't resent him so much."

"Him" being Drew.

I looked up, as if startled by a sudden loud noise.

"Whatever I feel for you has nothing to do with Drew."

I was angry and let it show. If Gabe knew me as well as Drew did, he would have known that I only use such a defensive tone when I'm aware I'm wrong.

"I think it has a lot to do with Drew. You're lonely. You're angry at him. If you betrayed him, I bet you feel like you'd just be making things even between the two of you."

I was quiet.

"And you wouldn't be wrong in making things even. Maybe I would want that, too, if I were in your shoes," he said. "But I'm in my shoes and I don't want to be someone's weapon of revenge."

"You're not that," I said.

"I know I'm that," he said. "I'm asking if I'm *just* that, or if I'm something more."

He was different from Drew. He wanted to understand how I felt, what I wanted. He pressed, he challenged. Drew did neither. Drew played the role of the oh-shucks, unobservant-but-well-meaning guy. He didn't ask what he meant to me, he didn't ask if I still loved him, if I was unhappy. He didn't possess the courage to want to know.

"You're more to me," I admitted, both to myself and to him.

"How do you know?" he asked.

If he was taking the risk of asking me such things, I could take the risk of being honest.

"I think about you all the time," I said. And I did. When I went to bed at night, I resorted to kissing the back of my hand, like a desperate teenager, imagining his lips. When I woke up in the morning, I picked out my clothes according to what would be most attractive—for him. The fantasies sustained me.

"What about Drew?"

"I don't really think about Drew," I said.

Whatever resentment I'd felt for Drew had given way to a sort of apathy. I wasn't angry anymore; I wasn't anything. I'd been under the impression that a marriage was in trouble when there was bitterness and rage. But, in the months that had passed since

Drew had moved in with his mom, I'd realized that a marriage was truly in trouble when there were no feelings at all.

"So what are we doing?" Gabe asked. He clasped his hands together, like he did at the conclusion of business meetings.

"I don't know," I said. "It's a question I've been going out of my way to avoid."

He sighed. The waitress came to take our order.

"We need a minute," I told her. She nodded and walked away.

"Life's short," Gabe said to me, looking at me intently, refusing to blink.

"It is," I agreed, holding his stare.

Not taking his eyes off me, he raised his hand in the air like a kid with an answer in elementary school, catching the waitress's attention. She returned to the table, little notepad in hand again.

"Can we just get the check?" he said to her.

She looked at him strangely, then nodded, put her notepad back in the pocket of her apron, and went to a register at the rear of the restaurant.

"Let's go to my place," he said. It was a demand—not an invitation. "I have leftover Moroccan takeout."

I'd expected his place to be the kind of swanky bachelor pad you see in movies featuring high-powered businessmen looking for love. In those movies, the guys always have commitment issues. They subsist on liquor and have a woman's bra strewn across some piece of furniture. They decorate to attract the bra-flinging women—modern, sleek, sharp edges everywhere. Their couches cost a few grand and aren't even comfortable, but that doesn't matter because this type of man is never home anyway.

Gabe's place was not like that, though. It was in Greenwich Village, so it cost him a penny prettier than any penny I'd ever see, but it was humble, wholesome even. He admitted that he didn't know a thing about how to make a home; he relied on the Crate & Barrel store on Madison for guidance, even knew the name of one of the employees—"Jeff with a G," so Geoff, a gay guy who moonlit as an aspiring ballet dancer. Gabe's couch was full of soft pillows. A throw blanket was resting on the armchair. It wasn't folded neatly, as if he'd recently used it, curled up in it to watch TV late at night. There wasn't a liquor bottle—or bra—in sight.

"I love the dining table," I said.

"Reclaimed wood from a barn upstate. Supposedly."

I wanted to linger there, in the dining area, for hours. I wasn't sure what would happen if we ventured toward the bedroom. I went into the kitchen, drew a finger across the marble countertop, as if checking for dust. I even opened his refrigerator, inspecting his daily life. There was a carton of orange juice and some white Styrofoam take-out containers.

"The Moroccan food?" I said.

He nodded. He was humored by me, my snooping.

"Want some?" he asked.

I shook my head. I had too many knots in my stomach to be the slightest bit hungry.

He walked toward me, entered the space I'd previously considered personal, my own. We'd never been so close before. I could smell his breath—musty, unfreshened, but not bad. I closed my eyes, either to prepare for him to kiss me or to play the childhood game of believing the entire world vanished if my vision went black. I was terrified and exhilarated simultaneously, the way you feel before a huge drop on a roller coaster.

He put his hands on my arms, as if to steady me. I thought of Drew, but only about how he was with his mom, in Jersey, so far from this, so far from ever having to know about this. He said he'd acquired his mom's early bedtime—seven o'clock. He wasn't even awake.

Gabe kissed my forehead first, left his lips there for a while, introducing them to my skin slowly. I tilted my chin up toward him, offering him my mouth. He took it—gently, with care. I'd never kissed someone with such full lips before, lips that could envelop mine. Drew's lips were thin. When he smiled, they disappeared completely.

"Do you have any idea how long I've wanted to kiss you?" he said, still just inches from my face. I pressed my lips together like I did after putting on balm or gloss.

"I have a pretty good idea."

I wanted to say more. I wanted to ask what this meant. I wanted to ask where it would go from here, *if* it could go from here. And, most of all, I wanted to ask, *Should we feel guilty?* because I knew he would comfort me by saying, *No.*

I was quiet, though. I wanted him to say the next words, make the next moves. Somehow, in my mind, this made me a passive participant, less at fault.

He took my hand and, for me, that would have been enough excitement for the night—to hold that hand until dawn. There was a single hallway leading to the one bedroom. He led us until I stopped him.

"I can't," I told him. I didn't want to cross the threshold, as if I held some superstitious belief about what may happen if I did, as if Drew would hear an alarm in his head the second I stepped into another man's bedroom. *Step on a crack, break your mother's back.*

"You're being awfully presumptuous, Ms. Overton," he said. He'd never accepted Morris.

"I just want to sleep—actually sleep—with you," he said.

It was a trick, I was sure. We'd get into bed with this lazy intention to "just sleep" and end up doing anything but that. Promising to behave ourselves would only make it more alluring not to.

"Sleep is good," I said, accepting the trickery. "It is a school night."

He took my hand and led me into his bedroom. He had a large king bed—unmade, which assured me he hadn't planned for this, hadn't anticipated talking me into this. Aside from the bed, there was a single nightstand on the right side of the bed—"his" side, I concluded—and a dresser with the top drawer opened slightly. There were no candles, none of the usual tools for romancing. Maybe he didn't do this all the time. Maybe I was a little wrong about him.

He straightened out the sheets, which were disarrayed and pulled over to the one side—the nightstand side, "his" side. He unbuttoned his shirt like it was nothing, like we had already shared some kind of domestic bliss. His chest was bare—he either trimmed the hair or there wasn't much there to begin with. His muscles were as defined as they'd been in my mind, putting to rest the cynic's notion that nothing is as good as you imagine it to be. Then he unbuckled the belt of his pants, let them fall to the floor. There he was, standing in front of me, in a pair of silk boxers—black. I sat on the bed, waiting for him to tell me what to do. He walked over to me, stood over me, one leg on either side of my two pressed-together thighs. Then he started unbuttoning my blouse, slowly, looking at me with each button as if to ask, *Is this okay?* I gave him small nods. When he was done, he rubbed his hands along my sides, up and over the front of my bra. He kissed me, his weight compelling me to lie back on the bed. We pressed against each other, his boxers and my skirt the only barriers to what we really wanted.

We must have done that—just pressed against each other and kissed—for an hour, maybe two. My mouth got dry, my chin and cheeks reddened by the stubble on his face. After one o'clock in the morning, he pulled me under the covers with him. I rested on his chest—now sweaty, even though restraint was all we'd exercised.

"What am I going to do tomorrow?" I asked. "I don't have anything with me. I can't wear the same clothes I wore yesterday. People will know. Cassie will know."

Cassie, the receptionist, the gossip every office has, there to provide the entertainment necessary for mundane hours to pass.

He felt my forehead with the back of his hand. "You feel feverish," he said. My mom used to love that Peggy Lee song—*you give me fever.* She'd play it when getting ready for dates.

"You should take a sick day. You can relax here," he said. "Eat those Moroccan leftovers in the fridge."

I liked the idea of lying in bed at his place, sipping his coffee from one of his mugs while wearing one of his football T-shirts. He was a Jets fan. More than anything, I liked that he trusted me to stay there. Either he knew I wouldn't snoop, or he didn't have anything to hide.

"And next time," he said, "bring a change of clothes."

TWENTY

Nurse Amy said most people have fewer side effects with Taxol. Apparently I'm not most people. I have "the weird breast cancer." And, thanks to Taxol, I also have joint and muscle pain, tingling in my hands and feet, and most enjoyable of all—diarrhea. I also have a horrifically bad attitude.

A lady at the infusion center gave me a book called *Getting Through Cancer* after I politely declined an invitation to her church. She just reached into her purse and handed it to me. Either she carries around copies on a regular basis to share with fellow patients, or she had me targeted as "a troubled person" and was waiting to pounce. I skimmed it. It's full of all kinds of hokey tips and Bible quotes. It says I should list five things I'm grateful for every day. It says that cancer is "an emotional journey." It says the grief of a diagnosis has the five stages of any heart-wrenching event—denial, anger, bargaining, depression, and acceptance. I am only familiar with anger.

There are days I want to take up Al on his offer for paid leave. Sometimes I can't stand being around normal, healthy people. Their worries are so petty, their laughs so careless, their priorities so mind-boggling. I overheard a distraught woman saying to her girlfriend, "I will just *die* if he doesn't call me," and I wanted to grab her by her neck and say, *No, you will not die.* That's just it—life goes on with all its silliness and stupidity while I'm dying. Perspective isn't always a good thing; sometimes it makes you feel fucking alone.

Last week at the bar, this husband and wife came in. I'd never seen them before. They were talkers, yammering on and on about how they used to live in Topanga Canyon and how they remember seeing Charles Manson around. They were just teenagers at the time and claimed he was "as strange as you'd suspect." The woman sipped on a Long Island iced tea while her husband pounded back scotch on the rocks. Then they turned the discussion to me.

"How long have you had cancer?" the woman asked.

I was wearing my scarf but, like Claire said, it doesn't really hide that I have cancer; it just makes my cancer a little prettier to look at.

"Diagnosed in September," I said.

"Breast?" the woman asked. It's strange how people assume bartenders are so willing to share details of their personal lives, as some kind of fair exchange.

When I nodded, the woman turned to her husband and said, "Mary St. Clair had cancer, remember?" And they had a little sidebar about Mary St. Clair while I cleaned out some glasses, trying my best to exit the conversation.

"She is totally cancer-free now," the woman said to me, an unwelcome invitation back. People do this a lot—use examples of their cancer survivor friends, lovers, neighbors, family members to insinuate that I have nothing to worry about. Al, bless his heart, mentioned his Aunt Pauline. Even JT said a "lady friend" of his beat breast cancer—twice. They don't know I have this rare and aggressive kind of breast cancer, though. If I die, they might think I was just weak, not up to the fight. I need to tell Al the percentages. He needs to know my odds aren't good. Because Claire may need him. The conversation will happen. I'm procrastinating.

As much as I hate my chemo treatments, I don't dread coming to the infusion center as much as I used to. I like Nurse Amy—even though I'm giving her a childish cold shoulder for getting my hopes up about the Taxol side effects. And I don't mind Paul. Some days I even like him. Because, unlike other people—at the bar, in the world—he doesn't offend me or annoy me or belittle my cancer. He knows this shit is real, even though he persists in smiling.

"I think cancer has made me a total bitch," I tell him while I get pumped full of the anti-nausea meds.

"That's one of the side effects they don't list."

Amy comes by to start my Taxol and I force myself to apologize to her for being edgy.

"I'm used to it," she says. "You're tired of all this. I understand."

"Paul doesn't seem tired of it," I say.

"Oh, no, I am," he says. "Trust me, I am."

Amy shakes her head in amusement at the two of us. We've become a duo—Abbott and Costello, playing off each other to pass the time.

"How's Claire?" he asks. He always asks.

"Distant," I say. "Still."

Since the lunch date, when I told her I could die, she's been giving me the silent treatment, using only monosyllabic words and grunts when I ask her a direct question. It's impressive, really, this monklike discipline she has. She's not making me breakfast anymore. She hasn't mentioned the road trip. The map of the United States is still tacked to her wall, but she has stopped putting pushpins into places of interest.

"She'll come around. It's hard on her, I'm sure," Amy says, before vanishing to tend to other patients.

"Chuck is pissed at me, too," Paul says. "He thinks I'm going to leave him."

Chuck is Paul's dog, a pit bull–Labrador mix, two years old. I give Paul a look. Is he really trying to make a joke out of my daughter's newfound hatred of me?

"I'm serious," Paul says. "He peed in the house the other day. He *never* does that."

He really does remind me of Drew sometimes.

I humor him: "Have you thought about what you'd do with Chuck if, you know . . . ?"

For Paul, the question is purely hypothetical. His chance of survival is above ninety percent. I've looked it up.

"I've thought about it. Hell, the day after I got diagnosed, I paid some online legal service to create a living trust for me. Chuck would go to my sister, Eileen."

A living trust. That's on my to-do list.

"She's Mormon. I don't love the idea of my dog being raised by a Mormon, but if I'm dead, I suppose it doesn't matter."

It bugs me sometimes, his lightheartedness. I know it's just his way of coping, or whatever, but it still bugs me.

"You're worried about Claire," he says. Unlike other people in my life, Paul knows the percentages, the odds. When I told him that most people with my cancer are terminal, he waved me off and said, "We're all terminal."

"Yeah. I mean, I have a friend, my boss at the bar, actually, who said, years ago, that he'd take care of her if something ever happened to me. I need to have a serious talk with him," I say.

"What about family?"

"There's someone," I say.

"Nearby?"

"New York, actually."

"You from there?"

Nobody out here in California knows the truth. Maybe Paul can be the first. Because I might die. Because even if I don't, I'm unlikely to see him again. Because we're in this infusion center where war stories are traded on a daily basis and secrets seem safe.

"Yes," I say.

He has no idea that, with that one-word reply, he now

possesses a bit, a piece, of me that nobody else does. He shrugs it off like it's nothing, because to him, it is.

"What brought you out here?"

"Change of life," I say, which is pretty much true.

"Well, maybe you should contact that person," he says, "in New York."

I swallow hard.

"Claire might like New York. Lots of things going on. You should make that part of your road trip."

He keeps talking because I don't say anything. This is another reason I like him. He gives me no silences that need filling.

"Considering she's barely talking to me, I'm not sure the road trip will happen."

"It will. She's just acting out."

"Claire never acts out."

"Cancer changes people," he says. A plain and simple truth.

My eyes well up like they sometimes do when I'm just sitting here thinking too much.

"We shouldn't even be talking about this," he says. "You're going to be fine."

"Right," I say.

"Right," he repeats.

Maybe I should tell him more, the rest of the story. He probably thinks that after cancer, nothing can shock him, but he is wrong. How will he see me—despicable, selfish, cowardly? Actually, the better question is how he could *not* see me as those things. Even with the added compassion that comes with cancer—compassion for the others in the secret club of suffering, those people who are all too aware that life is painfully short—he will see me differently. He will judge me. And he should.

I decide to stop at the bar on the way home from chemo. To talk to Al. It needs to be done. I need to have a plan for Claire, to put her mind at ease. I need her to stop hating me.

"Honey, I have to swing by the bar," I say, calling her on my drive.

"Fine, whatever," she says. "I'm ordering pizza."

She used to ask me if she could order pizza. It's like she's play-acting what it will be like when I'm gone, when I won't be there to give permission, advice, hugs.

"Okay, there's money in the kitchen—"

"In the drawer. I know."

Thankfully, the bar is quiet for a Thursday at five o'clock. It will get busy in an hour or so, after people flee their jobs. When I walk in, Al looks up from behind the counter and says, "You're not working today, Con." I've come in accidentally on a couple occasions, thinking I'm working. Chemo brain.

"I know," I say.

He looks worried now. I don't usually make social calls.

"I wanted to talk to you," I say. "Grab me a beer."

I take a seat at one of the tables. Al and I never sit at a table. We usually sit at the bar. He knows something is up.

"Are you quitting on me?" he asks, sitting across from me and sliding my beer across the table.

"No," I say.

"You can take time off. I told you that." He's gruff, prematurely defensive about whatever I have to say.

"It's not that," I say. "I'm doing okay on the work front."

He lets out a big exhale, seemingly from the bottom of his large gut, where it's been sitting for years.

"Do you remember when I was in that accident on the 405 and we had that talk?"

Al is in his late fifties. He claims to be an old man with a terrible memory, but I know he remembers.

He nods, slowly and deliberately.

"Do you remember what you said about Claire, about watching her?"

He nods again.

"It's just that, well, the chemo wasn't working. I'm on something new now, but it's not exactly a sure thing."

He narrows his eyes, like he's trying to focus his vision.

"It's actually really far from a sure thing," I say. "Like, I could die. Possibly."

He takes a long swig of beer and stiffens his posture.

"If you're asking if I'll still watch Claire, I will," he says.

I want more specifics, though. Where will he watch her? At his shitty apartment in the Valley? How will he make sure that she doesn't become a drug addict or a homeless person?

"You will?"

"Course," he says.

He must see the doubt on my face, because he exhales another long-trapped breath and tells me a story I don't expect:

"I had a daughter once, you know," he says. I don't know, so I just sit and listen.

"Back in Tennessee. Had a girlfriend, Genie. I was doin' lots of drugs. Hard stuff. Genie got pregnant, had the baby. Little girl named Sophie. Genie kept sayin' she was gonna leave and take Sophie with her if I didn't get my act together. I didn't think she would, but, you know."

"Jesus, Al."

"No idea where they went. I tried looking for a while. Used my last pennies to hire a private investigator. No luck. Maybe Genie changed her name."

Like me. Just like me.

"Genie's a strange name, ain't it?" he says.

He looks up at the ceiling.

"I don't know what to say." I really don't.

"You don't gotta say anything," he says. "You know, I came out to California after I gave up lookin' for Genie. I met JT at this biker bar, started talking about how I wanted to open up my own bar. JT loaned me the money, on pure faith. I paid him back and all. Years later, he mentions the lady renting his cottage needs a job. See how it all lines up?"

Al is one of those everything-happens-for-a-reason people. Who knew?

"Life is funny," I say, though "funny" isn't the right word.

"Anyway, Claire is like a daughter to me," he says. "That's what I'm sayin'."

He sniffles, pulls a paper napkin from the dispenser to wipe his nose.

"Thank you," I say. I reach across the table, place my hand over his. He glances away, at the bar.

"I'm not dying tomorrow," I say. "That much I know."

"You sure as hell better not," he says, turning back to me. Whatever tears he was about to cry are gone.

I don't hang around because I can tell Al wants to get back behind the bar, his barricade of sorts. There is sheer relief on his face when the after-work crowd starts to roll in. I should get home to Claire anyway. We need to make up, resume our road trip discussions.

When I pull into the driveway, I hear music. Loud music. And then I hear laughter, the laughter of multiple teenagers. Is Claire having a party?

"Claire," I shout when I open the front door. The music is blaring. It smells like pizza. There's loose cash on the little table next to the door, change from the pizza guy, probably.

"Claire!"

The teenage laughter stops abruptly, as does the music. They are outside, in the backyard. When I approach, one of them says, "Holy crap."

It's Claire and a trio of friends. I recognize Heather and Riley, the girls, gangly and awkward and pretty at the same time. And there's a boy. The infamous Tyler. I've seen him walking into school with Claire. How did they even get here? Were their parents stupid enough to drop them off on the pretense of a study session? There are two empty pizza boxes, lids flung open. Three paper plates flutter around on the ground. And there, in Claire's thirteen-year-old hand, is a bottle of wine.

"What the hell are you doing?" I ask.

I've never taken this tone before. I've never had to. Claire knew I was coming home. She wanted to be caught. She looks smug, pleased with herself. Judging by the terror in the other kids' wide eyes, they did not expect to see me. They have been rendered speechless.

"Sorry, Mom, just having some fun," Claire says flippantly. Heather, Riley, and Tyler look at her with something like awe.

I grab the bottle from Claire's hand and register that about three-quarters of it is left. It's not that she wanted to get drunk; she wanted to misbehave. *She's just acting out.*

"Guys," I say, giving each of the other kids a hard stare. "Out."

They practically stumble over each other on the way inside.

"Call your parents before I have to," I shout after them.

Claire and I stand five feet apart, facing each other, like in a Wild West showdown.

"Claire," I say, "this is ridiculous of you."

"Oh, *I'm* the ridiculous one?" she says.

"You are, in fact."

We sound like two petty teenagers. She is allowed, considering she is a petty teenager. I need to get ahold of myself.

"*You* are freaking ridiculous," she says.

I hate that word—"freaking." It makes me cringe that my daughter is on the verge of swear words, possibly past the verge when she's not around me.

"And dying on me is pretty freaking ridiculous," she says.

So that's what this is about.

"Fair enough," I say.

She rolls her eyes.

"Whatever," she says, and stomps inside.

I follow her, leaving the pizza boxes and paper plates outside. I'll get them later. Through the window by the front door, I see the other kids waiting on the driveway. They look petrified. I could get them all grounded for this. I won't, but they don't know that.

"Claire, come on, we have to talk about this," I say.

She stops in her tracks, turns around, arms crossed against her chest. She looks so small to me, so young, not at all like someone who could face life without her mother.

"Is talking going to change anything?" she says.

I'm quiet.

"That's what I thought."

She turns around again and marches to her room. She doesn't slam the door, which I take as a passive invitation to follow her.

She's lying flat on her bed, staring at the ceiling. She still has those adhesive-backed, glow-in-the-dark stars stuck to her ceiling. I'd put them there when she was nine or ten, when it was cool.

I sit on the edge of her bed and put my hand on her thigh.

"We don't know for sure if I'm dying," I say quietly.

She scoffs.

"And if I am, I'm sorry."

She can't scoff at my apology. She just stares at the ceiling.

"You have to know that I will endure decades of chemo if it means I can stay with you," I say. "I would do anything to stay with you."

I feel the tears coming, that just-ate-something-sour feeling in my throat.

"I talked to Al. He loves you, honey. You won't be alone if I'm gone. He will watch over you," I say, in hopes that this vague plan gives her equally vague comfort.

She snorts.

"Al would be an awful mother," she says. She's amused at the thought.

My lip quivers on its way to a smile.

"God-awful," I say.

"Can you imagine him buying tampons?" she says.

I can imagine this, actually. I can see his big, burly body walking down the aisle of a drugstore, shameless and committed to meeting his pseudo-daughter's every need. Claire hasn't even had her first period yet. I got my first around my fourteenth birthday—"late bloomer," my mother said. Claire will probably get hers soon. At least I will be around for that milestone.

"If I have to leave you, let's hope it's after you learn to drive, so you can buy your own tampons," I say.

She takes a deep breath.

"When do you meet with the doctor again?"

"Next week," I say.

She finally looks at me with those big blue eyes of hers. Her father's eyes.

"Just be honest with me, okay? From now on?"

I nod and lie next to her, wrapping one arm around her body.

Honest. It might be the most difficult request she's ever made.

TWENTY-ONE

Exactly a week after that restraint-filled night I spent with Gabe, I gave him every part of me, without hesitation.

"You're getting me too wound up," he said, as we lay together, bodies primed.

"I'd worry if I didn't."

"I've wanted this too long to control myself."

"Please don't control yourself," I said. Because, really, despite the mysteriously popular idea that a woman wants a man who can last for hours and tame his desires indefinitely, the ultimate compliment is a man who can't.

And that's how it started. I assumed it wouldn't last. But then it did. For a year. I, Emily Morris, was having an affair. It sounded so absurd—an affair.

Gabe started coming to my place because I didn't want to leave Bruce alone. That first time I spent the night at Gabe's, I came home to a puddle of pee in the kitchen and a guilty-but-mad look in Bruce's brown eyes. His food bowl was empty and a pillow on the couch was torn open, its white, fluffy insides strewn across the apartment. I told Bruce I'd never do it again. I promised. He smelled me more than usual, as if inspecting for the scent of another man, prepared to take his findings back to Drew. Man's best friend and all. But I think he was as resentful of Drew as I was. This would be our secret.

For the first couple months, the sleepovers were once or twice a week. We'd go somewhere for dinner after work, then end up at my apartment. He planned ahead, brought suits in dry-cleaning bags for the next day. It felt wrong, and thrilling in its wrongness. We arrived at the World Trade Center together, in his BMW, but made sure to leave five minutes between our entrances into the Berringer office. We did the same when we left at night, sending conspiring emails that read, *Okay, you go first. See you in a few.* Still, people at work had to see us together sometimes. Nobody ever said anything, of course. It's amazing what people will just shrug off.

Three months in, Gabe was spending every night at my apartment—except for Saturdays, when Drew came home. We didn't talk about Drew, didn't utter his name. We just agreed that weekends would be our time apart from each other. On all the other days, we played house—cooked meals, watched TV, walked Bruce in the park. If people recognized me out with a man they knew wasn't my husband, I didn't care. Maybe I wanted to get caught. Maybe I wanted a nosy neighbor to say something to Drew. I fantasized about the confrontation. Drew would yell and I would run out of the apartment dramatically and call Gabe, telling him he had to come get me. I would be the quintessential damsel in distress. Gabe would rescue me, take me back to his place in the Village, and we would stay there together until the end of time.

But that confrontation never happened. I began to think that even if a nosy neighbor did tell Drew, he wouldn't believe it. Even if he walked in on Gabe and me, he would pretend he didn't see anything. He had illusions to keep intact, for his own sanity.

Drew and I, we acted normal. Or what had become our normal. We talked on the phone during the week. I told him about work. He told me about his mom. She had gotten progressively worse. She couldn't walk without someone practically carrying her. She wore diapers day and night; she got one urinary tract infection after another from sitting too long in her own urine. Drew had taken her to the hospital twice for pressure sores on her back, the result of reclining in the same position on the couch for hours a day. When I saw her—on those weekend visits—I was convinced she knew I was cheating on her son, that her lack of smile upon seeing me was something personal. Then I realized it was just that her face had gone completely slack, the muscles not strong enough to hold any kind of emotion. She didn't have a smile for anyone, not even Drew. Her eyes were vacant, sinking farther and farther into her skull. Drew told me she'd asked for Dr. Kevorkian and he wasn't sure if she was joking or not.

We didn't have sex, and we didn't talk about why. I was sure Drew wanted to believe it was temporary, that all this would resolve itself in time. Just as he saw no point in me complaining about our circumstances with his mom, he probably saw no point in him complaining about our lack of intimacy. *These are just the cards we were dealt.* We weren't angry with each other. We were pleasant. I was in a better mood with Gabe in my life. Drew didn't question the improvement. He just seemed relieved we weren't fighting.

Gabe and I didn't talk about a future. He tiptoed around the issue on a few occasions, usually while lying in bed. He wanted me to leave Drew. That much was clear. He didn't outright ask, though, not at first. I placated him, told him I just wanted to be in the moment, enjoy each other without too many questions or expectations. "What are you waiting for?" he asked. I didn't know for sure. "When it's right to leave him, I'll know" was all I said. I thanked him for being so patient. He just said, "You give me no choice in the matter."

That tentative, let's-just-enjoy-this agreement lasted for months. And then Gabe became increasingly agitated. He would say things like, "Let's go to a play on Saturday. Oh, wait, my girlfriend sees her husband on Saturdays." Or, "If only I didn't have to live out of a bag during the week." In March, six months after that first night at his place, he said, "I think I'm falling in love with you." Then: "You're going to break my heart, aren't you?" I felt like I couldn't breathe, which meant either I was falling in love with him, too, or I was afraid I would break his heart. Or both.

There was this one night in June when I thought he would end it. It was a Friday. We had tickets to a comedy show that night. We did things like that—comedy shows, plays, movies—like we were a typical couple. I worried that we'd run into Marni somewhere. She was always out and about doing things. I hadn't told her about Gabe, not because I was afraid she would judge me (she wouldn't), but because I knew she would reiterate what Gabe said—I had to leave Drew.

We went to a bar near the theater for drinks before the show. It was annoyingly loud. Gabe took my hand as he pushed his way through the crowd of people to the back, where we found a little table. Our knees knocked against each other when we sat.

After one gin and tonic, he said, "I've been thinking."

I knew that wasn't good.

"We need to just be together, you and me," he said. "Officially."

Of course I'd thought about it. Multiple times. But leaving Drew? I didn't think I could do that. I didn't think I could accept myself as someone who did that.

I looked down at my drink, as if the ice cubes were little crystal balls.

"Em?" he said. He put his hand on my thigh. "We have to talk about this."

"Right now?"

"Is there a better time? I've been trying to talk about it since day one. My intentions have always been clear. I don't know what yours are."

What were my intentions? To stay in a bad marriage and have this thing—this *affair*—to keep me happy?

"I've been trying to give you space, but—"

"I know," I said. "You've been great."

It was a stupid thing to say: *You've been great.* That's what you say to summer interns who don't make the cut for fall hiring.

"Look, I respect that you're apprehensive," he said diplomatically. There was this tone he used sometimes that reminded me he was my work superior.

"I just don't want to hurt Drew."

"Don't you think you've already done that?" he said.

I didn't, in fact. I knew that for Drew, ignorance truly was bliss.

"He still wants us—me and him—to work. As delusional as it may be, that's what he wants."

"Of course he wants that. Why wouldn't he?"

I nodded, the way people nod when a doctor comes into the waiting room, after hours of anticipation and fear, to explain the extent of a loved one's injuries after a horrible car crash: a nod of reluctant acceptance.

"Still," I said. "It would crush him."

"What about you? Won't this crush you, continuing like this?"

Would it? I had thought, stupidly, that we could continue on like this forever.

He took his hand off my thigh with an air of irritation.

"Okay, then, it will crush *me*," he said. "Don't you know that?" Then: "Do you even care about that?"

"I do, but—"

He slammed a twenty on the table and stood.

"I'm so fucking sick of your 'buts.'"

We still went to the comedy show. Gabe stomped along in front of me to the theater. We took our seats without saying a word to each other. He didn't hold my hand. I can't even remember the headliner. It was a guy, someone famous. I was barely paying attention, but I laughed with gusto in an attempt to forget the discussion at the bar. Gabe didn't laugh at all.

We went back to my apartment after. He had his own place; he could have gone there. I figured he wanted to make up, apologize. He didn't say anything that night, though.

The next morning, Saturday, as he got ready to leave, he said, "I can't do this anymore."

I'd used those same words before, with Drew. I knew the desperation that created those words. The way my stomach lurched when he said them confirmed that I was on the verge of loving him and losing him. I knew I had to do something.

"I'll talk to him," I said. "Today." My head spun with the commitment. Here I was, ready to destroy a marriage based on nine months of sleepovers.

He looked surprised, then pleased, then doubtful.

"Today?" he said, calling my bluff.

"Yeah," I said. "Today."

As he packed up his things—an efficient routine he had down pat—I ran through what I would say to Drew. I wouldn't tell him about Gabe. I knew that much. I would use a script tried and true by others before me: *It's just not working. I'm not happy. You're not happy.* He wouldn't be shocked, or he shouldn't be. I'd let him have Bruce. He'd need the company more than I would. And besides, I couldn't keep Bruce at Gabe's place. It would be a constant reminder of what I'd left behind. Just the jingle-jangle of the tag on his collar would produce pangs of guilt.

Gabe looped his arm around my waist, pulled me close to him.

"Good luck," he said. He kissed me. "Call me later."

It was as if Drew knew what I was about to tell him and was ready to pull out all the stops. He came home, as usual, with his mother in tow. Or, rather, in his arms. He'd started carrying her up the stairs to our apartment. But, instead of flipping through take-out menus and talking about what pay-per-view movie to get, he said, "I have a surprise."

I do, too, I thought. By the sound of his voice, his was much different than mine.

"I arranged with someone at an agency to watch my mom tonight," he said.

"An agency?"

"Yeah, they have caregiving agencies. Anyway, it's expensive, but I want to take you out," he said. "On a date."

"Oh," I said. "Wow."

I definitely couldn't tell him that night. Gabe would have to understand.

"Dinner at Bellucci's," he said. Bellucci's was this Italian spot a few blocks away that had opened two years before. He'd been saying for two years that we should go there.

"What's the occasion?" I said, forcing a smile.

"No occasion," he said. "I don't know why I didn't think of this sooner."

I don't, either, I thought.

A girl named Hazel came to watch Drew's mom. She looked far too young—early twenties or so—for such a responsibility, but she nodded her head obediently when Drew gave her instructions, and then we left. We walked. It was a nice night, warm. Drew worried aloud about his mom. She'd had this cough for a few days, he said. I told him, "We'll only be gone for a couple hours," and he said, "You're right. God. Sorry."

There were a few tables outside, on the sidewalk. We sat at one of those. I ordered the gnocchi, he ordered the chicken parmesan, and then we just sat there. I pulled apart pieces of bread, ate them slowly.

"So," he said.

What did we used to talk about? I had no idea anymore.

"I've been cooking again," he said. "At my mom's house."

He'd stopped cooking completely after the restaurant closed, would only eat things that came directly out of boxes.

"That's great," I said. "Anything special?"

"I'm making my way through Julia Child's French cookbook, getting back to the basics."

"That doesn't sound very basic," I said. Flattering him was the least I could do. At least, if I left him, he had his cooking.

"Well, it's classic, I guess," he said. "Maybe that will be better for a future restaurant than something experimental, like tacos."

I didn't dare ask about this future restaurant. I just let the dream hang in the air between us.

"I'll cook you something. Next weekend," he said. "Any requests?"

"You pick," I said.

Awkward silence ensued, the kind you usually have during uncomfortable first dates, blind dates.

"How's work been going?" he asked.

"It's good," I said.

He nodded. "Good, good."

More silence.

My phone buzzed—Gabe—at the same time the waiter brought the dessert menu.

"You want anything?" Drew asked.

"Tiramisu," I said.

The longer we could stay at this restaurant, the more time I had to avoid reality.

At home, Drew pulled me close to him in bed, kissed my neck. I was disgusted with myself, knowing Gabe had kissed me just hours before. I didn't know how people could do this—carry on with two people at the same time. My mom had a few stints of juggling two or three guys. "They're all losers," she said, "but put them together, and it kind of works." Drew and Gabe weren't losers. They were both good guys, in their own ways. I was just greedy.

"Sorry," I said, resisting him.

"What's wrong?" I was surprised he asked.

"I just don't feel like it," I said.

He exhaled frustration.

My phone buzzed again. Gabe.

"You have to get that?" he said.

"No, it can wait."

Then I turned out the light and pretended to fall asleep.

I called Gabe the next day, after Drew and his mom left. I told him what had happened. He just said, "Uh-huh." I promised I wasn't deterred. I would tell Drew the following Saturday. It would have to wait until then. I had to do it in person. "Uh-huh," was all he said.

And then, that Wednesday, Drew's mom almost died.

She aspirated on something, the doctor said, and that turned into an infection in her lungs. Pneumonia.

I was at work when Drew called to tell me. I walked straight into Gabe's office to relay the news.

"I have to leave early," I said. "It's Drew's mom. She's in the hospital."

He looked up from his computer. He'd been cold with me, businesslike. He hadn't said it was over between us, but it felt like that was imminent.

"Do what you have to do," he said.

It's awful, that feeling of letting someone down completely.

"I'm going to end things," I said. "Now is just not the time. She's probably going to die."

"Okay," he said. "Keep me posted."

As if the status of our relationship were the same as the status of one of his business deals.

She was in the hospital for almost two weeks. It didn't look good at first, but then she improved. The doctor said she was "a stubborn thing." Drew muttered, "You're telling me."

On our way to her house after they discharged her, Drew said, "I probably won't be able to come home on weekends for a little while. She should stay put, in bed, until she's got strength back."

We talked about her as if she weren't right there, in the backseat.

"Okay," I said. "That's probably for the best."

"I'm sorry," he said, looking over at me while he stopped at a red light.

"I know you are."

I called Gabe, told him that Drew wasn't coming home on weekends for a while. I told him it was because I'd requested a trial separation. I lied, essentially. I felt bad about it until I heard the happiness in Gabe's voice.

"Now we're getting somewhere," he said.

I didn't know where that somewhere was, but I was willing to live with that uncertainty to feel loved by Gabe again. We resumed our sleepovers—every night, now including Saturdays. He still came to my place because I had Bruce. Drew continued calling nightly, so I'd have to do weird things like take the phone into the bathroom with me while Gabe was arranging dinner. Thankfully, the conversations were short. What was there to say?

Most nights, with dinner, Gabe and I split a bottle of wine. He'd always raise a glass and say, "To us." I'd repeat the toast and think, *Whatever we become.*

TWENTY-TWO

The day I found out I was pregnant began with a visit to the restroom at work. It was a Monday. When I came out of the stall, Cassie the receptionist was at the sink, applying one of her many layers of mascara.

"Hey," she said. "Do you have a tampon?"

I rummaged in my purse and found one. She took it, called me a lifesaver, and I went on my way. When I got to my desk, it occurred to me that I hadn't had my period since the end of July. July 20, to be exact. I remembered because Gabe and I went to this movie—*Sidewalks of New York*—on its opening night. After the movie, back at my place, we started to fool around and I told him I had my period. In the past, this usually stopped things. This time, he claimed not to care about the mess, so we did it anyway. It was the most vulnerable I'd ever felt with a man—streaks of blood on the towel we placed beneath us, his fingers red from touching me.

I told myself that lots of women had irregular cycles, that it was a fluke. But my period had always been on time. I couldn't remember one instance of its lateness. On my lunch break, I went to Duane Reade. I bought five tests, five different brands, just like the teenage girls do in after-school specials. Back at work, in the bathroom, I peed on the first stick and then waited.

The minutes of waiting felt like the eternity every fearing-to-be-pregnant woman says it is. In those couple minutes, I thought about the possibilities. If it was negative, I would consider myself fairly warned, thank a God I believed in sporadically, and vow to be more careful. If it was positive, I would cry. And then I would have to get on with life.

Two minutes ticked by on my wristwatch. I looked at the stick. A plus sign. I took out another stick, calmly, robotically. Two minutes later, that one gave me two lines—indicating two beings, me and the baby. The third, fourth, and fifth sticks all confirmed the same. Not one dissenter. I stared at them, in a line on top of the metal container used to discard pads and tampon wrappers.

When I left the bathroom and went back to my cubicle, Gabe was waiting there, leaning on my desk, arms crossed, a suggestive smile on his face. It would have been impossible for people not to know about us. He always looked too happy to see me.

"Hey, you," he said.

"Hey," I said, trying to pretend as if nothing were wrong. He knew me well, though.

"What's wrong?"

"Nothing," I said. "Actually, I'm not feeling that well."

His brows furrowed in genuine concern.

"Go home, then," he said. Then, in a whisper: "I'll bring you some soup later."

I nodded, unable to form actual words. I knew I would have to tell him, at some point. But I could buy time with a fake flu.

In our year of pseudo-togetherness, Gabe and I had never talked about kids—the desire for them, or lack thereof. But there was no question I would keep the baby. As much as those pregnancy tests scared me, I felt a jolt of excitement, too. I'd harbored the desire for a baby for years. Maybe I wanted a baby for the wrong reasons—to distract me, occupy me, give me purpose. But I wasn't sure what the right reasons were. Marni would have disagreed with me and dragged me to a clinic that day, which was why I didn't tell her. She still didn't even know about Gabe.

I'd have a few months before I'd have to tell Drew about the pregnancy, a few months before my belly would protrude and truths would reveal themselves. I wouldn't have to tell him right away that the baby wasn't his. I would have nine months to think about that confession, nine months before he would see the baby—with Gabe's brown skin.

Drew would assume it was his, conceived on that one night we had sex together—a miracle of sorts. Yes, we finally did have sex. It was a moment of weakness for me. He came home one Friday night in August—I told Gabe I had plans with Marni—and I got a little woozy with wine. I was feeling especially guilty lying next to Drew in bed, wondering what the hell I was doing with my life.

"You know, next month it will be nine years since we met," he said.

"Nine years? Wow."

"We should do something special. To celebrate."

"Yeah, sure," I said.

"We could have dinner at that restaurant we went to the day we got married," he said. There was excitement in his voice that made me nauseated.

"Old Homestead Steak House," I said.

"Have a couple martinis, appetizers, desserts—the works."

"Sounds nice."

"It'll celebrate the start of our tenth year—a decade!"

"Good idea," I said, trying to share his enthusiasm, or at least sound like I did.

He turned on his side, put his hand on my middle.

"I know things have been hard," he said.

I gave him a smile that felt weak, hoping it didn't look it. I don't know if it was remorse or pity or what, but when he peeled back the sheets that were covering my body, I didn't stop him. I felt I owed it to him. It didn't last long. He was inside me and, a minute later, he wasn't. I could have convinced myself it hadn't even happened except that my inner thighs were wet with him leaking out of me and my cheeks were wet with tears.

"What's wrong?" he said, using his thumb to dry under my eyes.

"I don't know," I said. I did know, though.

"I was thinking," Drew said, "maybe you were right."

I pulled the sheets back up to cover my body, all the way up to my chin.

"About what?" I asked. I thought—hoped—he was going to say I was right that we should split up, but then I remembered I'd never proposed such a thing, not out loud, at least.

"Maybe I should get her a professional caretaker, come home to you," he said. "It's been so long. She's not going to get better. We can't do this forever."

But, see, I'd found Gabe. I'd found a way to do exactly this—forever.

"How could we afford it?" I asked, using his own argument against him.

"I have to get a job. We'll make it work somehow."

There was a time when this was all I wanted from him—these words. They were stale now.

"I don't want to get my hopes up," I said. I was mean. I wanted him to be the one to give up on our marriage. I wanted him to be the one to quit. "Come to me when you have a caretaker and a job and a balance sheet that shows we won't be in debt for the rest of our lives."

He pulled away, back to his side of the bed, resumed staring at the ceiling.

"You don't have faith in us, do you?" he asked.

"These last few years have done a number," I said.

His only rebuttal was a long sigh.

I knew the baby was Gabe's. We'd taken chances—too many times. I should have gone back on the pill. I'd stopped taking it a few months after Drew moved in with his mother, telling Drew, "What's the point?" Gabe and I were responsible, at first. We used condoms, Drew's condoms. Then we decided to skip the condoms, because it felt better without them. He would just pull out, a method every man claims to have mastered. The first couple months, I was nervous. But then nothing happened and I felt invincible. This woman at work—Tricia—had been trying to have a baby for years. I figured it couldn't be that easy.

When I pictured telling Drew I was pregnant, I saw him smiling. He'd say something like, *That's awesome*. He wouldn't worry about logistics. He would be relentlessly happy, until I'd tell him about Gabe. Then his face would fall, every muscle in it giving up entirely. He would look confused and sad—not angry, though. There would be pain in his eyes, as if he'd just been knifed in the stomach by someone he thought he could trust. He wouldn't look down at the wound, though; he'd just look at me, asking how I could do this. I wouldn't have an answer.

I faked the flu for the rest of the week. I needed time to think, to contemplate the human growing inside me. I still called Gabe every day, just to hear his voice. He said he couldn't wait to see me, he missed me. He said we'd have to make up for lost time, as if that lost time were the duration of a year rather than just some days. My stomach ached—either subtle morning sickness or nervous nausea brought on by what I'd have to tell him when I saw him.

I went back to work on Monday. September 10. I set my purse on my desk, then went straight to Gabe's office. I thought I'd tell him right then, rip off the proverbial Band-Aid. But the way he looked at me rendered me speechless. He looked at me like he was witnessing the most beautiful sight in the world, taking it in, appreciating it in the way only poets can. He stood from his chair, walked past me so I caught the whiff of his cologne, and shut his office door, without care for who saw. Then he lifted me up—two hands on my waist—and set me on his desk. He lay me down so I knocked over a small wooden desk clock and the only picture he had in his office—of him and his mother, Lucy. He'd said she'd love me, that he couldn't wait for her to meet me.

He pushed up my skirt as far as it would go, to the very top of my thighs. He yanked down my nylon stockings. They tore.

"I've been thinking about this for days," he said, kissing my neck. My entire body tingled. I reached up and under his shirt, touched his skin.

"I like you like this," I said. I felt wanted—desperately wanted.

It was quick because it had to be. Anyone could knock on the door. Anyone could hear the heavy breathing, the creaking of furniture under the weight of bodies. When we were done, I took off my nylons, put them in his trash can, underneath some already-discarded papers. He pulled up his pants and, except for our flushed faces, it was like nothing had happened. He opened the door, said loudly, so everyone in the vicinity could hear, "Thank you for the update, Emmy. Check back in a couple hours if you get any more information."

I nodded obediently and left, some folders in my arms as props.

For the next few hours, he instant-messaged me on my computer. I had to turn the sound off so my coworkers wouldn't hear the constant ding of a new message. I sat close to the screen, blocking the view of the little arriving thought bubbles containing his words.

I already can't wait to see you again, he wrote.

You're so beautiful, he wrote.

I asked him where he wanted to go for dinner after work, told him I'd make a reservation—somewhere nice. We could stay the night at his house, for once. Drew had picked up Bruce when I told him I was sick. "I'll get him out of your hair," he'd said.

Let's just ditch work, he wrote.

Let's spend the day together, he wrote.

I crossed and uncrossed my legs. My panties were wet. I told him we couldn't just leave together in the middle of the morning—everyone would know.

I'll leave first. I'll tell them I have a meeting uptown. I always have meetings, he wrote.

You leave an hour after that, he wrote.

An hour will give me time to prepare a picnic for you, he wrote.

Central Park. Meet at the Christopher Columbus statue at noon, he wrote.

I watched the cursor flicker on the screen, considering.

Okay.

I walked up Sixth, toward the park. As I got closer, foreign languages flew around me every which way. The city was crawling with camera-carrying tourists, even on a Monday. They snapped pictures of art deco buildings that weren't special, but may have seemed so. When I got to the edge of the park, the horse carriage drivers bombarded me, asking if I wanted a ride, waving brochures in my face. I wanted to ask why it wasn't obvious that I lived there, that I was a New Yorker, that I didn't need a ride through the park because I could walk its paths every day if I so desired. I put my head down, shuffled past the crowds of tourists who were considering a carriage ride, and made my way to the mall.

I could see him standing there, next to the Christopher Columbus statue, from a good hundred yards away. He was holding a picnic basket in his right hand—a wicker basket, the kind you picture in your head when thinking of a "picnic basket." I wondered if he owned it, if he'd had it stashed in a closet at home for whatever reason, or if he'd gone out to buy it for this very occasion.

The forecast dictated rain later in the day. A few stray clouds hung in the sky, but I was convinced they would wait to break open until after our picnic. I felt like the universe was on my side.

He didn't see me coming; he was facing the other direction, watching a woman in workout attire walk briskly while pushing an empty stroller. The baby was strapped to her back, asleep. Gabe was smiling, and I wondered if it was at the baby, or if he was just smiling in anticipation of me.

I tiptoed right up behind him: "Boo."

He flinched. All New Yorkers knew to be slightly on edge in Central Park. We'd heard the stories.

He set down the picnic basket and put his arms around me, lifting me off the ground far enough that my shoes dangled off my toes, my heels bare. He took my hand and we walked down the path, the trees arching overhead, as if the branches on one side of the mall and the branches on the other side were desperate to touch each other. Every other park bench was occupied: one with a man in a business suit, maybe out of the office for a rare breath of fresh air; one with a woman who had a sketchbook in her lap; one with a couple and a toddler having a temper tantrum so loud that the couple couldn't bear to make eye contact with us. They were embarrassed, clearly, shushing the young girl and promising things—cotton candy, a stuffed animal, a horse carriage ride—to get her to shut up.

"They must be from out of town," Gabe said once we passed them.

"How do you know?"

"They're forcing an outing to Central Park when that kid is in a terrible mood."

The way he said it—*that kid*—made me uneasy about telling him about my kid, our kid.

"It's probably their last day here. Long weekend trip. From Rhode Island, I'd guess," he said.

Drew and I used to do this—watch people and guess their circumstances. The more outlandish, the better.

We didn't walk through the park; we meandered, the way lovers do, announcing with their slow stroll that they are in no hurry to be anywhere else. When we got to the Great Lawn, Gabe took a carefully folded, red-and-white-checkered blanket from the messenger bag slung over his shoulder and shook it out onto the grass. He sat and I did the same.

In the heat of summer, when kids were out of school and tourists were at their peak, the lawn was crowded with people tanning, throwing Frisbees, playing catch. On this day, we were mostly alone.

We were facing the Belvedere Castle, Central Park's oddest attraction. It looked to have been lifted by a crane from Victorian England and transported to America, dropped in the middle of the park with no discernible rhyme or reason. When I was a little girl, I asked my mom if a princess lived there and she said, with a snort, "There are no princesses."

"I always thought it would be nice to get married there," Gabe said, nodding up toward the castle.

I'd never heard of a man who dreamed about his wedding day.

"It would be," I said.

"People do it," he said. "Someone from the office went to a friend's wedding there."

"And I bet a thousand different strangers have pictures of it."

"True."

He took a bottle of wine out of the basket, along with a sleeve of crackers and a plastic-wrapped plate of cheese cut into little squares.

"I did the best I could with the hour I had," he said.

"Pretty impressive."

He poured wine into plastic cups—one for each of us. Thankfully, the cups were red, not see-through. I took a fake sip and set my cup behind me. I'd pour out some of the wine whenever he turned around. It was silly, but the only alternative I could think of to blurting out, *I can't drink, I'm pregnant.*

"So," he said, with a long exhale that warned me he had something on his mind. I'd hoped this would be one of those romantic outings when both parties maintain the illusion of having nothing on their minds besides each other.

"So," I repeated.

I nibbled on a cracker, nervously.

"We've been together a year now," he said.

Had it been a year? It all went by so fast.

"Have you and Drew talked about the trial separation? Like, making it a permanent separation?"

I gazed off at the castle, thought of the princess I'd imagined, her storybook life.

"Not exactly. Not yet," I said.

"I think it's time," he said, resolved. "You can move out and move in with me."

I thought of the teachers in school saying at the end of exams, "Time's up." I had to know this moment would come. Maybe it was meant to come. I was pregnant now, after all. It sounded idyllic—living with Gabe, having this child with him. I just couldn't imagine telling Drew. Maybe I could just end things with Drew without him ever knowing about the pregnancy. There were all kinds of ways to be a coward.

"I want that," I said.

"Good," he said. "So do I."

His sincerity made me understand the phrase "tugging at heartstrings." I felt that—the physical pull in my chest.

"I think about us sharing an actual life, taking vacations together, getting married one day."

Starting a family? I wondered.

"You have the imagination of a woman," I said. I was trying to be funny, but he was tight-lipped in response.

"I'm serious," he said. "What we're doing now isn't enough."

He had the ultimatum of a woman, too.

I fiddled with a cracker, turning it over and over in my palm like old men did with dominoes during afternoon games in the park. A dog barked behind us. When Gabe turned around to look, I tipped over my cup, let the grass drink my wine.

I had to make a choice, finally. I couldn't keep putting it off. Gabe would end it. And then I'd be left with Drew, unhappy again. It was a risk to choose Gabe, to hurt Drew. It was becoming clear, though, that I had to take it—not just for me, but for the baby.

I looked up at the sky, scattered clouds descending on me and Manhattan.

"Do you want a family?" I didn't realize how scared I was to ask until the question left my mouth.

"Of course," he said. He leaned back, weight on his hands, pressed firmly into the ground.

The relief, oh, the relief. That was it—I would leave Drew.

"Come here," he said. He reached out toward me, coaxing me to fall into him. I crawled across the blanket and let his arms envelop me. He made me feel small; he made my worries feel small. He lay back onto the blanket and eased my body down to join his. He was lying flat, gazing up at the sky. I pressed up next to his side, one leg swung over him, head on his chest.

We lay like that, intertwined like a couple of homeless people trying to stay warm, until a cloud broke open and a few raindrops fell. Then he said, "Let's go home."

We lay in his bed, in the middle of the afternoon, naked. We'd lost any sense of time, alternating between sex and naps for hours. It was luxurious, hedonistic, what I imagined a honeymoon to be. I've never been the kind of person to use the phrase "made love," but that's the only phrase appropriate for what we did in the middle of that afternoon.

"You know, if you had a life with me, I'd annoy you," I said, sitting up in bed. "Eventually, I mean."

He sat behind me, rubbing my shoulders, leaning in every few minutes to kiss my neck. If he was trying to convince me to be with him, to choose him, he was doing all the right things.

"Maybe," he said. "But I'm fairly certain my adoration of you would outweigh the annoyances."

He seemed so sure, so confident.

"Sometimes I clip my nails while I'm sitting on the couch. The noise will drive you crazy," I said. "And I'll blame you for things that aren't your fault. I'll have bad moods. I snore. Did you know that?"

He laughed. "I want to know all the details of you—even the ones you consider bad," he said. "And, yes, I know you snore."

I turned around. "Do I keep you up at night?"

"Nope," he said. "I just nudge you a little, ease you onto your side, and the snoring stops."

I turn back, face forward again, looking at the TV that isn't on.

"What if you feel this way—we feel this way—because this isn't real life we're living?"

He was quiet.

"This is a fantasy," I said, stretching my arms out wide to indicate I was referring to his bed, his home, us. "That's what all affairs are, aren't they? An escape?"

"This isn't an affair for me," he said. I'd offended him.

"I didn't mean it like that. It's more than an 'affair' to me, too," I said, putting air quotes around the offending word. "But if we're not sneaking around, if it's not so *thrilling*, maybe we'll feel differently about each other."

"Em," he said, coaxing me to turn around and face him. I did. "I never wanted thrilling. I'm not twenty years old anymore. I can't even tolerate roller coasters. I'd love to be boring together. Not bored—never bored. Just boring. Ordinary. Together. I'd love that."

I hung on that word—"love."

"Boring together," I repeated.

Maybe it wasn't cowardly to leave Drew. Maybe it was cowardly to stay. I'd told myself to sit through things, to wait it out, like an antsy child in the backseat during a seemingly endless car trip. I'd told myself the destination would be worth the journey. We would trudge through and count ourselves as one of the bruised and battered—but emboldened—couples who "stuck with it." I'd heard older couples tell stories of their own turmoil, how they stood by each other's side when leaving would have been easier—even better. I respected them, applauded them, looked to them as the example that my own mother could never provide. But I'd come to wonder if they deserved the accolades. Perhaps applauding them was just applauding cowardice.

Perhaps there is truth to the notion of two people growing apart.

Perhaps we don't want to say we're unhappy—out loud, to ourselves, to the world—because then we'd have to do something about it.

Perhaps the truly courageous thing is to leave.

"I've had my exciting times, Em. I'm ready to settle down," Gabe went on. "Somewhere, right now, my mother is thanking God."

I laughed, then changed the subject: "You hungry?"

"I am. You?"

"Starving. Should we go out into the world?"

"Let's stay here," he said. "Order in."

He got out of bed, put on his boxers. He ran into the kitchen and returned with a small stack of take-out menus.

"Tell me what sounds good," he said.

I picked Chinese. I had a distinct craving for oil and salt. He paced back and forth in front of the bed while he was on the phone calling in the order. I watched him and wanted him, every part of him. The late afternoon light through the window hit his body just so, shadowing each muscle. He was like a charcoal drawing of the perfect man.

If Gabe and I were ever unhappy, we'd admit it to each other. Somehow, I just knew that. That was the difference between what I'd have with him and what I had with Drew. Drew and I were living the common lie lived by all people who fall out of love, until one person musters the courage to be honest. I would have to be that person; he never would.

I wanted to tell Gabe, right then and there, as he finished repeating back the take-out order on the phone, that I'd decided.

I would do it. I would leave Drew and move in with him. I wanted to scream it. I wanted to jump up and down on the bed with excitement. I wanted to tell him about the baby, to paint a complete picture of the life we'd have together. But I told myself to be calm, to sleep on it—if sleep was even possible in the midst of exhilaration. I would tell him the next day, at a nice dinner: *So, I've decided.* Then nothing would be the same ever again.

"Food will be here in a half hour," he said with a smile.

He dove back into bed next to me.

"We should do this every day," I said, which was the closest I'd come that night to telling him what I'd decided.

He kissed my still-flat belly as if he knew what was within.

"You make me happy," he said, letting his lips linger on my skin.

"You make me happy, too."

His BlackBerry on the nightstand flashed red—there were messages, emails waiting. He didn't seem to care.

"Do you think it's possible for two people to *always* make each other happy?" I asked. It was one more question I needed him to answer.

"I wouldn't ask you to leave your husband if I didn't think it was possible," he said.

I sighed.

"Are you looking for a guarantee? Because I can't give you that. Nobody could—not with a clean conscience," he said. "I can promise you I've never felt this way before. About anyone."

"What else?" I asked, searching for something close to the guarantee he wouldn't give.

"I can promise you I'll be honest with you—even if you don't want me to be."

That was good enough, the most I could ask for.

"It's a risk," I said. "Love, in general, I mean."

"It wouldn't be meaningful if it wasn't."

I kissed him, the words *I want to take the risk* primed on the tip of my tongue. I withheld, though, exhaled the breath saved for that sentence into his mouth.

We ate chow mein and fried rice and egg rolls in bed, using chopsticks to pick out grains of rice when they fell into the folds of the sheets. He fed me, I fed him. We read each other's fortune cookies. Mine read: "A package of value will arrive soon." His read: "The past is gone. Tomorrow is full of possibilities." We played the adolescent game of adding "in bed" to the end of our fortunes.

"Tomorrow is full of possibilities in bed," he said with a satisfied nod. "Does that mean you'll spend the night again?"

"Maybe," I said, with a teasing smile.

"You should take the day off tomorrow, be waiting here when I get home."

I climbed into his lap, straddled him.

"I have a feeling I'm getting special treatment since I'm sleeping with the boss," I said.

"So? What of it?" he said. "You don't have clothes here. You should start moving some, see how it feels. I'll clear drawers for you."

This—the drawers—excited me to an embarrassing point of giddiness. I did my best to hide it, but I was sure my face was flushed.

"Sleep here. Bring some clothes back. We'll play house for the week."

I'd tell Drew I was still really sick, that he needed to keep Bruce with him at his mother's house. He'd probably insist on visiting me, caretaker that he'd become, but I'd tell him to stay away. *I don't want you to get what I have,* I'd say.

"I'll need at least two drawers," I told Gabe. "For now."

Still lying in bed, we ate spoonfuls of Neapolitan ice cream out of the carton. It had frostbite, the way ice cream does when it's been sitting in the freezer for months.

The sun set and I said, "This has got to be one of the top five best days of my life."

He said, "If it's any lower than number three, I've failed you."

He turned out the bedside light early—around nine o'clock. Even with all the resting, all the gluttony, we were tired. He had an early meeting, had to be at the office by seven to prepare a PowerPoint. He told me he'd be quiet in the morning, said he didn't want to wake me. He detailed the contents of his pantry so I knew my breakfast options. And then he kissed me good night and wished me sweet dreams.

"Right now I think reality is sweeter than any dream could be," I said.

It was hokey, but I didn't care. My heart beat wildly as I thought about the next night. I'd call around in the morning for a reservation somewhere fancy. I'd tell him about leaving Drew and he'd lean across the table, take my face in his hands, and kiss me hard. He'd be surprised about the baby, but happy. His face would light up. We'd spend hours imagining our future together. The restaurant manager would have to kick us out. And when we went to bed together that night, I'd say, *This is it—the number one best day of my life.*

TWENTY-THREE

I'm walking through the produce section of the grocery store, apples and bananas in my basket, when I see Drew. Right there, analyzing the yellow onions, trying to pick a good one, though it's impossible to see through all the layers. I'm frozen, standing on a square tile as if it is surrounded by thrashing ocean water. This tile, my lifeboat. He looks up, sees me. There is no flash of recognition on his face, no confusion. He puts two onions in his basket and disappears, turning the corner to another aisle. I drop my basket on the floor, apples rolling out, and leave.

I wake up in a sweat. The sheets are cold, sticking to my skin. I've been having these dreams—or nightmares, rather—more often lately. Sometimes I run into Drew, sometimes my mom, sometimes Marni or Nancy. People who knew me. It's always in an everyday place such as the bank, the post office, the grocery store. Sometimes they recognize me, in spite of the blond dye job. I still have hair in my dreams. A look of shock registers on their faces and I wake up with a jolt, like when I take an unintentional nap at the movie theater and flinch awake thinking I'm falling off a cliff. Sometimes, more often, they don't recognize me. I'm not sure which version of the nightmare is more disconcerting. Regardless, I can't sleep after.

I keep thinking about Claire's request for total honesty. If Dr. Richter has bad news, if the much-feared end is near, I need to tell Claire about New York, about what happened. I owe it to her.

When I go to see Dr. Richter, she repeats the same thing she did before starting me on Taxol: "It's not working as well as I'd hoped."

Hearing her words, I'm not so much sad as I am angry.

"The chemo is doing *nothing*?" I say, incredulous.

She tilts her head from one side to the other, as if she's evaluating the first sip of a glass of wine someone's just poured for her.

"The swelling in your breast has gone down a little, the breast tissue isn't as thick, the redness isn't as bad. So the chemo hasn't done *nothing*," she says, defensive of the drugs. I guess she has to be.

"So what now?"

"Well, I'd consider this a partial response to the chemo. I want to do the mastectomy and radiation, see how much we can get that way."

Her corny parting words this time: "Stay hopeful."

The Internet tells me that hope is for fools, that even if I get through this round of treatment, the cancer will likely come back somewhere else. I'll be playing a game of chemotherapy Whac-A-Mole until my body gives up completely.

I've been talking more and more to Paul. It's gotten to the point that we have each other's phone numbers and text when we're going to the infusion center. Chemo dates, Nurse Amy says. Paul's my first friend in California. Al and JT are different. They started as necessities and are like family now. I suppose I've gone all these years without friends because I haven't needed them. I've had moments of needing them, but those moments just pass. Cancer doesn't just pass. And if you don't talk to someone about it, you'll go crazy. I could see a shrink, but what I picture is someone speaking to me in a soft voice—as if anything above normal volume would disrupt my peaceful dying process—using a bank of psychological terms to explain away the basic fact that I'm fucking afraid of dying.

So I have Paul. And, occasionally, Nurse Amy. She's on vacation now—Hawaii. People's lives go on.

Paul finishes chemo next month and he should be in the clear, for good. It's hard not to resent him, and it's hard not to hate myself for resenting him.

"I wish I had prostate cancer," I tell him.

"That would make you a man," he says, "which would be far less appealing for me."

I'm never sure if he's flirting. Amy says he is. Whatever he's doing shouldn't be allowed in infusion centers.

"I don't even know why I'm sitting here," I say, disregarding his potential flirtation. "The chemo is barely doing anything."

"I bet the surgery and radiation kill it," he says.

"Maybe," I say. "And then it could come back. I might make it this year, but die next year."

"Isn't that true for anyone?"

It's a valid point. I hate when Paul makes valid points.

"I'm doing the genetic testing," I say, changing the subject. Nurse Amy's fill-in, an all-business Latina named Desi, comes to check on me. She doesn't make small talk. She must overhear us chatting, but she never chimes in. She doesn't get involved. It's a good skill to have in her line of work.

"Are you? That's a good decision, I think," Paul says.

I've hemmed and hawed about it before. I've been avoiding the test, but now, in the name of honesty with Claire, I have to do it. It's strange to think there's a gene for cancer, that I may have been destined for this. Could it be that I was walking around New York all those years ago, blissfully deaf to the ticking clock buried in my body, thinking that I had everything under control? I've put off the test this long because I don't know how I can live with myself if I have the gene, if I pass it on to Claire. But the thing is, if the Internet is right, I may not be living with myself that much longer.

"Claire should know," I say. "It's selfish of me not to find out."

"Ignorance is bliss, as they say."

"Until it isn't."

"When are you doing it?" he asks.

"This week."

"Look at you, taking the bull by the ol' horns."

"Reluctantly," I say.

Getting my affairs in order. That's what people say. I did a living trust online. It's not so difficult when you don't have a lot of things, and when you have only one person to leave them to.

"I'm also thinking about contacting that person in New York."

I figure if I have to be honest with Claire from here on out, I can use Paul as practice. I decided this morning that I would tell him the story—the messy, strange story.

"The infamous person," he says, an eyebrow raised.

"She should know," I say. "If I don't tell her and I die, she'll never know."

He lowers his eyebrow.

"Then contact *that person,*" he says.

"It's kind of complicated," I say.

"Complicated how?"

"Well, the person is Claire's father."

"Oh," he says, a little more intrigued. "I thought he was out of the picture."

I never said that, exactly. I just told him once, when he asked, that I had full custody of Claire.

"He is out of the picture," I say.

"I'm confused."

"He doesn't know about Claire."

He shifts in his chair, turns to look me in the eye. Normally we just talk to the air, facing forward.

"Go on," he says.

I finally let go of my breath.

"I used to live in New York. I left a week after 9/11. Came here to start over."

"Left the guy behind?"

The way he says it—*the guy*—rattles me, as if Claire's father meant nothing or, worse, as if he was an awful person, a drug addict, a convict, a deadbeat.

"It's not what you think," I say. I'm defensive even though I have no right to be. Paul doesn't know anything.

"I read in *The New York Times* that lots of people left the city after 9/11," he says.

Oh, Paul. He's trying to give me a pass I don't really deserve.

"I was pregnant with Claire." That's not the reason I left, or not the only one. It's all so convoluted now.

"I was married in New York," I say. "Drew was his name—my husband."

"Oh," he says. He shifts in his chair again, noticeably uncomfortable. Maybe, in his eyes, I am just a woman who left her husband. Like his ex-wife.

"So you just left without saying anything?"

This, the judgment, is what I feared.

"It's a long story," I say.

And then I tell him about Drew and me, from the time we fell in love to the time I fell out. I tell him about the night we met, about the fateful date I canceled to stay up talking to Drew until early morning. I tell him how we got married so young—too young. I tell him about our little apartment. I tell him about my career in advertising, about Drew's failed taco shop and his subsequent career in taking care of his sick mother.

"That's hard," he says, when I elaborate on the part about his sick mother.

"I know," I say. "It is. It was. But that's the thing. Love is supposed to survive hard. It's supposed to withstand hard."

"Ideally, I guess. That's not always the case."

There's a slight tension to his voice. I think of his wife leaving him after he was diagnosed. I think of how that was probably a long story, too.

"It gets worse," I say.

He grips the armrest like he's bracing himself. Maybe it's selfish to tell him all this, to attempt to exonerate myself like this.

"You know how I said I ditched a date the night I first met Drew? In college? That date was with a guy named Gabe," I say. "Well, years later, Gabe and I crossed paths again."

I make it sound happenstance, even though the truth is somewhat different. "Gabe and I ended up getting close."

I've never told this story to anyone. It feels just like that—a story, someone else's life.

"Oh," he says. I wish he would stop saying that.

"One thing led to another?" he ventures.

He's packaging up my story into something so ordinary, when there is nothing ordinary about what actually happened.

"To put it simply," I say, jumping, leaping, skipping over so many details.

"And then you got pregnant."

I nod sheepishly.

"Connie, Connie, Connie," he says. He doesn't know I used to be Emily. The more I tell him, the more I realize how little he knows. He's shaking his head disapprovingly, the way you shake your head at an adorable child sneaking an extra cookie off the kitchen counter. He's making light of it, for my sake but also his own, I think. Paul wants to like me, for some reason.

"Gabe was Puerto Rican—brown skin. If I had the baby, Drew would have known everything. It would have killed him."

"So you didn't tell either of the guys."

The guys.

I shake my head.

"And then you made a case for moving out here to start over."

This isn't how it went down, exactly, but I'm swept up in the momentum of his conclusions.

"And now I'm dying."

"Stop saying that," he says.

I've learned through this whole experience that some people cope by denying the possibility of death and some people, like me, cope by talking their way into apprehensive acceptance of it.

"Okay, well, regardless, I realize there are things Claire needs to know."

"What does she think happened to her dad? She must've asked."

"I told her he died in a car accident."

He grimaces. "Fuck," he says. I liked it better when he was saying "Oh."

"So you're going to have to contact the guy and then talk to Claire," he says.

"Right."

"What are you going to say?"

"To Claire?"

"To either of them."

"I have no idea," I say. "I suppose I'll start with apologizing for being a horrible person."

I say this earnestly, not in the hopes of getting him to contradict me, but he does anyway: "You're not a horrible person, Con."

But, see, he doesn't know the half of it. Or maybe he knows about half—just about.

He reaches over and gives me a hey-cheer-up nudge in the arm. Then we sit there in silence for what feels like an hour.

"You should Google 'How to talk to my baby daddy about his kid,'" he says finally.

Maybe it's the stress of all this, but hearing him say "baby daddy" puts me in hysterics. And when I start laughing, he starts laughing. We fold over in our chairs, tears in our eyes, IV bags swinging with our movement. A couple other patients glance up from their books and magazines to see what we could possibly think is so amusing while our cells are being killed, one by one. Desi walks by and gives us a look like a librarian gives teenagers making a ruckus when they should be reading. We recompose ourselves, our laughter dying down like a crackling campfire after everyone has roasted their marshmallows and retired to their tents for the night. Claire and I should go camping this summer—the two of us in sleeping bags under a huge starry sky.

"I've never told anyone any of this," I say when the laughter is gone.

"Why the hell did you choose me?" he asks.

Because you like me, for some reason. Because you always smile. Because you make me feel better about things.

"I don't know," I say. "Should I have spared you?"

"Nah," he says. "I judge you a little, but I'll get over it."

It's hard to hear that he judges me, even if it's just a little, and even if he'll get over it.

"I'm a coward, huh?" I say.

He looks over at me. "You've got poison running through your veins," he says. "That's pretty brave."

TWENTY-FOUR

Gabe had thick, expensive silk curtains. Burgundy. They were so long that the excess fabric gathered at the floor beneath the window. I overslept that morning because of those curtains. When I finally woke up in his bed, the darkness deceived me into thinking it was early—before six. But Gabe was gone, the sheets on his side of the bed pulled tight, his pillow sitting against the headboard just so. The clock said eight o'clock. It was the best sleep I'd had in months.

I lay in bed luxuriously, enjoying the feel of the six-hundred-thread-count Egyptian cotton sateen sheets against my bare skin. My stomach growled. If Gabe had all the ingredients, I'd make pancakes—a big batch. I'd freeze the leftovers so he'd have something to eat in the morning, while running out the door on the way to work. He always claimed coffee was his breakfast. When I protested, he said, "I put cream in it."

It was a little after eight o'clock when I stretched my arms up toward the ceiling, the way bad actors do in scenes showing them "waking up." I made my side of the bed, set my pillow against the headboard to match Gabe's. He was clean, something Drew wasn't. I wouldn't have to pick up after Gabe in the life I envisioned for us. I pulled back the curtains and the room filled with light. It was a beautiful day—not a cloud in the very blue sky.

Gabe's shower had one of those showerheads on the ceiling that dropped water like rain. We'd stood together underneath it once and I'd closed my eyes, pretending I was in the middle of a Costa Rican rain forest with him during a passing storm. The shower at my apartment was barely big enough for one person. I nicked myself while shaving on a routine basis because there was no bench; I just had to balance on one foot, my other foot stamping the shower wall while I attempted to shave as quickly as possible—without soap or gel. Gabe's shower had a bench. I took the time to lather up, to shave properly, to feel like a woman.

His robe was still damp from his own morning shower. I didn't mind; I wrapped it, and him, around me happily. I hadn't even heard him in the shower earlier. I hadn't even heard him get up. He'd kept his promise of letting me sleep, totally undisturbed. I twisted my wet hair up into a bun on the top of my head and went to the kitchen.

As luck would have it, Gabe had all the supplies needed for pancakes—even a raspberry syrup in the side of the fridge that had an expiration date of July 2001. I figured it would still be good. It smelled fine. I sent him a text message:

Making pancakes. Leftovers will be in the freezer to go with your coffee in the morning.

Then another: *I must really like you.*

I'd just gotten a phone with text-messaging capabilities. The technology, the anticipation, was new to me. I waited for his response, my phone sitting right next to the mixing bowl, lightly dusted in flour. It'd been a while since I'd done this—made breakfast, felt like someone's significant other. He wrote back:

I promise you I'll eat breakfast every day of my life if I get to eat it with you.

I smiled so big that I wondered what someone in the next building would think if they saw me through the expansive kitchen window. I covered my mouth, almost embarrassed by my own bliss.

He wrote again:

Going into my meeting. Will be thinking of you when I really shouldn't be.

I didn't write back because I wanted to be respectful of his work time. He had a big presentation. I knew that.

It was 8:30 A.M..

I finished one batch of pancakes while humming along to the remake of "Lady Marmalade" on the radio. I went back to the bathroom, found a comb in one of the drawers. It was a small comb, meant for short, male hair. I hung up the robe and waltzed, naked, to the bedroom. I sat on the bed, knees bent underneath me, my hair gathered in front of me, dripping onto my bare chest. I clicked on the TV and went to work on my tangles. I needed a haircut. My hair was getting long, unruly. I'd call the salon later that day. Maybe they could get me in for an appointment before my dinner with Gabe.

I was watching *The Today Show* on NBC. Matt Lauer was interviewing an author, a guy named Richard Hack who had written a book about Howard Hughes. I wasn't particularly interested. I was waiting for the weather report to tell me if the sunny skies would stay. Suddenly Matt Lauer interrupted the author and said they wanted to go live to a picture of the World Trade Center. Then someone off-camera told him they didn't have the image yet. Matt Lauer said there was a breaking story and they'd be right back. It was 8:51 A.M. according to the ticker on the screen.

I didn't think to change the channel, to check what other stations were reporting. I didn't think it was something serious. After all, newscasters called snow flurries a "breaking story." During the commercial break, I went into the kitchen for a pancake. I was eating it—no plate, just straight from hand to mouth—when Katie Couric and Matt Lauer appeared on-screen together at 8:53 A.M. They said a plane had just crashed into the World Trade Center. They had very little information.

I dropped the half-eaten pancake onto the bed and went closer to the TV screen, staring at the picture of the building with a hole in its side, smoke billowing out. It was the north tower—my tower, Gabe's tower. The hole was high up. The Berringer office was high up—on the 101st floor. I tried to count how many floors down the hole was. The towers were 110 stories each. I knew that much. The hole was seven, ten, twelve stories down? I was reluctant to know for sure.

I ran, still naked, to the kitchen, to my phone. I expected to find a text message from Gabe, telling me about this crazy accident that had happened, how they'd evacuated through the stairwells and were on the street, looking up at the scene in disbelief. There was no text message, though. I wrote:

Watching the news. You okay?

I waited. In the background, an eyewitness was talking to Katie Couric and Matt Lauer. She was calling in from a cell phone. It was hard to hear her. There were sirens in the background. She told them about the ball of fire she saw when she came out of the subway station to go to work at the Ritz-Carlton. She said pieces of the building were flying. She said the smoke was incredible. She said she couldn't see the top of the towers through the smoke. Katie and Matt told her that it was a plane that crashed into the tower. She didn't know it was a plane.

Finally, my phone screen lit up. But it wasn't Gabe. It was Drew calling. There was no sound—I'd turned off the ringer. I saw his number flash four times. He thought I was in the tower, at work. I couldn't bring myself to answer the phone. I was frozen, paralyzed. He left a voice mail. I didn't listen.

My mom called next. I let it ring again. Another voice-mail notification appeared. I couldn't respond to anyone. I wanted to reserve my phone for Gabe.

Em, I'm scared shitless. They're saying a plane hit the tower. Please tell me you're OK.

A text message. Marni.

Those were the only people who had my new number—Drew, my mom, Marni. And Gabe, of course.

I brought my phone to the bedroom, resumed my seat on the edge of the bed, knees bent underneath me. I turned up the volume on the TV, as if I'd understand more if it was louder. My phone screen lit up with another text message from Marni asking if I was okay. I wasn't, though. I wouldn't be until I heard from Gabe.

Drew tried calling again. He didn't leave a message.

Katie and Matt were questioning another eyewitness, a woman named Elliott. She was talking about the air being filled with hundreds of pieces of paper, like confetti, when, at 9:03 A.M., she screamed, "Another one just hit!" Katie and Matt gasped. The off-screen news crew gasped. Elliott's voice was shaky. She wondered aloud if there were air traffic control problems. Nobody knew then what the reality was.

They cut to a woman named Jennifer. She kept saying, "It was a jet." Al Roker said, "What are the odds of two separate planes hitting both towers?" Matt proposed that it might not be an accident, that it might be something deliberate. That's the word he used—"deliberate."

My phone lit up—my mom again. Then Drew again. My mom didn't leave a message. Drew did.

The towers—both of them—were slowly being consumed by fire, lines of red running down the sides, leaving behind black and plumes of gray. Eyewitnesses confirmed the towers were leaning. Katie said it was pandemonium. Matt wondered how people got out of the building, if the elevators were jammed. I tried Gabe again:

You got out, right? Please call me.

Maybe he'd left his phone at his desk. That's what I told myself. Maybe his phone wasn't working. Maybe no messages were getting through. I expected him to walk through the front door, to hold my naked body and tell me everything was all right. We'd both cry.

At 9:15 A.M., Katie said the planes were hijacked, that it was a terrorist attack. At 9:17 A.M., Matt said the potential for injury and death was high. At 9:20 A.M., they were already talking about what kind of military action to take. I shivered. I got under the bedsheets, pulled my knees to my chest, my wet hair on Gabe's pillow. Goose bumps rose up on my scalp.

The blue sky was going dark. The newscast was focused on whether or not military jets should be deployed to protect the rest of the city. They didn't know anything about the people in the buildings. They didn't know what had happened to Gabe.

Please call if you're there. I'm scared. I love you, dear friend.

Marni again.

At 9:30 A.M., George W. Bush came on and said, "Today we've had a national tragedy," as if the event were already in the past, as if it weren't still happening. He said the government would help the victims and their loved ones. But who were those people? Was Gabe a victim? Was I a loved one? Bush said we'd track down the terrorists. But we didn't know who they were, either. There was a moment of silence, and then he left the podium. People clapped. I didn't know why they clapped.

I held my phone in the palm of my hand, against my chest. It was wet with my sweat. As the moments went on, I looked at the phone with less and less hope and more and more dread. If that first plane hit the north tower around 8:45 A.M., Gabe would have been out by 9:30 A.M., wouldn't he? Maybe he was helping other people. Maybe he was walking the streets around Battery Park, dazed and confused. Maybe there was no way for him to get home. But, assuming he wasn't injured, he could walk—it was less than two miles for him to get from the chaos back to me. It would take him no more than thirty minutes. Maybe he was injured—on a gurney a safe distance from the disaster. I told myself to be patient. I told myself it was too early to conclude anything.

"Just wait," I said aloud. I was stroking my belly when I said it, assuring my unborn baby, my Claire.

At 9:42 A.M., the news coverage cut to the Pentagon, where

there was more fire and billowing smoke. Another plane crash, they said. I wanted them to go back to the towers.

At 9:59 A.M., they said big chunks of the south building had fallen away. A few moments later, they realized it wasn't chunks; it was the building itself, flattened, demolished. All that was left were huge puffs of white smoke, clouding where the tower had once been, engulfing the surrounding buildings. A street-level view showed people running, the smoke chasing them. Katie said eyewitnesses claimed to see people jumping out of the buildings. At 10:14 A.M., Katie said, "It looks like a movie."

At 10:17 A.M., they said they were worried about the north tower collapsing. Gabe's tower. At 10:28 A.M., it did. And that's when I cried my first tears of the morning. Up until that moment, I'd been dedicated to the lie that everything would be fine.

I looked at my phone again. Nothing. I wrote Gabe one last message:

I love you. So much.

I left the TV on, but pulled the covers up and over my head. I crawled closer to Gabe's pillow, hugged it as if it were him. I stayed like that, in that position, until the next day, when my stomach growled ferociously, my unborn baby asking me to feed her, reminding me that life goes on whether you want it to or not.

TWENTY-FIVE

When I woke up, the sky was an ashy gray and I knew that the day before was not just a bad dream. I turned off the TV. There was nothing new to know. I'd listened to the reports throughout the night, from under the covers. People were dead, so many people. They wouldn't know the exact numbers for days, weeks. Loved ones were tacking up MISSING posters on the streets—outside hospitals primarily, but also on streetlamps, walls, trees, store windows, subway signs, wherever a piece of tape would stick. I already knew what others would realize in a few more days—these MISSING signs were really obituaries, remembrances.

I looked at my phone. I had two voice mails from Drew, one from my mom. There was nothing from Gabe. He was gone—a fact that settled in as night turned to dawn. I had no need to post a MISSING poster for him. I wished I'd met his mom so I could call her, so we could console each other. Nobody knew about Gabe and me. Some presumed, I was sure, but nobody *knew*. I had no consolation.

I went to the kitchen, found the plate of pancakes right where I'd left them, batter still left in the mixing bowl for the second batch I never made. I picked up one of the cold pancakes, ate it mindlessly, trying to satisfy my annoying hunger. I opened the fridge, took out a carton of milk, drank straight from it. I was still naked.

I went back to my phone, considered the prompt alerting me to my awaiting voice messages. I listened:

Drew—concerned, but still composed:

Em? I'm—I'm watching the news. They're saying a plane just hit the tower—the north one. Is that your tower? I think it is. Fuck, I should know that. I tried calling your office, but the phone's dead. Call me when you're safe, okay? Okay, call. Please. Love you.

I saved the message. I wasn't sure why.

My mom—confused, totally confused:

Emily, can you call me? It looks like there was some kind of plane crash where you work. Gina from next door is here. Call when you can, okay?

Drew again—panicked this time, possibly crying:

Em, God, please tell me you're okay. I don't know what I would do if— God, please tell me you're okay. I love you, babe.

I started to cry. He was so afraid, so desperate, so convinced that he couldn't live without me, when really that was all he'd been doing for months. I wished, in that moment, that I was dead, that I could visit Drew as an at-peace spirit and tell him he'd be fine. Because he would. I knew he would.

And that's when it occurred to me that I could be dead. That they thought I was dead. More than likely, there was a MISSING sign for me, an obituary, a remembrance, somewhere on the streets of Manhattan. That's something Marni would do—post a sign. She'd use the prettiest picture of me she could find, maybe the one from when we'd had lunch together a few weeks before. It was a beautiful Friday, we were sitting outside at this new restaurant in Chelsea. The light was just right. She said, "Did you just get laid? You're glowing." I'd planned to tell her about Gabe and me that day, but she overtook the conversation with her own relationship woes. I figured I'd tell her at the next lunch. We were trying to make it a monthly thing.

I rubbed my thumb over the keys of the phone, thinking. It wasn't that I *could* have been in those towers; I *should* have been. I would have been if Gabe and I hadn't spent the night together, if Gabe hadn't told me to sleep in, take the day off. Some would call it luck or fortune; I didn't see it that way. I would never see it that way. I'd always see it as a bizarre twist of fate.

I brought the plate of cold pancakes into the bedroom, got under the covers, and set them next to me. There were eleven left, enough to get me through the day. After I ate two, I fell asleep. I was awakened a couple hours later by my phone buzzing. I reached across the bed for it with residual hope. I scolded myself for that hope. It was Drew, trying again. He had residual hope, too. On the third ring, I threw the phone at the hardwood floor. The battery popped out upon impact and a couple other small pieces scattered across the room, the phone itself coming to an anticlimactic rest at the threshold to the bathroom.

I didn't yet know what I would do—not exactly, anyway. I had no plan. All I knew was that the life I'd had was gone, that I was gone in a sense, that the people who knew me should stop looking. It wasn't that I didn't love them, but I was quite certain they shouldn't love me. I was quite certain they had to let me go. Maybe I was in shock. Maybe I was delirious with grief or hunger or anger or confusion. I would sleep until I knew for certain.

TWENTY-SIX

I stayed in Gabe's apartment for a week. I didn't want to go out into the world. It felt dangerous to me. I didn't know who I'd be in it now. It was different and so was I.

I wore Gabe's clothes—his NYU sweatshirt, a pair of soccer shorts that were too big for me even when I pulled the drawstring tight, and green wool socks. I read books from his shelf—business books, mostly. I wasn't interested, but I wanted to fill the hours. On his nightstand was a biography of John Adams, a bookmark stuck in twenty pages from the end. I read those twenty pages, finished it for him. I subsisted on what he had in his pantry and fridge and freezer—canned soups, dry cereal, stale crackers, peanut butter on toast, frozen dinners. I hadn't turned on the TV since September 12.

I decided I would leave. Because I could. Because I had to. That was it—I *had* to. There were other options, of course, but I discounted them. The city, resilient as ever, was starting to function again. I could tell by looking out the window, seeing pedestrians and taxis on the street. I would get one of those taxis to take me to the airport and I would buy a ticket to California. I would start over. I would be a better person.

I put the clothes I'd worn the day before 9/11 in the washer—my flowy white blouse, the skirt that hugged my hips just so. Then I remembered how Gabe had yanked that skirt off me in his office and I took it out of the washer. I wanted to keep it as it was. I just ironed out the wrinkles. I stepped into it and zipped it up to see if it still fit. After all, it felt like years had passed; not just one week. It did fit, but was a little loose where before it had been tight. I'd lost weight in that one week. I worried for the baby.

I found a set of matching luggage in the back of Gabe's closet, behind boxes of dress shoes. Behind the luggage was a safe, left unlocked, as if he'd known I'd need it. At least, that's what I told myself when I took out the cash inside—two stacks of twenties, one taller than the other—totaling almost five thousand dollars. I put thirty bills in my wallet, the rest in the overnight bag from the luggage set.

I packed the overnight bag with some toiletries taken from his bathroom, along with some granola bars from his pantry. I'd have to buy clothes at an airport shop, or first thing in California. I imagined myself in a sundress. I'd never worn a sundress in New York.

I cut up all my credit cards and my ATM card using the scissors from his knife set in the kitchen. I flushed the bits down the toilet. They disappeared. I flushed again for good measure.

I took out the trash, made the bed, washed the dishes, and put them back in their respective cabinets. I found a feather duster in the linen closet and used it on all the furniture. I swept the floors with a broom that had bits of past messes still stuck on its bristles. I didn't know why I did any of this, why it mattered to me. It just did.

I sat on the bed, in his NYU sweatshirt and soccer shorts and wool socks, next to my packed bag and my purse. The sun set. I still had the curtains drawn, but I could tell when the sun was there and when it was not. I knew I wouldn't be able to sleep. I just sat there, until a small sliver of light through the curtains told me it was morning.

Just after eight o' clock, I changed into my skirt and blouse and slipped on my heels. I hung my purse over one shoulder, the overnight bag over the other. I felt like I was forgetting something, but then realized I had nothing to forget. This wasn't my home.

I stood in the doorway, staring at the apartment for a moment, as if I were reluctant to say good-bye, as if I'd created hundreds of wonderful memories there, within those walls. In reality, I was mourning the fact that I didn't get to.

I cleared my throat, anticipating my need to hail a taxi. I hadn't spoken a word out loud in a week. I wondered if I'd be able to.

I started to pull the door shut, then decided to turn the inside lock. I wasn't worried about other people breaking in. I wasn't worried about Gabe's property; it all seemed so worthless now. My only worry was that I might try to come back.

TWENTY-SEVEN

Claire's due date was the end of April, but she took her sweet time. May arrived and she still hadn't. I couldn't afford to take any time off work, so at forty weeks' pregnant, I lugged my huge belly to the day-care center and the steakhouse in Malibu. It was at the steakhouse, in the middle of the dinner rush, around six o'clock, on May 9, that my water broke as dramatically as you see in the movies. I was in the kitchen, picking up just-plated food to bring to a table, and the telltale puddle appeared between my legs. A waitress I worked with, Tina, said, "Well, shit."

My plan all along was to just drive myself to the hospital, but Tina insisted on taking me. I barely knew her; she'd only been working at the steakhouse for a few weeks. She drove my car instead of her own. "In case you have the kid on the way," she said with a look of mild disgust.

I'd expected labor to be a days-long ordeal, especially since it was my first child. But, no. It was fast and furious, as if Claire had decided she'd waited long enough and wanted out immediately. That's like Claire—determined, intent, stubborn. There wasn't even time for drugs or an epidural. I screamed through the most intense pain of my life and then she was in the world, crying her tiny lungs out.

When the nurses put her in my arms for the first time, I lost my breath. It just left me. It wasn't only the miracle of this human being on my chest that took it away, but the realization that I'd made a grave error. It was so blatantly obvious: Claire wasn't Gabe's; she was Drew's.

It shocked me, truly. Most newborns don't even look human, do they? They look shriveled and swollen simultaneously—like plump raisins. I didn't think she would have distinguishable features for months. And if she did, I thought they would be Gabe's. I was so sure.

I cried uncontrollably, shaking so badly that one of the nurses—a round, fifty-something black woman—came to the bedside to steady Claire, cradle her head as it bobbed each time my chest heaved.

"I know, it's emotional," the nurse said, stroking my hand. I don't remember her name. She was kind to me, committed to being at my side because nobody else was. Tina had taken a taxi back to the restaurant right after she dropped me off.

"She looks just like him," I said.

His bright blue eyes, his sharp nose. There was no doubt.

"Does she?" was all the kind nurse said.

The nurse helped me position Claire on my breast. She latched right onto my nipple and I just stared. At the time, I saw the uncanny resemblance to Drew as some kind of punishment. I'd have to look at Claire every day and think about what I'd done, who I'd left behind. But over the years I've realized that she doesn't look like him so I *have* to remember him; she looks like him so I *can* remember him.

Dr. Richter calls on a Tuesday to say she has good news.

"You don't have the gene," she says.

Most people think you only need to sit when receiving bad

news, but my knees buckle at this news, too. No gene. My cancer is random, like most things in life.

"So there's no chance I can pass this on to Claire?" I say. I'm tentative. Dr. Richter is not a big fan of speaking in absolutes. I'm afraid she'll say, *Well, there is a slight chance . . .*

"No, Connie," she says, surprising me, "there is nothing you can pass on."

I've never heard her so bubbly. She must know, as a mother herself, how much this means to me.

"Is there any chance the test is wrong?" I say.

"You don't have the gene. This is one test that is pretty black-and-white."

Claire and I are talking again, though she seems guarded, wary. It's like she's steeling herself for whatever is to come. On Sunday, we go to Zuma Beach instead of our usual beach. It's farther up the coast, at the north end of Malibu. During summer it's packed with people, cars parallel-parked haphazardly along the highway. Now, though, in February, it's deserted. The long, wide stretch of sand is just for us.

I've thought about how to start this talk with Claire:

I have a couple things I need to tell you about your DNA. First, you don't have the gene for breast cancer. Second, you have a father in New York.

In the moment, though, I just opt for:

"I want to talk to you about some things."

She stops in her tracks. She's worried, noticeably. She thinks there's a new cancer update, a proverbial turn for the worse.

"It's not about the cancer," I say. "I mean, it is and it isn't."

"Mom, just tell me," she says impatiently. Her arms are crossed over her chest—not in an angry way, but like she's bracing herself, like she's learning how to soothe herself, without me.

"I talked to Dr. Richter earlier this week and I don't have the gene for cancer," I say.

"Oh, okay," she says. She's not exactly sure what this means.

"So you can't inherit it from me," I say. Then: "It's all random."

"Random," she repeats. "I guess that's good?"

"I think so," I say. "If I had the gene, you would have a high chance of getting cancer one day."

"But you don't," she says. "So if I get cancer, it will be random."

"Random," I say.

She resumes walking and I follow her.

"Is that it?" she says. The wind tousles her hair. She started letting it grow out when she found out I might die. She's cold, hands hidden inside the sleeves of her oversized sweatshirt. She's still so skinny and flat-chested, like I was at her age. Her naïveté is obvious in the shape—or lack thereof—of her body. All that will change soon. Hormones will make her a different person than the one I see now. Tears come when I consider not meeting that girl, that woman. I swallow them back, feel them drip down my throat.

"There's something else."

She stops again, a few feet in front of me. She faces me, but doesn't step closer. She wants news at a distance. She can't handle it up close. I don't blame her.

"I've been thinking," I say. "If I'm gone, there's something you need to know."

She moves her mouth just slightly, starts to say something, probably, *You won't be gone,* but she stops, silenced by this mysterious thing she needs to know.

I always thought I'd tell her one day, but I imagined it would be when she was older—in her twenties or thirties, even, after she'd had her own complicated experiences with love, when we had transcended the mother-daughter dynamic to pure friendship. Life has rushed me, us.

"What is it?"

She's tentative, unsure whether or not she wants to know. The look on her face is the same as when I took her to the famous haunted house in the Valley last year for Halloween. She clung to me as we approached, said, "You first."

I go to her. The wind is picking up, tossing around grains of sand.

"It's about your father," I say, just letting the words dangle there in the ocean air between us.

She squints at me.

"What about him?"

All she knows is the story I made up. The only true part of that story is the blue eyes.

"He didn't die like I said."

She squints harder, because of the sandy wind or because of confusion. It's like she's trying to find something minuscule—some little lie, some little truth—on my face.

"He didn't die at all."

She starts gnawing on her thumbnail, a nervous habit she got from me.

"He's alive?" she says.

"As far as I know."

"Where?"

"In New York."

"New York?" She says it like it's Nepal.

"That's where I used to live."

She doesn't say anything, just hugs herself, so I go on: "His name is Andrew Morris. I used to call him—everyone called him—Drew."

I've decided she doesn't need to know about Gabe, about the affair. Not now. If I live long enough, I'll tell her one day.

"I don't understand," she says.

I put my hands on her upper arms, nearly completing a thumb-to-index-finger circle around them. She doesn't release her grip on herself, though.

"I'm sorry I lied to you," I say.

She gives me the look I've been dreading, the look that says she's not sure she trusts me, the look that says she doesn't know who I am.

"He's been alive this whole time?" she says.

It's still sinking in, this truth.

I nod.

She wriggles herself out my grasp and releases the grip on herself, drops her arms at her sides like they weigh a hundred pounds each.

"Are you freaking kidding me?"

She shrieks these words as she backs away slowly, as if I'm wielding some kind of deadly weapon.

"Claire," I say. "I'm sorry."

She's standing several feet away from me.

"You're not sorry," she says. "You never would have told me if you weren't dying."

She shouts the word "dying."

"Is this, like, your attempt to confess all your sins?" she says. "Am I supposed to just forgive you?"

She's screaming.

Every step I take toward her, she takes one back.

"Claire," I say. "Stop, let's talk—"

"No," she says. "You don't get to do that."

"Claire."

"Does he even know about me?" she shouts.

When I hesitate, she says, "Are you serious?" Then: "That is so fucked up."

She runs through the sand toward the car. I go after her.

"Claire," I say when I catch her. I'm out of breath, gasping, leaning on the hood of the car. She's waiting at the passenger's-side door, probably hating the fact that she can't just drive herself away from here.

"Just take me home," she says. "And don't talk to me."

It is fucked up, Drew not knowing. Claire isn't wrong, and I shouldn't have expected that she would just blindly accept how my past choices have affected her present. What was I thinking, harboring that expectation? I honor her wishes. We don't talk. I want so badly to talk, to try to explain, as futile as it may be. She stays in her room. I can hear her on the phone with her friends. The way she describes the situation makes me sound heartless. Maybe I am.

I have to tell Drew. Somehow. The idea of calling him makes my throat clamp shut, though. I've called him before. The week after I brought newborn Claire home, there was that gang shooting on our block and I panicked. I thought maybe I'd just go back to New York and tell everyone I had a moment of insanity, a psychotic break. They would blame it on 9/11, excuse it. I dialed Drew's cell phone number, a sequence that remains imprinted on my brain despite active attempts to forget it. Sometimes, still, I dream of the numbers, see them lined up before me. He picked up on the third ring. It sounded like he was in the middle of a grocery store or a mall. There was so much ambient noise. I hung up immediately. He was going on with life, on the assumption I was gone. I couldn't just go back to him. The very next day I saw that classified ad for the tiny cottage house in the canyon.

There was another time, too, right after I had that unbelievable run-in with Jade at the crafts fair. I was in the middle of a shift at the bar and I thought of Drew, so suddenly that I wondered if it meant something. There was a pay phone right outside. I figured I'd use that, not my own phone or the bar's phone—just in case. I stood in the phone booth for a good five minutes, trying to remember the last time I'd been in one. In college, I guessed, though I couldn't retrieve a specific memory. They're like upright coffins, aren't they? Someone had etched a heart into the metal phone box—*A+M Forever* scrawled inside of it. Drew and I had etched *D+E Always* into a tree trunk on campus the year we met. I wondered if A and M kept their promises to each other.

I dialed his number slowly, each push of a button exaggerated and dramatic. When it started ringing, I froze. I could hear my heartbeat. What time was it in New York? After seven o'clock. Dinnertime. After two rings, there was the click of a pick-up.

"This is Andrew," he said.

Again, I hung up. I stayed standing there, hand still on the phone. Andrew? Did he say that because he didn't recognize the incoming phone number? Was he trying to sound professional? Did he have a profession that would require him to sound professional? Did his new girlfriend or wife prefer "Andrew" to "Drew"? Or, was that just the name he chose to use now?

It occurred to me: perhaps we both became new people.

I didn't call again. The pay phone was removed a couple months later—by the city or the phone company or whoever is in charge of the fate of pay phones. There's just a square of dirt where it used to stand. There were other times I wanted to check on him, but I didn't dare call from a traceable line. And now there's the Internet in all its glory, so much more useful than it was when I first came to California.

Four years ago, I created a fake Facebook profile—under the name Jane Smith—so I could browse. Just a few clicks and there was Drew—looking the same, smiling, some kind of lake or ocean in the background. I visit his page every now and then, the same way you visit a blog you remember liking once and always forget about. He remarried, which comforts me more than it saddens me. I don't know when he remarried. It just says MARRIED TO LISA SHAW next to a little heart icon. Lisa Shaw. She didn't take his name. I like that he's with that kind of woman. His photos are private, so I can't see Lisa Shaw, or their children, if there are children. He only shares his personal life with "friends." I am not his friend. After fourteen years, sometimes it's hard to believe I ever was, let alone that I was much, much more than that.

I've found Marni on Facebook, too. She's married—in spite of herself. She's childless and working at a Manhattan ad agency, which reminds me that not everything in life goes haywire. Nancy, not surprisingly, doesn't have a Facebook page. Neither does my mom. Google has nothing to say about them, either.

I text Paul to ask him if Facebook is an acceptable way to contact Claire's father.

He writes: *Remember when I said you're not a coward? I take it back.*

Ha. You see my true colors now.

Let me know how it goes.

I click "Send Message" on Drew's page. A box appears. This box is for friends messaging each other about an upcoming party or their date last night. It's for reminders like, *Hey, you left your sweater at my house. I'll bring it when I see you on Tuesday.* It's for casual conversation. It's not appropriate for what I have to say. And yet it will have to do, because, like Paul has finally realized, I'm a coward.

I type:

Dear Drew . . . or Andrew . . . or Andy:

It makes me sad that I don't know what you go by anymore. To me, you were always Drew.

You're probably wondering who this is. You don't know a Jane Smith. That's what you're thinking, right? My profile name is fake and my one photo, of the sun setting at a beach near where I live, doesn't offer many clues. Even if I told you it was in California, that wouldn't help. You might not think you know anyone in California. But you do.

My name is Connie Prynne, but it used to be Emily Morris.

Yes, your Emily Morris.

How do I say this? What happened on September 11 didn't kill me—not physically, at least. I'm alive.

If you don't believe me, try this:

You have a mole on your lower back, placed as if to mark the very end of your spine.

On the day of our wedding, your mom brought a bouquet of carnations. I knew the shaking in her hands was getting worse because I could hear the flowers rustling in the plastic as she tried to hold the bouquet steady during the ceremony.

We adopted Bruce when we were right out of college, clueless but full of love.

Our first and last apartment was on Irving Avenue. We had a neighbor named Jim. He had pet parakeets and wore the same windbreaker every day.

Do you believe me now?

There's only one real purpose to this message: To tell you about Claire. She turns fourteen in May. It was time to tell her about you, her father.

I don't know how to explain why I left New York. I had to. If you have questions, I'll answer them. We weren't happy—you and me. We both know that, don't we?

Anyway, I'd just found out I was pregnant, then 9/11 happened. I left. I gave birth here, in California, the place I call home now. She looks just like you.

I would have called, but I didn't want to catch you off guard. Or maybe I didn't want you to hang up on me. This way, you can take your time with what I've said and respond—or not—as you see fit. I can only imagine what I put you through. I'll understand if I never hear from you.

—Em
818-555-0198

I don't mention Gabe. And I don't mention the cancer because I don't want that to be the reason he responds, if he responds. I read it through one time. Then again. And again. The cursor seems to blink at me faster and faster, with greater urgency. I hit "Send" and the message disappears. I close my laptop, place it back on the coffee table. I stare at it and wait. I've already decided that I won't tell Claire I sent the message. If he doesn't respond at all, I'll act like I never contacted him. She'll resent me and what I've done—*that is so fucked up*—and I'll have to live, or die, with that.

TWENTY-EIGHT

It's not like Claire to oversleep. Maybe she's exhausted from yesterday, from the disastrous trip to the beach. I, for one, didn't sleep at all last night. I was up thinking about Claire's hatred of me while simultaneously waiting for Drew to respond to my message. It says "Read" next to the message, so I know he's seen it.

I go to her room and knock lightly on the door.

"Claire?" I say.

Claire never misses school. Come hell or high water, she goes to school.

There's no answer.

"Claire?" I say again.

I turn the knob quietly, push the door open. And there is her bed, carefully made. No Claire.

I text her.

Where are you?

I go through the motions of a normal day, trying to trick myself into believing it is a normal day. There has to be an explanation. After I shower and eat my cereal, there's no response, though.

Claire, this isn't funny. Call me.

I call Al. He hasn't heard from her.

"Is her backpack there?" he asks.

I go check, rifling through her room. "Doesn't look like it," I say.

"Well, then, she's taken off somewhere," he says.

Al would probably be a good parent. He has the "calm, cool, collected" thing down pat.

"Don't worry, Con," he says. "She's at that age. I'm sure she's fine."

Al doesn't know I told her about Drew. Al doesn't even know about Drew. What am I supposed to say to him? *You know how your girlfriend took your daughter and left you? I did the same thing.*

After eight o' clock, I call the school. They say Claire isn't in homeroom. I thought for sure she would be. Like I said, Claire never misses school. I call Heather's mom and Riley's mom. They haven't seen her or heard anything. They both say, "But Claire's such a good kid," which just makes me think she didn't leave on her own accord; someone took her, like in a *Dateline* episode. I don't have Tyler's mom's number, but Riley's mom does.

"Ty isn't here, either," his mom says, with less worry in her voice than I think she should have. She sounds relieved almost, maybe assured that Claire is with him, that this is some kind of teenage scheme as opposed to abduction.

"Any idea where they might be?" I ask.

"God, I don't know," she says.

"They can't be far. They can't drive."

I don't even know how or when Claire and Tyler convened. Was it last night?

"I bet my older son is involved," she says, still too calm for my liking. "Let me call him and I'll call you back."

I wait an agonizing five minutes before she calls.

"I was right," she says with satisfaction. "I promised Trevor a new paint job for his car and he came clean."

I don't care about your bribing tactics, lady.

"He says he picked up Claire last night and took them to the beach."

"The beach?"

"He says they wanted to camp there."

"Is that even legal?" I say, then catch myself: "Never mind, what beach?"

"The one at the end of Topanga Canyon."

"I'm on my way."

"Thanks," she says, as if I'm doing her a favor, as if this isn't any kind of emergency. "Tell Ty he's in big trouble."

The beach parking lot is mostly empty considering it's a Monday morning. At first I think I'm at the wrong spot. I don't see them. But then, down by the shore, two silhouettes come into view. They're sitting cross-legged, facing the ocean. The wind whips. They must have been freezing last night.

They don't hear me coming because of the sound of the waves. When I appear, it must seem like I came out of nowhere. They're both startled. They stand at attention like military cadets.

"Mom," Claire says.

She probably thought it would take me longer to find them. She wanted me to worry, to feel the same panic she felt when I told her I was dying, the same rage she felt when I told her about Drew.

"How did you—"

"Doesn't matter," I say. "I'm glad you're both safe."

Tyler looks embarrassed. I'm sure Claire put him up to this. It's easy to blame the boy, when you're the mother of a girl, but this has Claire written all over it.

"We didn't have any tests or anything at school today," he says, trying to make it okay.

"It's my fault," Claire adds.

She must really like this Tyler boy. She's abandoned her feud with me to defend him.

"Let's just go," I say.

Claire and Tyler look at each other, waiting for me to reprimand them and deliver a punishment. I don't have the energy for that.

"Oh, and Tyler, I'm supposed to tell you you're in big trouble."

I drop off Tyler at his house at the other end of the canyon. He thanks me profusely and then tells Claire to call him later. He likes her. The way his eyes flick from side to side when he attempts to look straight at her gives it away. Surprisingly, I don't hate this kid. He seems harmless and a little dumb.

"Is he your boyfriend yet?" I say to Claire, breaking the silence of our car ride.

"No," she says. "Just my friend."

"That's what you think," I say. "He likes you."

"Whatever," Claire says.

I see her smile, though, slightly.

We are silent again until Claire realizes we're not headed home and says, "Where are we going?"

"I have my last chemo treatment today," I say, "and since you're apparently a flight risk, you're coming with me."

Paul is at the infusion center when we show up. He's done with his treatments, so I'm not sure what he's doing here.

"Surprise!" he says.

He has a book under one arm, and a bottle of sparkling water. I always bring sparkling water to my treatments.

"You came to sit with me?" I ask.

Throughout this hell—or "journey," as some like to say—I've envied the people who have visitors, loved ones who pull up a chair next to them. There's this older guy who comes with his thirty-three-year-old daughter who has stage four breast cancer. Sometimes he naps, sitting upright. Sometimes he reads his newspaper. Sometimes he holds his daughter's hand. Sometimes he argues with her about politics. No matter, he's there.

"I did," he says, "but I see you have company."

Claire gives a shy wave.

"Oh, this is Claire," I say. "She wasn't supposed to come, but she ran away from home and I just found her, so this is her punishment."

He disregards these details and just says, "The infamous Claire."

Claire looks at me like, *Who is this guy?* I haven't mentioned Paul to her before. We don't really talk about my chemo treatments. In her mind, they happen, but in some alternate universe.

"I'm Paul," he says, when he realizes she has no idea who he is. He seems a little hurt, like maybe he thought he was a bigger part of my life than he is.

I go to my usual chair. Paul and Claire sit on either side of me. Nurse Amy isn't working today. It's Desi, the mute, again. She hooks me up without fanfare, without recognition of this being my final treatment. Nurse Amy brought me a cake the last time she saw me. A cake!

"Last one," Paul says, as if reading my mind.

"For now," I say.

"Ever," he says. He winks at Claire.

"I need to go to the bathroom," Claire says.

"Are you going to run away again?" I ask. I'm teasing her, mostly, but she's not in the mood.

"I didn't *run away,*" she says. "I just needed some space."

Before I can tell her that she should take space in the backyard next time, she pushes herself out of the chair and walks to the bathroom slowly, like she's in no hurry, like she's hoping my chemo will be over by the time she gets back.

"I told her about her father," I say to Paul when she's out of earshot.

"Oh," he says. Paul and his "oh."

"It didn't go so well."

"Probably came as a bit of a shock."

"A bit," I say.

"Have you heard from him?" he asks.

I check my phone again, just in case.

"No," I say. "I should have expected that, though."

"Maybe he doesn't go on Facebook very often," he says. "I *never* go on Facebook."

"He saw it," I say. "He even changed his profile picture." The picture now is a close-up of him smiling on what appears to be a ski slope. I can't help but wonder if he posted it as a message to me, a hey-I'm-really-happy, fuck-off message. That's probably what I would do, if I were him.

"Maybe he's thinking about it," he says. "Give it a few more days."

"He probably hates me," I say.

"Probably," he says. My stomach drops when he says this. "But he can't hate Claire."

Claire comes back from the bathroom and takes her seat. She pulls out her phone and starts texting away. Tyler, probably.

"So, Claire, have you planned out the summer road trip yet?" Paul asks.

I've told him I'm not sure the road trip is on. He's trying to play peacemaker for us. Claire looks at me, her eyes asking the same question I have: *Are we still doing that*?

"Uh, kind of, not really," Claire says.

"You two gotta get on that," Paul says. "You *are* going, right?"

Claire and I look at each other.

"Come on, you're going," Paul says. He nods his head once, like a genie granting a wish.

"I'm in if you are," I tell Claire.

We've both pissed each other off over the last several weeks. I'm willing to extend the ol' olive branch.

"I'll think about it," she says.

She's holding the power for now. I get it. She resumes texting.

When I'm all finished, when Paul and I have exhausted our small talk, we walk out together, the three of us. Paul follows us to our car.

"You're done," he says.

It doesn't feel like I'm done, though.

"Yep," I say.

"So I guess this is it," he says.

He's referring to us, the regularity of our togetherness. He's fishing for a future.

"Yep," is all I say.

"You know, I can give you a ride to and from the hospital when you have your surgery."

I hadn't even thought about needing a ride. It unnerves me that Paul has.

"My personal chauffeur?" I say nervously.

"At your service." He bends at the waist, a playful bow.

I will need a ride, so I say, "I might take you up on that."

Claire gets in the car, bored with us.

"Please do," Paul says.

He probably wants me to hug him, but I'm not really a hugger. Instead, I give him an awkward wave. He stuffs his hands in the pockets of his jeans and walks away. I'm a little wistful watching him go.

"That guy likes you," Claire says, the second I close the door and start the car.

"Paul?" I say.

"Yes, Paul," she says, like I'm an idiot.

"Nah," I say.

She just shakes her head. We're halfway home when she pulls her knees up to her chest and looks over at me.

"Why would you leave my father and then spend the rest of your life single?" she says.

The question catches me off guard.

"Don't you want to fall in love?" she says.

Young people and their romanticism.

"You're my priority, sweetie," I say, "not love."

"That's sad," she says.

More silence, then: "So you're not going to, like, ground me?"

"I don't think so," I say. "I think we're even."

She scoffs. "Hardly."

We pull into the driveway at home, but she doesn't get out. I take this as a cue to stay where I am.

"Ty says I should try to find him, my father," Claire says.

"Oh," I say. Paul's favorite refrain.

"Why did you leave him?" she asks with a seriousness that implies she'll understand the reasons I give.

"You know what happened on September eleventh?" I ask her. I don't mention the year. Nobody ever mentions the year.

"Yeah." From her history classes, she knows.

"I died on September eleventh," I say. "In a way. I died, in a way."

"Like, you couldn't be there anymore?" she says.

"Something like that."

"So you came here."

She inhales a big breath.

"Was he a bad guy or something?"

"No, nothing like that."

"Didn't you miss him?"

"Sometimes," I say.

"Am I like him?"

"You look like him. You're optimistic like him. You have a kind heart like him," I say. "You're smarter than both of us."

She smiles.

"Do you think he'd want to meet me?"

"He'd be a fool not to," I say.

"Maybe we could figure that out somehow," she says.

She's thought about this already, I can tell. It pains me a little because I don't know if it's possible. I don't know if Drew wants anything to do with me, and her by association.

"Yeah, sweetie, maybe."

She opens the door and gets out. I stay for a minute, sorting the coins in my cup holder. Just then, like magic, my phone rings. The caller ID shows the 917 area code. New York. It takes only a second before I recognize the shapes, the order, of the numbers. I swallow hard, consider letting it go to voice mail. But then I consider that this may be the one time he calls, my one chance.

"Hello?" I say, gripping the steering wheel, knuckles white.

"Emily?" he says.

He used to call me Em.

"Emily?" he says again.

And then I start to cry.

TWENTY-NINE

"It's really you?"

Those are Drew's first words, spoken not with wonderment, but with bafflement and maybe a little anger.

"It's me," I say meekly.

"I can't believe this."

"I know."

"I can't believe this," he repeats. He's definitely angry. Of course he is.

"We held out hope for you, for days and days," he says.

"We put up signs. We had a funeral." He doesn't say the word "funeral" as much as he spits it. It's always pained me to wonder about the funeral—who was there, what they said.

"I'm sorry. It's crazy. I know."

"All those tears wasted while you were living in *California*?"

"Look, I—"

"And with my *child*, no less?"

"Drew, I know I'm an awful person."

He snorts like this is the biggest understatement he's ever heard in his life.

"I can't believe this," he repeats again.

There's a female voice in the background—probably his wife. Lisa Shaw. He must be covering the phone with his palm. There's muffled whispering.

Then: "I have to think this through. I gotta go."

And just like that, he hangs up. I sit in the car, holding the phone to my ear. Then I put it down and cry some more.

I don't tell Claire about the call. I don't want her to take it personally if he never calls again.

But then he does call again, exactly a week later. I'm at the bar. Al sees my face go white and says, "You okay?" I tell him, "I gotta take this," and then I disappear into the back office.

"I'm not calling to talk to you," Drew says. There is no *Hello* or *How are you?* "You are dead to me, by your own choosing."

The Drew I knew never would have said something like this. He's changed.

"I'm calling because of Claire," he says.

I want to defend myself, but what is there to say? I have to let him have his anger. I can't take that from him. I've already taken so much.

"That's the only reason I reached out," I say. "For Claire."

I remember all over again what it feels like to be "the wrong one" of the two of us, the one who isn't as moral, isn't as patient, isn't as kind.

"I mean, you're sure she's my child?" he says.

I'm offended, though I have no right to be. After all, I was so sure, for so long, that Gabe was Claire's father. I won't tell him about Gabe. That would make things worse.

"I'm sure," I say.

"What did you tell her about me?" he asks.

"That you died," I say. There's no use sugarcoating it.

"Fake deaths—your go-to, huh?"

He's definitely changed. If he would have talked back to me like this years ago, called me on my shit, taken ownership of his own, maybe our marriage could have survived, maybe I'd still be in New York. Maybe.

"She knows now that you're alive," I say.

"You and me, coming back to life," he says with a disbelieving grunt.

"I'm sorry," I say.

"That's beside the point," he says. "We want to talk to her. On the phone."

We—him and Lisa Shaw.

"Okay," I say, though this collision of worlds feels anything but okay.

"We will call her next Saturday. Around noon your time."

He says it like it's an appointment. Lisa Shaw is probably scribbling it in their family day planner.

"Sure," I say, even though I'm supposed to be in bed, avoiding stress, on Saturday. My mastectomy is this Wednesday.

Paul comes to the house on Wednesday morning to take me to the hospital. It's only when he's inside, perusing my picture frames, that I realize how few people I've allowed into my house in fourteen years. I'm uncomfortable watching him examine my life. He's smiling at Claire's kindergarten picture when I emerge with my packed hospital bag.

"You ready?" he says.

I'm not, but we go.

Claire wanted to come, but I told her absolutely not. She's staying at Heather's until I'm out of the hospital so she can go to school like normal. Paul rambles the whole way to the hospital, saying how "mastectomy" is a terrible name for a procedure. "They should call it a cancerectomy," he says, "focus on removing the cancer, not the boob."

When we get there, Paul asks if I want him to come into the pre-op room with me, but I say no. I tell him to go home, but he insists on camping out in the waiting area. The last thing I remember is a woman in scrubs drawing an *X* on my shoulder with a felt-tip pen, marking the diseased side. The world goes black sometime when they're rolling me to the OR.

When I wake up, it could be a few hours later or a few years later. I'm shivering violently. A nurse says, "Poor thing," and throws a warm blanket on me. I open my eyes. I'm in a small curtained space, machines beeping. The surgeon appears, standing over me, saying they took a lot of tissue, six lymph nodes. Before I was diagnosed, I wouldn't have even known I had six lymph nodes in my armpit. The surgeon disappears as quickly as he appeared and the nurse returns.

"Do you want us to get your husband?" she says.

"He's not my husband."

Dr. Richter says my margins are clear. She says that means they didn't see any cancer cells at the outer edge of the tissue that was removed, meaning they probably don't have to go back in to remove more. "Unless it reappears somewhere else," she says. Dr. Richter and her caveats.

They release me from the hospital on Friday afternoon. Paul carries my bag and escorts me out. He asks if I feel lopsided and I tell him it's too soon for jokes. He says, "Let me know when it's not. I have a bunch."

When we get to the house, he walks me inside. He lingers. He wants me to ask him to stay, to watch a movie or have tea or something.

"I'm really tired," I tell him.

"Right, right," he says. "I'll leave you be, then."

He looks so disappointed that I find myself saying, "I'll call you in a couple days." It's a commitment I'll regret later, but what's done is done. He seems pleased.

The nurse was very clear that I shouldn't remove my bandages until my follow-up appointment in one week. But, standing before the mirror in my bathroom, I'm curious. Once, when scolding Claire about something I can't even remember, I said, "Curiosity killed the cat," and she looked at me quizzically and said, "But, Mom, I'm not a cat."

I'm not a cat.

One of the corner edges is slightly upturned. I pick at it. I can always reapply the bandage. I just want a peek.

I pull it off, slowly. And then there I am, my new self. A dark red horizontal line, a railroad track of stitches, is across half my chest. When I was younger, I longed for larger breasts. That longing seems silly to me now. My healthy breast, small as it is, looks perfect compared to what is no longer there.

My mother had huge breasts. I'd stare at them when she changed in front of me, wondering when I would have my own. She said to me, "You're just so thin. You'll probably always be flat-chested. Don't blame me. Obviously wasn't my genes." So my breasts came from my father's side of the family. I can't know that for sure, of course; I never met him, never will. My mother never knew her father, either. Claire will break the cycle.

I run my fingertips gently over the sewed-up incision, picture the scar that will be. I don't think the scar will bother me as much as the fact that my nipple is gone. It's not just that I no longer look like a woman; I no longer look human. Dr. Richter said I could consider breast reconstruction—nipple included!—but somehow I feel like it's better to accept what is. To resist the urge to cover up the truth with something fake. For once. And, besides, if I'm granted more years of life, I shouldn't care about a stupid nipple.

"Does it hurt?" a voice says.

I cover my former breast and whip around to see Claire standing behind me.

"I didn't hear you," I say, horrified that she's seen what she has.

"Heather's mom just dropped me off."

She's staring at my chest.

"It doesn't scare me," she says.

Even so, I close the door to the bathroom, create a barrier

between us. I stick the bandage back on, along with my T-shirt—an oversized one, a freebie from Claire's soccer league. When I open the door, she's sitting on my bed, feet dangling.

"Sorry, honey."

"I'm just glad it's gone," she says.

"Me, too."

"I wonder what they do with it," she says.

I laugh. "That's a good question." I can't help but picture a bin of cancerous breasts, marked with a yellow HAZARDOUS WASTE sign.

"Does it hurt?"

"It stings. It's still kind of numb. I've got pain meds, though. And the nurse gave me some exercises to do so I don't get too stiff," I say.

She nods like she approves of this plan.

I sit next to her on the bed. I haven't told her yet about Drew. He's calling tomorrow and I haven't told her.

"I have some news," I say.

She looks at me expectantly, eyebrows raised.

"I wanted to wait until after the surgery—"

"Mom. What is it?"

"I talked to your father," I say.

She looks more surprised than excited.

"And he wants talk to you. On the phone. Tomorrow."

"He does?"

"Yeah. I mean, if you want. It's up to you."

She stands, paces, gnaws at her thumbnail.

"What do I say?"

"Whatever you want to."

"Whatever I want to," she says, tapping her bottom lip with her index finger. I've never seen her so nervous. "I guess I'll start with hello."

Claire and I sit at the kitchen table, staring at the phone between us as if it's a hand grenade. I'm not as anxious as I thought I would be. The pain meds take the edge off. My wooziness just exacerbates how surreal this feels.

"You ready?" I ask.

She has a list of questions to ask her father. She's ready.

At exactly noon, the phone rings. Claire picks up.

"Is this Claire?" Drew says, his voice friendly and kind. Nothing like it was with me.

She says, softly, "It's me."

We're on speakerphone, but I don't say anything, don't make myself part of their conversation.

"How are you?" Drew says. He's talking to her like she's younger than she is, his voice a little too cheery. If he has children, they must be small. He has no experience with teenagers.

"I'm good. How are you?"

"Good."

And then they are silent and Claire looks at me, her eyes big and worried. I just smile and mouth, *It's okay.*

"So your mom says you're almost fourteen?"

"Yep. In May."

"Wow," he says. "What do you like to do for fun?"

This sounds like an uncomfortably forced interview.

"Well," she says, "I'm class president."

"Really? That's awesome."

She tells him how she gets straight A's, and I'm proud. He must be relieved to know I did something right. She tells him how she wants to be mayor one day—an ambition I didn't know about, an ambition she may have made up for the purposes of this call. She tells him how we live near the beach, how she's never been out of California. He responds like this is all incredibly fascinating and I'm grateful for that, for his enthusiasm.

He asks if she has any questions for him. She does. She consults her paper. She asks what he does for a living, which is an odd first question, but who am I to judge? He says he's a chef, that he owns a French restaurant. It makes me simultaneously sad and happy that he stuck with it. She asks if he's married and he says he is, to a "wonderful woman" named Lisa. She asks if he has kids and he says he does—Wyatt is three and Winter is one. He clarifies that they are her half-siblings and she says, "I always thought it would be cool to have one of each—a brother and a sister." He says, "Right. Cool."

She asks if he has any pets. He says they have a cat named Felix. I want to ask, *What about Bruce?* but then I remember that he must have died years ago. She asks Drew how we met. It's a question she asked me, before this call, but she must want to hear him tell the story. He confirms what I told her: we met in college, and it was love at first sight. She says she wants to go to college someday. He says, "You're certainly smart enough." She blushes. She asks if he likes New York and he says, "It's home." She asks if he thinks she'll like New York, and my heart seizes for a second. Is she picturing her life there—without me? He says, "New York is exciting. The city that never sleeps." She says, deadpan, "How do you never sleep?"

They agree to talk again soon, make it a weekly thing.

"And, I don't know if my mom told you, but we're thinking of doing a road trip," she says. "This summer."

My heart seizes again. Claire didn't tell me she was going to bring this up, probably because she knew I'd say something like, *Let's wait on that.*

"This summer, huh? She didn't mention it," he says.

"Maybe, when we come to New York, we could meet," Claire says. She bites off part of her thumbnail. I can see the muscles in her jaw contracting as she chews on it.

"Wow, um, yeah," Drew says, noticeably flustered.

I'm sure he wants to meet her. He's probably flustered at the notion of me being there. I don't blame him. I can't imagine standing face-to-face with him again.

"Or not," Claire says. She slouches. "It's just an idea."

"No, no," he says, recomposed, "let's plan on that."

She sits up straight again. She won't look at me. She doesn't want me interfering with this plan of hers by shaking my head in disapproval.

"Really?" she says.

"Yeah. Let's figure out the dates when we talk next time."

"Cool," she says.

"Cool," he says.

They stumble over pleasantries—"It was nice to talk to you," "Have a good rest of your weekend"—before hanging up.

"You're conniving, Claire," I say.

She finally looks at me, smirks.

"I know."

THIRTY

Compared to chemo, radiation is a cakewalk. I'm in my last week of it. I go Monday through Friday, after dropping off Claire at school. Unless there's traffic and I'm a few minutes late, thus losing my place in the schedule and having to wait twenty minutes or so, I'm in and out in fifteen minutes—like a quick run to the post office to buy stamps. Rico, the radiation technician, escorts me behind a huge white door—eight inches thick, four feet wide, DANGER written on it in big bold letters. Despite the warning, I go in each time unfazed. When the choice is cancer or something else that could be harmful, you choose the something else. You take the risk so you can live a little bit longer, so you can be cancer-free, so you can see your daughter grow up.

On the other side of the DANGER door, I lie on the table—arms over my head, gown wide open—beneath an intimidating machine called a linear accelerator. And I do my best to stay still—to play dead, ironically—because if I so much as sneeze, moving even a few millimeters, the rays might shoot at my heart. The machine does its click-clacking thing and then it is over in just a few minutes and Rico says, "See you tomorrow."

The way Dr. Richter describes it, radiation is an attempt to burn away the cells so nothing new can grow back. It makes me think of that fire that tore through Topanga Canyon a few years ago, leaving behind black earth reminiscent of the surface of Mars. But, before long, green blades started to shoot up through the soil. Nature is persistent. Cancer may be persistent. Paul says I have to get used to not knowing what the future holds.

I've been talking to Paul daily. We haven't seen each other, just talked. I think we have a mutual understanding that this is what we'll be—phone friends—until he says, "Why don't you and Claire come over for dinner?" I'm on speakerphone when he says it. Of course, with my luck, Claire hears and shouts, "We'll be there."

Paul lives a few miles inland, in Woodland Hills. It's a small one-story house, a rental, the lease signed hastily after his wife left him. He talks about her a lot, his wife. Not in a nostalgic or longing way, but in a way that confirms he's human and has feelings. Sometimes I talk to him about Drew, about my guilt. Drew and Claire are chatting weekly, as they promised each other. She doesn't let me listen in anymore. She goes to her room and shuts the door. I wonder what they talk about. I wonder if she's told him that I never remarried, never even dated a single person. I wonder if she's told him about the cancer. I wonder if that would please him, if he would think, *Serves her right*. Probably not. Drew was never as mean as me. All Claire has told me is that he's "nice" and she can't wait to meet him. Yes, the meeting is happening, whether I like it or not.

Paul's house has twinkly, clear lights along the roofline. The front door is wide open, the sound of music audible from the sidewalk.

"Why does he still have Christmas lights up?" Claire asks.

It's May.

"Paul is just that kind of guy."

Claire walks right through the open door and I follow her. Paul is in the kitchen, wearing an apron, standing at the stove. His dog,

Chuck, sees us before he does. He barks crazily and we kneel down, put out our palms. Chuck sniffs and stops barking, concluding we are friendlies.

"He's my welcoming committee," Paul says, turning around. "He does a terrible job."

He puts a lid on the pot and comes to greet us. He hugs me without hesitation, as if he's forgotten that we're not that kind of friends.

"Your hair!" he says.

I look like Sinead O'Connor circa 1990. My hair started to grow back a few weeks after my last chemo treatment. It was soft fuzz at first, like a baby's, and then coarser. It's coming in brown, as it should. Claire thinks this is odd, since she has known me only as a blonde. I tell her sometimes hair grows back a different color, because that's a true fact according to the Internet and I feel sheepish telling her that I was attempting to disguise myself all these years. I'm still sorting through which details to give her, which lies to reveal.

Paul's hair has completely grown back. It's dark, dark brown—almost black. His eyebrows have filled in, too. I admit, he's handsome with hair.

"You look great."

"Doesn't she?" Claire says with a scheming smile. Claire, always scheming.

For dinner, he makes some kind of Indian curry dish. He keeps refilling my wineglass. He says, "I figure if I get you drunk, you won't be able to tell that my cooking is terrible." Claire says, "But I can tell." We laugh.

We let Chuck lick our plates when we're done. Paul says he doesn't believe in dogs not eating people food.

"What's the point of having one if you can't spoil it?" he says.

"I miss having a dog," I say. For years, I've been so diligent about avoiding references to the past. It's strange to let down that guard.

"You had a dog?" Claire says.

I nod. "Bruce."

"Bruce?"

"He just looked like a Bruce," I say, remembering.

Paul refuses to let us help with dishes. As he scrubs away at the sink, Claire leans over to me and says, "You seem so happy, Mom."

Cynic that I am, I want to tell her she'll realize when she's older that alcohol can create an illusion of happiness for the short time it circulates through your body. But then I stop to consider that maybe I actually am happy.

"Do I?" I ask.

"Yeah, really happy," she says.

"I am, I think."

Paul brings a container of chocolate ice cream and three spoons to the table.

"Classy," I say.

"I aim to please."

We take shameless scoops, the three of us. I am happy. Yes. I am.

"You must be getting excited for your road trip," Paul says to Claire.

She beams. "I am!"

"What's the itinerary?"

I've let Claire plan the whole thing.

"Route 66 all the way to Chicago," she says.

"Then pass through Ohio to get to D.C.," I say.

"Then New York to meet my dad for the first time."

Dad. She's been calling him that. *Dad*. It's only when talking about this trip and meeting him that she sounds younger than she is, like a five-year-old excited about unicorns.

"I bet he can't wait to see you," Paul says.

He gives me a look. He knows how nervous I am about the whole thing.

Even though I've sobered up, Paul insists we stay the night. I say, "No, really, that's okay," but then he promises pancakes in the morning and Claire says, "Mom, let's just stay." So we do. He has a guest room. Claire and I share a bed. I roll on my side and she curls up right behind me, her breath on the back of my neck.

"Don't snore," she says.

"You better get used to it. We're sharing beds in some of the hotels on our trip."

She groans.

"Mom?" she says.

"Yeah?"

"I know you say Paul is your cancer friend," she says.

"Yeah?"

"But you don't have cancer anymore."

"No, I don't," I say, hoping that's true.

"And neither does he."

"No, he doesn't," I say.

"So what now?" she presses.

"Claire," I say. "Go to sleep."

When I wake up the next morning, I hear voices in the kitchen—Claire's and Paul's. I get out of bed and do my best to straighten out the wrinkled shirt I slept in. I walk quietly down the hallway, wanting to spy on whatever budding friendship Paul has with my daughter. They are laughing. I peek around the wall and he is standing behind her, instructing her on pancake-flipping.

"She's alive!" Paul says when I appear.

Claire flips a pancake flawlessly and gives Paul a high five.

"Just in time," she says.

We sit at the kitchen table. It's small, but still too big for Paul's cramped kitchen. We pass butter and syrup between us. We comment on the niceness of the day outside. The sun glares through the window above the kitchen sink.

When we're done, I do the dishes while Paul and Claire look at a map of the United States on his iPad, plotting the points of our road trip. She says she'll text him to let him know where we are on our route. Claire welcomes people into her life so easily. I envy and fear that about her.

"Okay, Claire, you ready to go?" I say.

She looks disappointed, but says, "I guess."

Paul walks us out to our car, Claire still chatting with him the whole way. He opens the passenger door for her to get inside.

"You're cool, Paul," she says with a confirmatory nod.

"As are you," he says. He shuts her door and then walks around to my side.

"Thanks for everything," I say. "You're too nice to me."

"One of my many flaws."

He holds our eye contact, challenging me not to look away. I can't help it, though. I shift my gaze to the ground, staring at my unpainted toenails sticking out of my sandals.

"Connie," he says, "I want to take you out sometime. Like on a date."

I keep looking at my feet.

"You waited to ask until my hair started growing back, huh?" I say.

"Duh."

He touches my chin with his index finger, raises it so I'm looking at him.

"What do you say?"

I don't know if the hangover has weakened me or what, but I say, "I guess that would be fine."

He laughs. "Wow, that kind of enthusiastic response is what every man hopes for."

"Sorry," I say. "Let's do it. After the road trip?"

I need some time to prepare myself. It will be my first date since 2001.

"I'll plan something fun."

If I'm honest, this promise of something fun makes my stomach flutter. If I'm honest, there's a chance I'll back out. If I'm honest, I don't think I will.

"Okay," I say.

"Okay," he repeats.

With nothing left to say but good-bye, he pulls me against him and wraps his arms around me. His growing-in stubble rubs against my cheek.

"You two be safe," he says. "Don't pick up any hitchhikers."

"Thanks," I say, daring to look at him, smile.

When I get in the car, he goes to the edge of his lawn to watch us go.

"It's so obvious," Claire says as we pull away. She waves at him.

"What?" I say, looking in my rearview as he gets smaller and smaller.

"He, like, loves you."

If you think grown women don't blush, you're wrong.

THIRTY-ONE

Less than a week before we leave on our road trip, I meet with Dr. Richter to see how my latest scans look.

"I'm afraid I have some bad news," she says. I haven't even sat down yet. It's like she can't keep this in, can't let me have one more moment of false hope.

"What now?" I say.

I try to appear blasé, like I'm immune to bad news. I'm not, though.

She exhales. For the first time, Dr. Richter looks weary.

"It looks like the cancer has popped up in your right lung," she says.

Popped up. All I can think of is the toaster waffles Claire eats for breakfast.

"This isn't uncommon," she says. As if that makes it better.

I know all too well what this means. Once the cancer has spread from its original site, it's stage four. Only eleven percent of people survive five years. Eighty-nine percent of people die. There will be more chemo, possibly more surgery, if it's even operable. I'll lose my hair all over again. Claire will be devastated. Paul will be devastated. We'll all wonder why.

"I'm going on a road trip with my daughter," I say. This is what matters, not the treatment plan that I'm sure Dr. Richter wants to discuss.

"Okay," she says, though her tone suggests she's not sure it's okay.

"Is that a problem?"

"Well, I mean, I'd advise you to start chemo as soon as possible," she says, "but I know life sometimes has to come first."

Yes, life must come first. Life must come before death.

I sit in my car outside Dr. Richter's office building for a good ten minutes. I'm not going to tell Claire about this, not now. I'll tell her after the trip. Same with Paul. I was starting to imagine some kind of future with him. Now it appears foolish that I imagined some kind of future, period.

There's one person I want to see right now. Al. Big, burly Al. When I show up at the bar, JT is there, too, having a whiskey. I get teary-eyed just seeing the two of them.

"Well, look what the cat dragged in," JT says.

They either don't notice the tears in my eyes, primed right on the ridge and ready to roll down my cheeks, or they don't want to know why I'm sad.

"Hi, guys," I say.

Al gets me a beer from the tap, sets it in front of me.

"What's up, little lady?" Al says.

They're in good moods, probably both a little buzzed. Al doesn't drink much on the job, but he does when JT is around.

"Just wanted to stop in," I say.

I dismiss my impulsive plan to tell Al about the cancer coming back. It would be selfish, venting to him because I know he'd keep it together. He doesn't want to know. JT doesn't want to know. Somehow, over the course of this decade and a half, I've acquired people who care about me. Those people are still celebrating that the cancer is gone. I can't ruin that for them.

"You crazy girls are hittin' the road in a few days, right?" JT says.

I nod. JT is going to watch over the house while we're gone—get the mail, water the plants. I haven't told them that we're meeting Claire's father on this trip of ours. I can't bring myself to share that story, with Al especially. He got left, just like Drew. I don't know if he could see me the same again, let alone forgive me. See, I'm still a coward. I'm still withholding truths. Old habits and all.

"You going to be okay without me?" I ask Al.

I mean while we're on the trip, but also when I'm gone for good.

"I'll manage just fine," he says.

And he will. He managed fine for years before I showed up asking him for a job.

"You give me a ring if you have car troubles," JT says.

JT is good with cars. One of his many talents.

"I will," I say.

"We'll miss you," Al blurts. Maybe he says it because he can see I'm upset about something; maybe he says it because he's buzzed. He's never said anything like it before.

"How much have you guys had to drink?" I say. I can't take it right now, the sentiment.

"Too much," Al says.

They both laugh. I down my beer quickly and stand.

"You goin' already?" JT says.

"Sure am," I say. "I still have a couple more shifts before we leave. Try to hold it together, you saps."

In my car, I let the tears go. That's always a safe place, the car. By the time I get home, I'll be composed. For Claire. Everything is for Claire.

Claire and I rent an SUV because it has enough room for all our stuff, along with the in-a-pinch option to put down the backseats and create a bed. I thought about getting an all-American, made-for-a-road-trip Mustang convertible, pictured the two of us riding with the top down, but Claire said, "Mom, that's not practical."

We pack a few weeks' worth of clothes and a year's worth of snacks. "Priorities," Claire says. I check my packing list repeatedly, tote it around like a kid with a security blanket. Misplaced anxiety, that's what the shrinks call it. This trip will be the longest Claire and I have ever been away from our tiny cottage house in the canyon. And this trip will bring me face-to-face with Drew after nearly fifteen years. Anxiety is to be expected.

Claire takes a picture of the packed-up car with her phone. She's documenting the trip, sending updates to Paul and Tyler and her girlfriends.

"Ready?" she says.

No.

"As ready as I'll ever be."

And we are off.

Our first stop is the Grand Canyon. We drive in just as the sun is setting and race to park the car so we can run to the rim and get our first view. We both gasp at the same time. Even if you've seen it in pictures, even if you've prepared yourself for it be incredible, even if you've told yourself that you aren't as easily impressed as all those other people, the Grand Canyon still does what everyone says it will—take your breath away.

The next day, we walk down into the canyon, blissfully ignoring the fact that we have to walk back up. I lag behind Claire on the return trip. My body is weaker than I let her know, fatigued from all it's been through. My cells aren't sure if they're coming or going, living or dying. I imagine each individual one debating which side of the fence to jump to. Sometimes it's tempting to just give up.

We camp two nights in the Grand Canyon. The two of us

barely fit in our little tent. We turn our sleeping bags so we can open the front of the tent and stick our heads out to look at the speckled sky. Claire sees a shooting star. I don't see it.

"I made a wish," she says.

"What is it?"

"I can't tell you or it won't come true," she says. "Duh."

"I bet it was about Tyler," I say. I hope it's about Tyler and not about me and my cancer. I hope Claire's not thinking at all about me and my cancer.

"He kissed me," she says.

"Really?"

My first kiss was when I was her age, exactly. It was during a game of spin the bottle. I don't even remember the boy's name.

"The day before we left. He just did it out of nowhere."

She seems baffled by the whole thing.

"That's sweet," I say. "Did you . . . like it?"

"Mom!" she says.

And I know that means she did.

From the Grand Canyon, we drive six hours to Albuquerque. We wander around Old Town and I buy Claire a turquoise ring. Our motel has a pool of questionable cleanliness, but we spend most of our time there because it's hot and there doesn't seem to be much to do in Albuquerque.

It's eight hours to Oklahoma City, but the drive feels longer because of the monotonous miles of farmland. Claire naps on and off. We stop for greasy food at a mom-and-pop diner.

"Paul says hi," Claire says, alternating between holding her unwieldy hamburger and holding her phone. She starts texting.

"He does?" I say. I miss him, kind of. "Tell him I say hi."

"You know, you can text him, too," she says.

"I'm not much of a texter," I say. The truth is that it scares me to have a person to share everything with. I haven't had that since New York, since Gabe and Drew.

"You need to get with the times, Mom," she says, texting away.

"You're going to hurt your neck staring down at that thing all the time."

She rolls her eyes in that way only teenagers can.

There isn't much to do in Oklahoma City, either. All I can think about is the bombing. Drew and I were glued to the news the day it happened in 1995. We couldn't make sense of what we were seeing—the large hole taken out of the building, all those people dead. We had no idea we'd be even more horrified just a few years later. Claire doesn't know anything about that bombing. It didn't make it into her history book, apparently. I'm curious to see the memorial, driven by a masochistic urge to pick that metaphorical scab and feel sad for a bit. Instead, we go to the National Cowboy & Western Heritage Museum. And the next day we go to the Frontier City amusement park to ride roller coasters and eat cotton candy. At one point I feel like I'm going to throw up. I don't.

After another eight-hour drive, we're in St. Louis. We take the 630-foot ride to the top of the Gateway Arch and visit the memorial where Lewis and Clark set out on their history-book-making expedition. We go to the St. Louis Zoo and have dinner at the Fountain on Locust. According to the back of the menu, it was built as a car showroom in 1916, part of Locust Street's historic Automotive Row. It has one of those black-and-white-checkered floors that make you dizzy if you stare long enough.

We get seats at a wooden booth against the wall, order vanilla milkshakes served in fountain glasses, with the extra milkshake leftover from the blending process in stainless steel tumblers.

I lean across the table and say, in a conspiring whisper, "Let's tell them it's your birthday."

"Seriously?" There's disapproval in her tone. Suddenly she's the adult and I'm the teenager.

"Whatever, I'm doing it," I say, sticking to my new role. She shakes her head.

We celebrated her birthday last month, in our usual way: pizza and ice cream cake. I want to celebrate again, though. If I only get a certain number of actual birthdays left with her, I want to celebrate them over and over and over again.

On my way to the restroom, I tell the waitress about the special occasion. I give Claire a thumbs-up on my way back. She just rolls her eyes like, *Grow up, Mom*.

"I still can't believe you're fourteen," I say, biting my maraschino cherry off its stem.

I imagine the cancer festering in my lung. I figure I have a year, maybe two. According to the American Cancer Society website, people with stage four inflammatory breast cancer are given twenty-one months. *Given*, as if it's some kind of present: *Here you go, you have twenty-one months of life*.

"I'll be fifteen before you know it." She finger-combs her hair behind her ears. It's getting longer, her hair. She says she wants to donate it to cancer patients when it gets long enough. She says that will be her "platform" when she runs for class president in high school. She starts high school in fall, a shock. "I'll call it Hairitable Donations," she says. Clever girl.

"I'll be driving this time next year," she says. It sounds like a threat. It is one, I guess.

"Driving!" I say. I attempt a smile, though the whole idea of this terrifies me. I hope I can be one of those cool mothers when it comes to teaching her to drive, not too anxious, not slamming my foot into the floor, pressing the imaginary brake.

"I should start saving for a car," she says. "Babysitting's where it's at. Heather is making bank."

"You'd be good with kids," I say.

Chances are, I won't see Claire become a mother. She'll be a much better mother than me, I bet. I won't get to see who she chooses as a husband. Chances are, it won't be Tyler. She will have many loves and many heartbreaks and I won't get to be there. There's an it's-not-fair tantrum going on in my head. I would stomp my feet and scream if I could.

The waitress I tipped off and a group of four coworkers sing while presenting Claire with a giant sundae that looks to be composed of mostly whipped cream. Claire stares at the candle long and hard, as if contemplating something of great importance. Then she blows and they clap politely before going back to their ususal duties.

"Big wish, huh?" I say.

"That one," she says, "was for you."

We spend two days in Chicago. We take the bridge over the river and walk the Magnificent Mile, ending up at the edge of Lake Michigan. We see "the Bean" in Millennium Park, eat deep-dish pizza, take the L to Wrigley Field to walk around the neighborhood. Drew and I went to Chicago once—a spontaneous weekend adventure to see the Cubs play the Mets. Drew liked the Mets, hated the Yankees. He was always rooting for the underdogs. It was June. A thunderstorm passed through and we spent three hours waiting in the stands with the other diehards, drinking Old Style beer and eating peanuts. We were so drunk by the time the game started. I don't even remember who won.

Claire declares Cincinnati her favorite stop. She likes the Over-the-Rhine neighborhood. She reads from her phone: "It's believed to be the largest, most intact urban historic district in the United States."

"Maybe you'll live here one day," I muse.

"I can't imagine leaving California," she says.

"I used to say that about New York."

We're walking through the riverfront park. I never thought of Cincinnati as having a water feature. There's so much of the country, of the world, I don't know.

"Are you nervous?" Claire asks. "To go back?"

"Yes," I say.

She sits on a bench and I sit next to her.

"I don't think he hates you, if that helps," she says.

It does help, but this might be wishful thinking on her part.

"I mean, we don't talk about you all the time, but I was telling him how you let me plan the whole trip and he said, 'Your mom sounds pretty cool,'" she says. "I don't think he would say that if he hated you."

I hang on the words: *Your mom sounds pretty cool.*

"Maybe," I say. "I would hate me."

She gazes out at the river.

"*I* don't hate you," she says. "And you always say I'm a good judge of character."

It's true, I do say that.

"You're biased," I say.

She taps her fingers on the bench like it's a piano.

"Did you have a different name in New York? Like, who were you there?"

Who was I? I was a little selfish, a little idealistic, a little sad.

"Emily," I say, "that was my name."

She scratches her head. "The lady, at that craft fair, when you bought me that bracelet?"

I can't believe she remembers.

"Yes, she recognized me," I say. "She was my boss."

"Were you a bartender there, too?"

I laugh.

"No, no. I was a writer at an ad agency, and then I was an administrative assistant at this big company," I tell her.

This big company in the World Trade Center. Yes, the buildings that crashed down. I was supposed to be there. I faked my death. It's obvious Drew hasn't told her these things about me yet. That restraint, that kindness, is what suggests that maybe she's right—he doesn't hate me.

"I can't see it," Claire says. She knows me, and will only ever know me, as a bartender trying to make ends meet.

"I know," I say. "Sometimes I can't, either."

From Cincinnati, we drive to Washington, D.C. We arrive at night because of traffic. We've picked a nice hotel for this part of the trip because I've heard horror stories of being in "the wrong area" in D.C. Our room has a view of the Washington Monument, all lit up. And if we stick our heads out the window and turn them just so, we can see the White House, also lit up, in the distance.

By the end of the next day, after strolling through the National Mall and touring the Museum of American History and Museum of Natural History—Claire likes to read all the placards, mind you—I reach a level of exhaustion that only a bottle of wine can fix. I wait until Claire falls asleep watching a movie on TV and then I slip out and down to the hotel bar.

"Rough day?" the bartender says, filling my second glass. I don't do this very often at Al's Place, make conversation with the patrons. This guy is young, hopeful for tips.

"I actually had a great day," I say.

My head is starting to feel totally detached from my body, my thoughts and worries floating in the ether.

"Tomorrow, though," I say, "tomorrow may be a doozy."

Tomorrow, we go to New York.

"Well," he says, "no use thinking about it right now."

He sounds like Paul.

I pay my bill and leave an extra twenty as a tip.

THIRTY-TWO

We are on the New Jersey Turnpike, approaching Newark Airport, the last place I was Emily Morris. I feel like I'm going to puke again. I've puked once already, when I pulled over in the middle of nowhere in Pennsylvania. I told Claire I had to pee. I wish I could blame the nausea on last night's bottle of wine, but I know it's not that.

My palms are sweaty on the steering wheel. Drew is expecting us around four o'clock. That's in two hours. We're going to his house—an Upper West Side address between Riverside Park and Central Park, estimated at one million dollars according to the Internet. Either his restaurant is extremely successful or he married very well. I can't resent him either way.

"I'm nervous, too," Claire says. I didn't say I was nervous. She just knows.

She rubs her palms on her thighs.

Of course, the one time I wouldn't mind traffic on the New Jersey Turnpike, there isn't any. We pass Newark, memories of Drew's mother flooding my head. We're so close to Irvington, where I grew up, where my mother may still live. I won't find out. I've thought about it, and I just can't.

"We're early," I say to Claire, whose face is an inch from the window, taking in the approaching city. She'll never know the World Trade Center as part of that skyline. What is there now—the Freedom Tower? As if any of us could be truly free from that day.

Cars back up on the George Washington Bridge, as predicted. I tell Claire we're crossing the state line between New Jersey and New York. She's been obsessed with that on this trip—state lines, how you can be in one place one second and another place the next.

Before I know it, I'm on the Henry Hudson Parkway, remembering my cab ride out of the city with Angel Rivera like it was yesterday. I take the exit for Ninety-fifth Street.

"Is that Central Park?" Claire says, pointing down Ninety-sixth at the seemingly out-of-place, confounding cluster of green amid all the smog and concrete.

"Sure is," I say. "We have an hour before we have to be there. You want to walk around?"

The park hasn't changed a bit—a fact that both comforts and astounds me. I'm right back to the last time I was here, with Gabe, on that day we had the picnic beneath the castle, the day before I was going to tell him about the baby, the day before I was going to leave Drew, the day before he died. Claire and I pass the Great Lawn. Two kids are playing Frisbee among the ghosts of Gabe Walters and Emily Morris. Of course, Claire says she wants to see the castle, so we do. There's a line because there is a line for everything in New York, and by the time we make our way back into the daylight, it's time to go.

The last time Drew and I saw each other was right after I found out I was pregnant, when he came over to pick up Bruce because he thought I was too sick to walk him. Drew, ever dutiful, always doing the "right thing." It's baffling to me now, the way I resented him. I miss Emily Morris in some ways, but I see her as so naïve, so trapped by her own illusions. I guess that's the perspective that comes with age. I shiver and wonder how much more perspective I'll be allowed. How many years. Will I get the chance to prove that Connie is different, better? Maybe Drew will realize that. Maybe there is hope.

According to the all-knowing Internet, Drew's one-million-dollar apartment is in a 1929 prewar building. There's a doorman, which my mother used to say was "only for rich assholes." My heart pounds in my chest as we take the creaky old elevator to the second floor, my sweaty palm clutching the brass railing. I asked Claire if she wanted me to come up with her and she said yes. I'm surprised Drew didn't instruct her to have me drop her off and come back, like this is some kind of playdate. Does that mean he wants to see me? What is he going to think when our eyes meet? What will I think? In this moment, I'm not sure I'll recognize him. His face is blurry in my mind.

"Do I look okay?" I feel stupid the millisecond the question leaves my mouth.

Claire doesn't hesitate: "Beautiful," she says. Whether it's a lie or an exaggeration, I don't know and I don't care. It's what I need to hear.

"What about me?" she says.

She's wearing a moss-green dress I bought her for this occasion, with a pair of heels—her first pair. They're white, with two thick straps across the front of her foot. I can hardly call them heels; they're elevated a half inch off the floor. It's obvious she feels more grown-up in them, though.

"Beautiful," I tell her. "Really beautiful."

We stand outside his door. It has an old-fashioned knocker, a metal lion's head. I wonder if Drew or his wife is looking through the peephole. I compose my face just in case.

"Go ahead, sweetie," I say.

This is for her. All of this is for her.

She knocks tentatively, looking at me as she does. I hear footsteps approaching, then the flipping of a lock. The doorknob turns.

And then, right there, is my past, instantly familiar. His eyes—those eyes—meet mine for a quick second before they dart down at our daughter.

"Hi," she says.

"You must be Claire."

ACKNOWLEDGMENTS

If you're like me, you read the acknowledgments for a small glimpse into the author's life and how the book came to be. So, here's your glimpse.

I've been writing books since I was in elementary school. When I gained enough skill and foolishness to submit novels to agents, I met with a lot of rejection. My mom always said, "It will happen. It's just a matter of time." I scoffed and rolled my eyes, but she was right. Mom, thank you for believing in me when I thought it was ridiculous to do so. And thank you for being such a voracious reader—of not just my writing, but of books in general. I hope we trade novels back and forth for decades to come.

Dad, thank you, too. You're big on not giving up, and I have to think that had something to do with this book existing in the world beyond my computer's hard drive.

Over the years, I've been rejected by many agents, and I kept a list of ones who were at least nice about it. Andrea Somberg was first on that list. So, when I finished my first draft of this book, I sent pages to her. Much to my surprise, she responded immediately and wanted to read the whole thing. A few days later, we were chatting on the phone, and she was so complimentary of the story that I was blushing like a schoolgirl. Thank you, Andrea, for holding my naive hand through all of this. My anxiety appreciates your fast response to e-mails.

Thank you to everyone at St. Martin's Press, especially my editor, Brenda Copeland, and her assistants, Laura Chasen and Michelle Ma. Brenda, you made me realize the true value of an editor. As a writer, when you finish a book, you think it's truly done. You can't see how it could be better. So, when you get an editor's notes, it's a shock to the system. There is so much insecurity and self-doubt. You were there to encourage me through all that. Next time, I'll look forward to your much-needed perspective, instead of fearing the revisions it entails. Also, thank you for making me aware of my problematic obsession with em-dashes. Did you see I snuck a couple into the dedication? You're welcome.

Also, I may be a decent writer, but I suck at self-promotion, so thank you to my publicity team, led by Katie Kurtzman and Brittani Hilles.

To all my early readers (Eurie, Megan, Meredith, Huong, Lauren, Jess, Jay, Steph, and Toni, to name a few), thank you for taking the time. I know some of that early stuff was cringe-worthy.

To Ken Medina, my middle school English teacher, I don't think you realize the impact you had. You made me really love reading. You made me believe I could be a writer (and you convinced me that was a valid path).

Thank you to my sister, Ashley, for the talks about staying true to my creative self. I'm not sure how two physical therapists produced a writer and a photographer, but here we are.

Going with the cliché of saving the best for last, thank you to my loving, left-brained husband. He describes himself as "not a reader," yet he will reread my novels over and over again and brainstorm solutions to problems with me. He also catches weird errors ("I thought this character's hair was brown. Here you say it's blond"). Chris, in many ways, I don't know what I (or my characters and their variable hair) would do without you. I'm sure you didn't know what you were getting into marrying a sensitive, introverted writer, and yet you stand by me and continue to make audacious claims like, "You're perfect for me." All I can say in return is that you're perfect for me, too.